TOMÁS ELOY MARTÍNEZ was born in Argentina in 1934. During the military dictatorship (1976–82), he lived in exile in Venezuela where he wrote his first three books, all of which were republished in Argentina in 1983, in the first months of democracy. But it was his later books, including *The Perón Novel, Santa Evita* and *The Tango Singer*, that made his international reputation. In 2005 he was shortlisted for the International Man Booker Prize, and until his death in January 2010 he was a professor and director of the Latin American Program at Rutgers University.

FRANK WYNNE has won three major prizes for his translations: the 2002 IMPAC for *Atomised* by Michel Houellebecq, the 2005 Independent Foreign Fiction Prize for *Windows on the World* by Frédéric Beigbeder, and the 2008 Scott Moncrieff Prize for *Holiday in a Coma* by the same author. He is also the translator of many other books, including *An Unfinished Business* by Boualem Sansal and *Kamchatka* by Miguel Figueras, which was shortlisted for the 2011 Independent Foreign Fiction Prize.

PURGATORY

Tomás Eloy Martínez

Translated from the Spanish by Frank Wynne

BLOOMSBURY
LONDON · NEW DELHI · NEW YORK · SYDNEY

This work has been published with a subsidy from the Directorate General of
Books, Archives and Libraries of the Spanish Ministry of Culture

This book has been selected to receive financial assistance from English PEN's Writers
in Translation programme supported by Bloomberg. English PEN exists to promote
literature and its understanding, uphold writers' freedoms around the world, campaign against the
persecution and imprisonment of writers for stating their views, and promote
the friendly co-operation of writers and free exchange of ideas.

Bloomsbury Publishing Plc
50 Bedford Square
London WC1B 3DP

www.bloomsbury.com

Bloomsbury Publishing, London, New Delhi, New York and Sydney

A CIP catalogue record for this book is available from the British Library

ISBN 978 1 4088 2202 9

10 9 8 7 6 5 4 3 2 1

Typeset by Hewer Text UK Ltd, Edinburgh

Printed and Bound by CPI Group (UK) Ltd, Croydon CR0 4YY

In memoriam Susana Rotker, ten years after.

. . . what is fleeting remains, it endures.

FRANCISCO DE QUEVEDO
'To Rome Buried in Her Ruins'

Contents

I

Treating shadows like solid things

'Purgatorio', XXI, 136

Simón Cardoso had been dead thirty years when his wife, Emilia Dupuy, spotted him at lunchtime in the lounge bar in Trudy Tuesday. He was in one of the booths at the back chatting to two people she didn't recognise. Emilia thought she had stepped into the wrong place and her first impulse was to turn round, get out of there, go back to the reality she had come from. Fighting for breath, throat dry, she had to grip the bar rail for support. She had spent her whole life looking for him, had imagined this scene a thousand times, and yet now that it was happening she realised she wasn't ready. Her eyes filled with tears; she wanted to call his name, run over to his table and take him in her arms. But it took all her strength simply to hold herself up, to stop herself from crumpling in a heap in the middle of the restaurant, from making a fool of herself. She could barely summon the energy to walk over to the booth in front of Simón's and sit in silence waiting for him to recognise her. As she waited, she would have to feign indifference though her blood pounded in her temples and her heart lurched into her mouth. She gestured for a waiter and ordered a double brandy. She needed something to calm her, to still the fear that, like her mother, she was losing her faculties. There were times when her senses betrayed her; she would lose her sense of smell, become disoriented in streets she knew like the back of her hand, drift off to sleep listening to silly songs that, she didn't know how, seemed to be coming from her stereo.

She glanced over at Simón's booth again. She needed to be sure it was really him. She could just see him between the two strangers, he was sitting facing her, talking animatedly to his companions. There could be no doubt: she recognised his gestures, the curve of his neck, the mole under his right eye. It was astonishing to discover that her husband was still alive but what was inexplicable was that he had not aged a day. He seemed stuck at thirty-three, even his clothes were from a different era. He was wearing bell-bottoms – something no one would be seen dead in these days – a wide-collared, open-necked shirt like the one John Travolta wears in *Saturday Night Fever*, even his long hair and his sideburns were relics of a different age. For Emilia, on the other hand, time had passed as expected and now she was ashamed of her body. The dark circles under her eyes, the sagging muscles of her face were clearly those of a woman of sixty, whereas on Simón's face she couldn't see a single line or wrinkle. In the countless times she imagined finding him again, it had never occurred to her that age would be an issue. But the disparity between their ages now forced her to reconsider everything. What if Simón had remarried? It pained her even to think that he might be living with another woman. In all the years of waiting, she never doubted for an instant that her husband still loved her. He had probably had affairs – she could understand that – but after the hell they had endured together, never for a moment had she imagined that he might have replaced her. But things were different now. Now, he looked as though he could be her son.

She studied him more carefully. It frightened her how inconsistent this appearance was with reality. He looked half as old as the age – sixty-three – that surely appeared on his passport. She remembered a photograph of Julio Cortázar taken in Paris late in 1964, in which the writer – born at the beginning of the First World War – looked as though he might be his own son. Perhaps, like Cortázar, Simón had fine wrinkles visible only close up, but his comments, which she could hear, were defiantly youthful, even his voice sounded like that of a young man, as though time for him were an endless loop, a treadmill on which he could run and run without ageing a single day.

Emilia resigned herself to waiting. She opened the Somerset Maugham novel she had brought with her. As she tried to read, something curious happened. Coming to the end of a line, she would run into an invisible barrier which stopped her going on. Not because she found Maugham boring; on the contrary, she loved his writing. It was similar to an experience she had had watching *Death in Venice* on DVD. In an early scene, as Dirk Bogarde sits, troubled, on the Lido watching Tadzio emerge from the sea, the scene had cut back to the conversation in Russian – or was it German? – between the bathers and the strawberry sellers. At first, assuming the director was giving an object lesson in critical realism, deliberately repeating the holidaymakers' vulgarities, Emilia waited for the next scene only for the sequence of Tadzio emerging from the sea, shaking himself dry, to stubbornly reappear once more to the delicate strains of Mahler's Fifth. Two nights later, when she should already have returned the film, Emilia played the DVD again and this time was able to watch it through to its poignant conclusion. She was aware that age had made her more dull-witted, but it was something she felt sure she could rectify with a little more attention.

The voices of the strangers in the booth behind her were irritating. She wanted to concentrate on Simón's voice, anything that distracted from it seemed unbearable. In a restaurant where it was rare to hear anything other than a nasal New Jersey drawl, the strangers' approximate English was peppered with interjections and technical words in some Scandinavian language. They were talking about Microstation map-making software, a program also used at Hammond, where she worked. Unwittingly, one of the two began to recite the clichés every cartography student learned in their first lecture. 'Maps,' he said, 'are imperfect reproductions of reality, two-dimensional representations of what are in fact volumes, moving water, mountains shaped by erosion and rock falls. Maps are poorly written fictions,' he went on. 'Too much detail and no history whatever. Now, ancient maps were *real* maps: they created worlds out of nothing. What they didn't know, they imagined. Remember Bonsignori's map of Africa? The kingdoms of Canze, of Melina, of Zaflan – pure inventions. On Bonsignori's map, the Nile rose in Lake Zaflan, and so on. Rather than orienting explorers, it disoriented them.'

The conversation shifted from one subject to another, a ceaseless torrent of words. Emilia remembered Bonsignori's map. Was she imagining it, or had she seen it in Florence or in the Vatican? The voices of the two men grated on her nerves. She could not quite make out their words, they seemed to reach her ears tattered and ravelled. A sentence that seemed about to make sense was suddenly interrupted by the roar of a fire truck or the animal wail of a passing ambulance.

One of the strangers, a man with a hoarse, weary voice, suggested they stop beating about the bush and talk about the Kaffeklubben expedition. Kaffeklubben? thought Emilia. Are they crazy? That tiny godforsaken island to the north-east of Greenland, that Ultima Thule where all the winds of the world veer towards perdition? 'Let's try and organise the expedition as soon as possible,' the gravelly voice insisted. 'In Copenhagen people think there's another island even further north. And if it doesn't exist, there's nothing to stop us imagining it—'

'*Let's think more about that, let's think more,*' Simón interrupted them. Emilia started. Though she recognised his voice, there was little trace of the Simón she had known in these words. Here was a man who spoke English fluently, who articulated final consonants – *think, let's* – with an English diction beyond the scope of her husband, who could never even manage to read an instruction booklet in a foreign language.

What makes a person who he is? Not the music of his words nor his eloquence, not the lines of his body, nothing that is visible. This was a mistake she had made more than once, rushing down the street after some man who walked like Simón, who trailed a scent that reminded her of the nape of his neck, only to catch up with the man, to see his face and feel she had lost Simón all over again. Why can't two people be identical? Why do the dead not even realise they're dead? The Simón deep in conversation barely three feet from where she sat was exactly the same man as he had been thirty years ago, but not the man he had been ten minutes earlier. Something in him was changing so quickly she did not have time to catch up. Dear God, could he be slipping away from her again, or was it her? Was she losing him? Don't leave me again, Simón, *querido*. I won't leave your side. A person's true identity is his memories, she reassured herself. I remember all his yesterdays as though they were today, she said to herself, and everything he remembers about who I was is still a part of who he is. Remind him, draw him out, don't lose him.

Emilia got to her feet, walked over, stopped in front of him and looked into his eyes.

'*Querido, querido mío*, where have you been?'

Simón looked up; held her gaze, smiled, untroubled, unsurprised, said goodbye to the Scandinavians then turned again and looked at Emilia as though he had seen her only yesterday.

'We need to talk, don't we? Let's get out of here.'

He offered not a word of explanation, did not ask how she was, what she had been doing all these years. He was nothing like the polite, attentive Simón she had shared her life with long ago. Emilia paid for her brandy, slipped her arm through her husband's arm and they walked outside.

For years, everything Emilia did had been in preparation for the moment when she would see Simón again. She forced herself to keep fit, to be beautiful as she had never been. She went to the gym three times a week and her body was still limber, firm except around her waist and in her face where she had found it hard not to put on weight. Since moving to Highland Park, New Jersey, she had slipped into a regular routine, one that seemed sensible to her: the meals and showers taken at the same time every day, the patience with which the minutes came and went, just as love had come only to go again. Sometimes, at night, she dreamed of lost love. She

8

would have liked to stop such dreams, but there was nothing she could do about things that were not real. Before she went to sleep, she would say to herself: the only thing that matters is what is real.

At Hammond, she had forty minutes for lunch, though half an hour was usually more than enough. The other cartographers brought sandwiches and ate in the empty offices, amusing themselves toying with vectors, creating imaginary rivers that flowed down Central Park West, railway lines that ran along the New Jersey Turnpike between exits 13A and 15W. She watched them move their homes to distant locations, to the shores of temperate seas, because, if he chooses, a cartographer can distort the way of the world.

When she was twelve, she too had drawn relief maps of cities, adopting a bird's-eye view. Maps in which houses were flattened, the ground was level. She dreamed up Gothic cathedrals, cylindrical mountains with slopes sculpted by the wind into curves and arabesques. She transformed broad shopping streets into Venetian canals, with tiny bridges arching across the roofs; created unexpected deserts dotted with cacti in church gardens, deserts with no birds, no insects, only a deathly dust that desiccated the air. Maps had taught her to confound nature's logic, to create illusions here where reality seemed most unshakeable. Perhaps this was why, having hesitated between literature and architecture, when she finally got to university she had felt drawn to cartography, in spite of her difficulty understanding Rand McNally cylindrical projections and remote sensing using microwaves. As a student, she proved a skilled draughtswoman but a poor mathematician. It took her nine years to complete the course which Simón, whom she was to marry, finished in six.

9

She met Simón in a basement on the avenida Pueyrredón where Almendra, a local rock band, played their hits – 'Muchacha ojos de papel', 'Ana no duerme', 'Plegaria para un niño dormido' – to their adoring fans. The moment Emilia's fingers brushed Simón's by chance, she sensed that she would never need any other man in her life since all men were contained within him, though she did not even know his name, did not know if she would ever see him again. This chance brush of fingers signified warmth, completeness, contentment, the sense of having felt a thousand times what she was actually feeling for the first time. On this stranger's body was written the map of her life, a representation of the universe just as it was set down in a Taoist encyclopedia two centuries before Christ. 'The curve of his head is the vault of heaven, his delicate feet are the lowest earth; his hair, the stars; his eyes, the sun and moon; his eyebrows Ursa Major; his nose is like unto a mountain; his four limbs are the seasons; his five organs, the five elements.'

After they left the gig, they wandered the streets of Buenos Aires aimlessly. Simón took her hand so naturally that it was as though he had always known her. They arrived, exhausted, at a bar only to find it was closing up and it took them a long time to find another one. Emilia phoned her mother a couple of times to tell her not to worry. They were unsurprised to find they were both studying cartography and that both thought of maps not as a means of making a living but as codes which allowed them to recognise objects by means of symbols. It was a rare thing in young people, and they were barely twenty-five, but they were at an age when they did not want to be like others and were astonished to discover they were like each other. They were also surprised to discover that even when they said nothing, each could guess the other's thoughts. Though Emilia had nothing to hide, she felt embarrassed at the idea of talking about herself. How could she explain she was still a virgin? Most of her friends were already married with children. There had been boys at school who had fallen for her, two or three had kissed her, fondled her breasts, but as soon as they had wanted to take things further, she had always immediately found something that repelled her: bad breath, acne, greasy hair. Simón, on the other hand, felt like an extension of her own body. Already, on that first night, she would have felt comfortable undressing in front of him, sleeping with him if he had asked. The thought did not even seem to have occurred to him. He was interested in her for what she said, for who she was, though she had barely told him anything about herself. He seemed eager to talk. He had dated a couple of girls in his teens, mostly because he felt that he should. He had not made them happy, nor had he been happy until, three years earlier, he had found a love he had thought would last forever.

'We met the same way you and I met,' he said. 'We were at an Almendra concert in the Parque Centenario, and when Spinetta sang "Muchacha ojos de papel", I gazed into her eyes and sang the chorus to her: "*Don't run any more, stay here until dawn.*"'

'You should always use that as a chat-up line.'

'Over time the song lost its charm; these days I think it sounds corny. But it worked with her. Everything between us was perfect until we decided to move in together. We'd been thinking about it for months. It would have saved us both a lot of money.'

'You didn't want to do it just to save money.'

'Of course not. We were soulmates, at least that's what I thought. We were working in the same office, drawing maps and illustrations for newspapers. Graphic artists were pretty well paid at the time. My family lived in Gálvez, a little town between Santa Fe and Rosario, and hers were from Rawson in Patagonia, so we were both alone here in Buenos Aires. Neither of us had many friends. Then one day her father called and asked her to come home. Her older sister had cancer – Hodgkin's lymphoma – and she'd had a relapse. She was weak from the chemotherapy and needed someone to look after her. I went to the bus station with her; she cried on my shoulder right up to the minute she had to get on the bus. I cried too. She promised she'd call as soon as she arrived, said she'd be back in two or three weeks, as soon as her sister's course of chemotherapy was finished. I felt devastated, it was like my whole world had crumbled. She didn't call the next day, I waited a whole month and she didn't call. I was desperate to see her, but I didn't know what to do. Back then, Rawson seemed so remote it might as well have been on another planet. I couldn't bear to be alone in my tiny apartment. I spent most of the time wandering the streets, reading in cafes, walking until I was exhausted. All this was during the first weeks after Péron came back from his long exile; there were marches and demonstrations all the time. I got so depressed that, when the cafes closed, I didn't know what to do. I was so preoccupied I started making mistakes at work. They would probably have fired me, but there was nobody else in the graphics department. In the end, I couldn't bear the silence any longer so I went to the telephone exchange on the corner of Corrientes and Maipu intending to call every single family in Rawson with her surname. As it turned out there were only six, but none of them had ever heard of her. This seemed weird, because Rawson is a small town, and everyone pretty much knows everyone else. I waited another month, but still there was nothing: no letters, no messages, nothing. In the end, I decided to ask for time off work to go to Patagonia. I figured that once I got to Rawson I'd have no trouble finding her. I took the bus – a twenty-hour journey along a flat deserted road that somehow seemed to symbolise my fate. The minute I arrived, I started searching for her. I went to the hospitals, talked to oncologists, checked the lists of patients who had died recently. No one knew anything.'

'It breaks my heart just listening to you,' Emilia said.

'That's not the worst. Every night I'd tour the bars, I'd go in, sit down, order a beer and play "Muchacha ojos de papel" endlessly on the jukebox in the hope that the song would make her appear. One night, I told the whole story to the guy behind the bar, I showed him the photo of her I kept in my wallet. I think I saw her in Trelew, he said. Why don't you try there? Trelew was a slightly bigger town about fourteen kilometres west and the people there seemed more wary. I visited all the places I had in Rawson, but this time I also asked in the prisons. I don't know how many times I made that tour in every town in the surrounding area, in Gaiman, Dolavon, Puerto Madryn. When I got back to Buenos Aires, I was sure that she'd be there, waiting for me. I never saw her again.'

'You're still waiting for her.'

'Not any more. There comes a moment when you finally resign yourself to losing what you've already lost. You feel as though it's slipping through your fingers, falling out of your life, you feel nothing will ever be the same again. I still think of her, obviously, but I don't wake up in the middle of the night any more, worrying that she's lying somewhere ill, or dead. Sometimes I wonder if she really existed. I know I didn't dream her. I still have a blouse of hers, a pair of shoes, a make-up bag, two of her books. Her name was Emilia too.'

Emilia and Simón were married two years later. Simón gave up working for the newspapers and joined the map-making department at the Argentina Automobile Club where Emilia had been working for some months. They were happy, and happiness was exactly as she had imagined it would be. They talked easily about things that would have made other couples uncomfortable, and upon this mutual trust they built their home life. If she did not discover the same intense pleasure in sex she had heard her friends talk about, she said nothing, assuming that this too would come in time.

Only after Simón disappeared on a trip to Tucumán did she begin to feel racked with guilt that she had not made him happy. She felt painfully jealous of the other Emilia, for whom Simón was perhaps still searching. There were nights when she woke up with the feeling that her husband's whole body was inside her, sounding her deepest depths, until it reached her throat. It was a pleasure so physical it made her weep. She would get up, take a shower, but when she went back to bed the spectre of the beloved body was still there, emblazoned within her.

Finding him again thirty years later unsettled her. In the past, when she had still been searching for him, she imagined that when she found him, they would quickly slip back into their old routine and carry on with their lives as though nothing had happened. But now, a sort of abyss separated them, a chasm made deeper by the fact that Simón had not aged a single day while she bore the full weight of her sixty years.

Emilia had felt no sense of foreboding when she got up that morning. She liked to lie in bed, to stretch languidly, to linger for a while before heading out to work. It was the best part of the day. After she showered, she would carefully apply her make-up, despite knowing that she was doing it for no one. As the day wore on, the lipstick would fade, the mascara fall from her lashes in tiny flecks. At least once a week she went to a beauty salon to have a new set of sculptured nails applied. She had replaced the previous nails – an orange and violet mosaic pattern – two days earlier and the new ones had a delicate pattern of blue wavy lines. She always breakfasted on toast and coffee, glanced at the headlines in the *Home News*. Her only friend was Nancy Frears, a librarian at Highland Park. Chela, her younger sister, lived in San Antonio, Texas, with her husband and their three children, and though they called each other on birthdays and at Thanksgiving, they hadn't seen each other for years. A couple of summers earlier, when Emilia had had her hernia operation, it had been Nancy, not Chela, who stayed with her, helped her shower, tidied the apartment. She could, of course, have found friends who shared similar interests, but she was loath to change the life she lived. A couple of geographers from Rutgers University she sometimes ran into on the train she took to Manhattan had invited her to go to the movies or to dinner. She enjoyed chatting with them on the train, but did not want to take the friendship further. To Emilia, sharing a movie with someone was like sharing a bed. In cinemas, people cry, they sigh, they reveal the flayed flesh of their emotions. She had no desire to be on such intimate terms with the geographers from Rutgers. With Nancy, on the other hand, she didn't mind. Nancy's friendship was like a cat or a comfortable eiderdown. Besides, for Nancy, Emilia represented a pinnacle of refinement she could never attain; when they were together she constantly felt she was learning something new, even when Emilia read her poems she did not understand or took her to little art-house cinemas to see classic Mizoguchi films.

Nancy's favourite quotation was a line from Ezra Pound she had chanced upon in the library. She was drawn to the hidden meaning she sensed in the cadence of the line: *How 'came I in'? Was I not thee and Thee?* It had a mysterious lilt; she asked Emilia to help her decipher it, and without even changing the order of the words, they managed to shed some light on it. 'What is it about this line you find so moving?' Emilia wanted to know. 'What is unsaid, but hinted at in the folds between the words.' Sometimes her friend was not so stupid.

Nancy had survived a stultifying marriage. Sid Frears, her late husband, had been a travelling salesman selling synthetic adhesive who left her alone for months at a time. After fifteen years of marriage, pancreatic cancer had carried him off. Nancy had not the slightest interest in changing her life. Sid's life insurance policy, invested at a fixed interest during the boom years, ensured her an annual income of $22,000. She decided she did not need to work. Her only work was voluntary: from 9 a.m. to 3 p.m. on Saturdays, and 10 a.m. to 4 p.m. on Tuesdays and Thursdays, she worked at the library. 'What would I want to go out to work for?' she said. 'So I don't feel alone? I'm not that kind of person, Millie. I like my own company. I read *People* magazine every week, I listen to the Beach Boys, and if I want to fart, I fart. There's no one to complain.'

More than once, Emilia caught her staring at the photo of Simón on her beside table. Comparing him to Sid and shaking her head. 'You had a good thing going there, huh, Millie? Was he good in bed?' Emilia would have liked to tell her that sex with Simón in her imagination was better than it had been in reality, but this was something she would tell no one, something she did not dare admit even to herself. Sometimes, when they got back from bingo, Nancy would gaze at Simón's broad forehead, his pale, honest eyes, his firm nose.

'He looks just like Clint Eastwood in *Dirty Harry*, don't you think, hon? If he hadn't died, he'd look like Clint in *The Bridges of Madison County* now.'

On the Friday when Emilia met Simón at Trudy Tuesday, she had left home at 7 a.m. as she did every morning. It took her forty minutes to drive from her apartment on North 4th Avenue to the Hammond offices in Springfield industrial park. She worried about avoiding the inevitable accidents on Garden State Parkway, the storms that could break suddenly over a two-mile area while in the distance the sun was still shining. Like a taxi driver, she drove with the radio tuned to 1010 AM, which kept her up to date on traffic tailbacks.

The suburbs were endless, indistinguishable, and if, as she sometimes did, she allowed her mind to wander she would somehow end up driving through a strip mall with branches of Wal-Mart, Pep Boys, Pathmark and Verizon Wireless laid out in an arc, beneath louring skies of identical clouds with identical squawking birds. Only the leaves of the walnut trees showed any imagination, distinguishing themselves in autumn as they fell.

Sometimes at the office, as her screen glowed with the colours of maps, print priorities and legends, Emilia would sit daydreaming about Simón whom she had not seen die. The death of a loved one is devastating. How much more devastating, then, was the death of someone you could not be sure was dead? How can you lose something not yet found? Emilia had seen the glimmer of an answer in a poem by Idea Vilariño dedicated to the man who abandoned her: *I am no more than I now / forever, and you / now / to me / no more than you. Now you are not / and some day soon / I won't know where you live / with whom / or whether you remember / You will never hold me / as you did that night / never / I will never touch you / I will not see you die.*

Some years previously, someone had told her about a group of geographers who spent their winters in Nuuk, Greenland, mapping the effects of global warming and she had imagined Simón was on that expedition. It was a foolish fantasy, but for a few months, it had been a consolation. In the notebook where she jotted down her feelings, she wrote something that still pained her today: 'If he came back, I would be able to see him die.'

During the Trial of the Juntas against the military leaders of the dictatorship, three separate witnesses claimed to have seen Simón's body in the courtyard of a police station in Tucumán, his body showing clear signs of having been tortured, a bullet hole between his eyes. Emilia was in Caracas during the trials and did not know whether to believe the story or not. The witnesses seemed genuine, but their testimonies differed. She had been with her husband when he was arrested, her own testimony would have been very different from theirs: they had been arrested by mistake and released two days later, Simón a couple of hours before Emilia. She had seen Simón's signature in the prison register indicating that he had left. Her father, Dr Orestes Dupuy, had checked the fact with the military governor himself.

To Emilia, her version was an indisputable fact. It was because she believed it that she did not set foot outside their San Telmo apartment in Buenos Aires for months, waiting for her husband to come home, waiting for him to call. She felt a terrible emptiness, spent the days staring out the window as the hours passed, learning by heart the relief map of the buildings, the shapes of the people moving behind their curtains. Her father had tried to persuade her to move back to the family home, but Emilia wanted things to be exactly as they had been when Simón was there. Every morning, she went to work at the Argentina Automobile Club, every evening when she came home, she made dinner, never forgetting to set two places at the table.

From time to time, she got distressing letters from people who claimed to have seen Simón on a street in Bogotá or Mexico City and demanded money in return for more information. There were phone calls, too, from people who told her that Simón was dead. These contradictory stories left her unable to sleep. She was still hopelessly in love and, what was worse, she realised it was a love that had no purpose, no object. Almost a year after Simón's disappearance, by which time his name was barely mentioned, Emilia decided to distract herself and after much hesitation went to the Cine Iguazú to see Ettore Scola's *A Special Day*, a film about a mother of six living in a seedy tenement building and her neighbour, a homosexual radio announcer, who care for each other as best they can while all the other tenants have left to go and take part in the parade to honour Hitler's visit to Rome in 1935. The film had been running for about an hour when the air conditioning cut out. The afternoon was so humid that now the images were shrouded in a vapour that made them seem unreal. The air in the cinema became unbreathable, there was a sound of whistling, of feet stamping. Some of the audience got up and left. A woman who seemed to have just arrived came over and sat in the seat next to Emilia so abruptly she knocked over her handbag. As Emilia leaned down to pick it up, the woman hissed: 'They murdered your husband in Tucumán just like they did mine. My husband died under torture. Yours got five bullets in his chest and one between the eyes to finish him off. We can't go on like this, like nothing's happened.' 'I don't believe you,' Emilia said. 'You're just a subversive.' 'I'm doing you a favour,' the woman insisted, 'I'm not asking you to do anything. In this country, we're all dead already.' At that moment, the house lights went out again, the air conditioning came on and the film started up. Somebody in the row behind them whistled. The woman got up and was lost in the darkness, Emilia moved to another seat where she sat, her whole body rigid, until the film was over.

More than once she had heard people tell her father that political subversives – who had been all but wiped out – were prepared to tell people anything they wanted to hear if they thought they could win them over to the cause. Obviously, this woman was one of them and, although Emilia dismissed what she had said as lies, she was haunted for a long time by the image of Simón's body lying broken in a courtyard like a dog. She couldn't stop herself picturing him lying with a bullet hole in his head, black with flies and with soot from the chimneys of the local sugar mills. The image went with her everywhere, as though her whole being was subsumed within this dead man whom no one had mourned, no one had buried. But she remained convinced Simón was still alive. Maybe he had lost his memory, maybe he was in a hospital and unable to get in touch.

Three days later, she was woken by the telephone.

'It's Ema,' said a distorted voice.

'Ema who?'

'Ema, the woman from the cinema.'

'Oh, you,' Emilia managed to say. 'Those things you said, they're not true. I read the police report again. My father checked the facts himself.'

The voice on the other end of the line suddenly became bitter, mocking.

'And you believe your old man? If he had his way, we'd never get out of this ocean of shit. There are thousands of women like you and me. Husbands who have disappeared, sons who never came back. We've lost so many . . .'

'Simón is alive. We're not involved in anything, so there's no reason for them to do anything to us. I haven't lost anyone.'

'Oh, but you have. And you'll spend the rest of your life wondering why your husband never came back. And when you finally accept the fact that he's dead, you'll still wonder where they buried him. I would give anything just to be able to kiss my husband's bones.'

Trembling, Emilia put down the phone. She didn't know what to think. A few days earlier, taking the bus home, some woman had dropped a leaflet into her lap. As the woman had looked like a beggar Emilia paid no attention. She was about to give back the flyer when the woman got off the bus and disappeared into the crowd. Absent-mindedly, Emilia read a paragraph: 'Between 1,500 and 3,000 people have been massacred in secret since the passing of the law forbidding the reporting on bodies being discovered.' It was lies. All the newspapers said the *exiliados* were telling lies about the country. The flyer was proof. She ripped it in two and threw it on the ground.

At work that morning, in the mapping department of the Argentina Automobile Club, she was overcome by an intense feeling of unease. She hated this Ema. *Your father is a shit.* How could this woman say such things? No one questioned the integrity of Dr Dupuy. On his deathbed General Perón himself had heaped praise on him: 'Read Dupuy,' he had said. 'He has written the most accurate analysis of my actions in government. And not just mine: he has proved himself the finest analyst of all governments.'

Since 1955, her father had been publishing *La República*, a privately circulated magazine keenly read by people of influence. Every word came from reliable sources; it was an invaluable guide to protecting one's assets from the constant devaluations of the peso, for anticipating the rate of inflation. The financial pages of the international press agreed. 'Only sound business deals come from the pages of *La República*.' Not only did *La República* announce forthcoming military coups, it fanned the flames that fostered them. Dupuy personally wrote the editorials linking decadence to democracy and extolling the spirit of the nation. His editorials never explained whether the 'spirit of the nation' changed, whether it was immutable, or what it consisted of. The 'spirit of the nation' was handed down unchanged from one government to the next.

In the family mansion on calle Arenales where Emilia was born, her father had been an imposing figure who rarely

22

addressed himself to her or her sister Chela. He would ruffle their hair, ask how things were going at school and, sometimes, if they were sick, would suddenly appear to talk to the doctors. Next to him, their mother seemed like a little girl.

In late March 1976, Emilia was drawing a map of the San Rafael glacier when she heard on the radio that the new military junta was planning to rebuild the country, reform the economy and – obviously – safeguard the spirit of the nation. The new junta announced all-out war on left-wing subversives and all those who refused to conform. Argentina had to be of one mind. There was no room for dissenters, for the half-hearted, for anyone who was seen to be different.

Three nights before what was called 'the revolution', Emilia had gone to her father's study to take him the guest list for her wedding. Dupuy had asked her to take his waste-paper basket, empty it into the furnace and make sure everything was reduced to ashes. Stuck to the bottom of the bin was a page of handwritten notes. As she peeled it away, Emilia read the first lines: 'What would Argentina be without the sword, without the cross? Who would wish to go down in history as the man who deprived the spirit of the nation of one of these twin bulwarks?' When she went back with the waste-paper bin, Emilia gave him back the page she had rescued from the flames.

'Forget you ever saw this,' her father warned, not bothering to look up.

'I thought the bit about the spirit of the nation was nice.'

'Nice? Don't talk such drivel. These are grave, important matters. The spirit of the nation is at stake and it can only be saved by force of arms. This country is Catholic and military. It is Western and white. Those who forget that "and" do not understand anything.' He gave a dismissive wave. 'You clearly don't understand anything. You'd do better to concentrate on your duties as a wife.'

Emilia and Simón were married in the church of Nuestra Señora del Carmen on April 24, one month after the coup d'état. The time of the ceremony was twice changed to foil any possible terrorist attack. Rather than entering by the main doors of the church and walking up the aisle, Emilia emerged from the sacristy on her father's arm. In the front pew Simón's two sisters, who had come up from Gálvez that morning, were wearing very low-cut purple-sequinned dresses, stilettos and pink hats. They wagged their heads like partridges, proud of their ample cleavage. They licked their thumbs and index fingers before making the sign of the cross, droning *amen, amen*, louder than the priest himself.

When they came up to congratulate their brother after the ceremony, Simón told them how happy he was they'd come and asked them not to leave, but afraid they might miss their bus, they dashed off, carrying their hats and their shoes in either hand. Emilia and Simón did not stay long at the intimate reception thrown by the Dupuys either. They had been loaned an apartment in Palermo with balconies looking out over the forest. There was a fire burning in the grate and a record player with Beatles and Sui Generis LPs. Emilia loved 'Michelle' and asked Simón to play it over and over.

When they lay stretched out in front of the fire and Simón kissed her throat, his fingertips searching for her breasts, she froze. Her blouse was damp with cold sweat. Until recently, she had abandoned herself to his embrace, pushed his hands into her pants so Simón could feel her wet desire. At such times it seemed to her that those lips too

24

could speak, as though her whole body could talk dirty, but on her wedding night, her vagina remained closed, her thighs as rigid as glass rods.

'Don't be nervous. It doesn't matter,' Simón said. 'Let's just lie here and listen to the music. The apartment's got three bedrooms. If you'd rather be alone, we can sleep in separate beds. It's just one night. We've got the rest of our lives together.'

'I'd like to listen to "Michelle" again,' said Emilia. 'I'm fine. It's just nerves. I'll get over it. I'm nervous because I love you so much.'

In the years that followed, Emilia would remember that duplicitous sentence many times. Couples regularly say things to each other that are hypocritical or clichéd. Though it was true that as she said the words she did love Simón, her love felt irrelevant. Her overriding feeling was one of uncertainty, as though the whole world were drawing away from her, as though nothing – no substance, no smell, no scene – would ever be as it had been before.

'Actually, let's not listen to "Michelle" again,' she said, 'it makes me sad.'

'Are you sad?'

'No, what makes you think that? It's the song that's sad.'

There was a comedy on television. Simón said maybe if they took their minds off things, focused on something else, they might get back to the way they felt before they were married. Might even forget that they were alone. He turned off the music and turned on the television. On the screen, a pale comedian was sitting on the floor of a cage on a pile of straw, wearing a black leotard through which his pitifully thin chest and his protruding ribs were clearly visible. From nearby cages came wild shrieks and roars. The comedian was obviously the only visible exhibit in a zoo – and clearly the least interesting, since people sneered, walked past his cage not even stopping to look at him, eager to see the lions or the monkeys. As the cage grew dark and light again, the sign outside changed to indicate the number of days the man had been fasting: *35 days, 40 days*, and so on.

Simón explained to Emilia that this was a comic version of Kafka's short story 'A Hunger Artist'. Every time the lights came up, fewer and fewer people stopped to look at the hunger artist. Visitors walked straight past his enclosure to look at the animals on either side. 'Let me out of here!' the actor screamed. 'Stop torturing me!' The screen faded to black and the words '*62 days later*' appeared to the sound of canned laughter. Simón, who remembered the story, told Emilia that in Kafka's version, the artist is proud of his record-breaking fasts and his main reason for staying in the cage is that he does not really like eating. Curiously, this version was even more Kafkaesque. On day 73, a guard came over and peered into the cage, poking the damp pile of straw with a stick looking for the comedian. Unable to see him, the attendant pressed his ear to the cage. A childlike, almost inaudible voice from the straw screamed, 'Get me out of here! I'm disappearing!' There was another burst of canned laughter. Eventually, a truck pulled up towing a wagon in which a restless panther was prowling. 'There's an empty cage here,' the driver says. 'Get it cleaned out, we've got a panther we need to house.' Some people in the audience started shouting, 'You can't put a panther in that cage! There's a starving man in there!' while others yelled, 'Go on, put him in the cage! Let him eat the bastard!' Hands on his hips, the truck driver said, 'Where is this hunger artist then? I want to see him!' He threw open the cage, took a pitchfork and began sifting through the straw on the dirty floor. The camera zoomed in on a tiny heap of straw and the actor appeared, no bigger than an ant, screaming, 'Don't stamp on me!' his voice so shrill, so faint, that only the microphone could pick it up. 'Don't trample me! I'm one of the disappeared!' The sketch ended with a close-up of the sole of a shoe hovering menacingly over the actor as the audience applauded, roaring with laughter.

The sketch left them feeling even more depressed. They decided to sleep in separate rooms and kissed each other good-night without passion. In the morning they were due to take the 10 a.m. flight to Recife for a two-week cruise down the Brazilian coast – a wedding present from Emilia's father.

They had been on the cruise for several days when, over breakfast, they heard that the actor in the sketch had issued an unqualified apology to the viewers and the authorities. 'Sometimes my jokes are in bad taste,' he said, 'and this time I have stupidly contributed to the campaign of vilification against our country. I am unworthy to live among you. The people of Argentina are a peaceful people, and I failed to respect that peace. To joke about the disappeared is to play into the hands of the subversives.' One of the ship's officers, who had seen the apology on television, mentioned it over breakfast. 'The poor bastard had circles under his eyes so black that they looked like they were painted on,' he said. '*Hijo de puta*,' commented a deeply tanned older woman sitting next to Emilia. 'People like that don't deserve to live. If I were a man, I'd kill every last one of them.' Everyone went on eating breakfast in silence.

The inchoate love Emilia had felt on her wedding night cured itself the following day in the narrow uncomfortable berth of the cruise ship put out of Recife. When Simón's hand brushed her belly as he stowed the luggage, she felt a smouldering desire she had kept buried deep inside her ever since she had her first period. Now, finally, she could satisfy it without virginal coyness or Catholic guilt. She fell back on the berth and begged Simón to rid her once and for all of her cursed hymen. But Simón did not feel the same urgency. He wanted to prolong the moment, to separate it into languid fragments of desire, to enter Emilia's body with his every sense. 'Let's take it gently, *amor*,' he said. 'It's your first time.' She was impatient and couldn't understand why her husband wanted to delay the moment of penetration. 'No, not gently, do it now,' she urged him. Was this Christian? She wanted nothing in that moment as much as she wanted to be hurt, defiled, broken. When she had been a little girl of seven or eight, the family cook had explained to her that losing her virginity would be like dying. That the pain she felt would be the same pain she would feel when she died, but that with it would come all of God's pleasures.

She allowed Simón to undress her; to discover for the first time the pinkish birthmark, round as a ten centavo coin, on her right buttock; to linger over the small folds of cellulite that had appeared on one of her thighs – while still she was a virgin, she had thought to herself, a twenty-nine-year-old virgin with cellulite – to trace with his tongue the almost invisible line of hair that ran from her navel to the centre of her being. Her eyes were closed when he, now naked, parted her lips with his tongue and mingled his saliva with hers. Feeling his gentleness, smelling his scent, Emilia's heart began to race, she had never felt it pound so hard, she didn't think it could take much more, but it was beating harder still when Simón slipped his tongue between her thighs.

'Don't . . .' she said. 'It's salty.' He looked up from between her legs and smiled. 'How do you know it's salty?' Then, without waiting for an answer, he buried himself in her depths until her inner labia gripped him. 'Now, please . . .' Emilia whimpered. 'Give it to me now, please.' Simón penetrated her gently, moving towards her hymen, more gently than she had imagined. She heard a brief moan and then the surge of his ejaculation overcame him.

'I'm sorry,' he said. 'I wanted it to last a lifetime.'

'It doesn't matter,' she reassured him. 'We can do it again in a little while.'

'I've hurt you. You're bleeding.'

'Good . . . I'm supposed to bleed. I won't even feel it tomorrow. And besides, like you said, we've got our whole lives together.'

After a while, Emilia shifted towards him, kissed his throat, behind his ear. Without saying a word, she took his penis and stroked it delicately.

'I can't,' Simón said. 'It's got a life of its own, this thing. Sometimes it stays limp like that for hours.'

'It's OK, it's OK, don't think about it. You can do it.'

Simón rummaged in a suitcase, took out a cassette deck and pressed Play. From the machine, in spite of the poor quality of the recording, came a sequence of simple piano chords of extraordinary purity, music that sounded like nothing else in the world.

'When I'm alone, Keith Jarrett's improvisations get me excited. With you, they'll get me even more excited.'

'It's beautiful,' Emilia smiled. 'You're saying he's improvising this?'

'From beginning to end.'

'It's so perfect. He must have the whole melody memorised.'

'No. This is Jarrett's great discovery. He turned up at the Köln Opera House without the faintest idea of what he was going to play. He was tired, he'd spent a whole week playing concerts and he was surprised to find that the music came to him in waves. Before that night, he was a great jazz pianist, but that night he created a genre all his own. His music is a constant, an absolute. The coughing from the audience, the creak of the piano, nothing is prepared. Maybe Bach or Mozart created galaxies like this, improvised harmonies that drift now through the darkness of time, but none of them have survived. That night at the Köln Opera House can never be repeated. Jarrett himself couldn't do it. It's an evanescent concerto, born to live and die in that very moment. It will become a commonplace, a cliché, to be listened to by lovers like us, but the human race will go on needing it.'

They lay back on the berth. After seven minutes, Jarrett began to moan as though fucking his instrument. Simón's penis remained inert.

'Let me hold you,' Emilia said.

She went on stroking him with one hand while slowly caressing herself with the other. After a moment, his moan joined Jarrett's.

After the phone call from the woman from the cinema, Emilia spent the morning wondering what to do. She could barely bring herself to concentrate on the maps which she was supposed to be working on, converting them from 1:450,000,000 scale to 1:450,000. She longed to talk to her father, but she was afraid of how he might react. He had become increasingly volatile and unpredictable. That afternoon, in the family home on calle Arenales, she finally confided in Chela. As always, her sister told her mother, who told Dupuy, who came to see her some two hours later trembling and angrier than she had ever seen him. He stood, glaring at Emilia.

'How can you be so naive? Don't you understand that we are at war? That your family could be attacked by subversives at any moment? You should have told me what happened in the cinema the moment it happened. You have no right to make a fool of me in front of my friends. I won't tolerate such behaviour.'

'What did I do? So, I didn't mention it for a couple of days. I'm not psychic. I don't know what's going on.'

'No, and you don't know how to look after yourself either. It was a trap. They were trying to get information out of you, trying to inveigle their way into this house. They want to blow our brains out, all of us.'

'So what am I supposed to do if this woman calls again?'

'She won't. She was picked up in a cafe near your place. She'd been spying on you, she was armed. A patrol surrounded her and when they told her to surrender her weapon, she tried to resist. They tried to stop her, but she shot herself.'

Two months after seizing power, the president came to her parents' house for dinner. He was accompanied by his wife, her stiff, swollen legs covered by a long skirt, and by the chaplain of the Military Vicariate. Since Emilia was his eldest daughter and had just come back from her honeymoon, Dr Dupuy condescended to invite her on the condition that she and her husband refrain from making any political comments. This peremptory command unsettled Simón who did not want to go. Outside the family house was a confusion of cars and soldiers in service uniforms.

It was a warm night in mid-May and the president, invariably described by the newspapers as ascetic, seemed exultant, almost triumphant. He greeted Emilia with a dispassionate kiss on the cheek, offered his hand for Simón to shake without looking at him, all the while relating the successes of the day. When he spoke, he enunciated each syllable as though mistrustful of his listeners' intelligence. From time to time, he gave Dupuy a sidelong glance and the doctor nodded his approval. Except for photos from the 1930s, Emilia had never seen a man wear his hair so plastered down with hair cream. The monsignor flirted with Simón. As he expounded on the meaning of the symbols on the golden chasuble he was to wear for the first time for the Corpus Christi procession, he toyed with the crucifix pinned to his chest. His shrill, bird-like voice was remarkable and he fell silent only when the president began to explain how, in less than two months, the government had managed to reduce inflation by more than 20 per cent.

'The National Reorganisation policies are beginning to take effect,' he said with the punctiliousness of a teacher. 'We have managed to keep salaries under control and the union protests are over—'

'Not before time,' the president's wife interrupted. 'Troublemakers and drunks, the lot of them. The minute they got their wages, they'd spent their last centavo in the bars. Well, now they'll learn what it means to behave decently.'

'Praised be the Lord,' said the chaplain.

The champagne moved the conversation on to subjects more likely to appeal to the ladies. All of them, including Emilia, used the same perfume, Madame Rochas, as though it were a sign of distinction. Chela and her mother discussed whether Lancôme creams were better than Revlon. The president's wife settled the matter.

'I've always favoured Lancôme,' she said, 'from the very first time I used it. I wouldn't use anything else now.'

'Why do any of you need to use creams at all?' the chaplain interjected. 'You all have such wonderful complexions.'

Ethel, the mother, smiled appreciatively. 'It's quite clear, Monsignor, that you are interested only in spiritual beauty. We women are forced to make do with what scant beauty God has blessed us with.'

'I have friends who went to Europe who told me that they have fabulous creams over there that we've never even heard of,' said Chela.

'They'll get here. Everything in its own time, *niña*,' said the president. 'Argentina used to be cut off from the world but we're going to open the doors to imports so that our industries learn to compete.'

'I'd really like to visit Europe,' said Chela.

'Who wouldn't?' the president's wife sighed. 'My dream is to meet the Holy Father; every day, he grows more like Pius XII. He has such a gentle, such an aristocratic manner about him, and such strength of character.'

The monsignor brought his hands together and raised his eyes to heaven.

'The Lord never fails those who love Him. Your dream will come true sooner than you think; plans for just such a trip are already well advanced.'

'Every night, I pray to God to keep the Holy Father healthy. Once we've dealt with the extremists, the first thing we'll do is go to Rome to give thanks. But just now we can't go anywhere. We have to look after our home.'

Dinner was served and the monsignor, seated at the head of the table, said grace. He prayed for a swift victory for the nation's armies and, his beatific smile almost caressing the president, intoned: 'Through me, and through the arm of our *comandante* Our Lord Jesus Christ, bless the process of national purification which makes it possible for us to eat in peace.'

'Amen,' said the president. He lifted his untouched glass of champagne. Everyone else did likewise. 'To peace.'

For a while, no one spoke. The president's wife praised the asparagus soufflé and the spider crab which Dr Dupuy had had shipped all the way from Tierra del Fuego. The chaplain accepted a second helping and, eyes half closed, savoured the food.

'Congratulations, my dear doctor. This is delicious.'

Dupuy accepted the compliment with a chilly smile and turned to the president.

'Did you have a good day, señor?'

He made a small gesture which the waiters immediately understood. They were to serve another round of Dom Perignon. Though in private, Dupuy addressed the president informally, he was careful to observe protocol when others were present. Behind the president's display of strength, he knew, the man was sensitive and insecure.

'I can't complain. I spent the morning addressing the World Advertising Congress and I've rarely heard such an ovation. The business community is thrilled by what's happening here. They say that in a couple of months we've managed to get the subversives on the ropes. We've flushed the rats from their nests. We inherited a country in chaos, now we live in an orderly society.'

Ethel felt compelled to intervene.

'Every night I prayed to God that you and your men would take power quickly. The Argentinian people were horrified to see the country in the clutches of that brainless burlesque dancer. We were afraid that by the time you came to power, the country would be in ruins. I've been terribly impressed by how quickly you've restored order. Even Borges – a man of few words – said how proud he is of the army that saved the country from Communism. I heard him on the radio only a couple of hours ago.'

'Ah, yes. I had lunch with Borges and a number of the intelligentsia. My advisers invited them so we could discuss cultural matters. Only one of them proved intractable – though it was the one person we least expected – a priest, a certain Father Leonardo Castellani.'

'I thought he was dead,' said Dupuy. 'He must be at least eighty.'

'Seventy-seven I was told. I see you know the man.'

'Not really. I've read some of his writings. He translated a section of St Thomas Aquinas' *Summa Theologica* and wrote a number of rather good crime novels. He was told that the Jesuits would punish him and indeed he was expelled from the order and sent into reclusion in a monastery in Spain. It was only a few years ago that the Vatican permitted him to say Mass again.'

The president had barely touched his food. He was so thin, the other *comandantes* called him the Eel. It was a nickname that did not displease him. Even as a young cadet, he had been slippery, cold, inscrutable. Though he had not sought it, he had accepted the highest office in the land for the sake of the military. Even now, at the height of his power, he was still an eel, noted for his secrecy, his cunning, his good luck.

'I had no idea the priest would prove so turbulent. I shall have to rebuke my advisers for inviting him. From the moment I saw him, he did not strike me as a man of God. He has a glass eye. A frozen, cadaverous eye. Over dessert, he had the gall to suggest that I release a former student of his from prison, someone named Conti. He ranted and raved like a man possessed.'

'He always was possessed,' Dupuy offered.

'He started shouting that this student of his was a great writer who had been tortured half to death after his arrest.'

'My God. What did you tell him?' This from the wife with the swollen legs.

'I told him the truth. I told him my government is at war against Communist subversives, but it does not resort to torture or to murder. Professor Addolorato, who was sitting on my right, managed to save the day. "How could you even think of bringing such an outlandish accusation to this table, Father?" he said.'

'Addolorato is a fine man,' his wife agreed.

'You don't know how grateful I am to him. The priest was about to launch into another diatribe, but Addolorato told him to calm down. "We are all living through troubled times," he said, "let's not distract the president with such trifling matters." '

Simón stopped eating and, for the first time, joined in the conversation. Dupuy and Ethel were afraid he would say something rash. And indeed he did.

'Torture, *comandante*, is not a trifling matter, regardless of the ends for which it is employed.'

The president twisted his mouth into an expression of disgust, but it was Dupuy who reprimanded him.

'This is none of your business, Simón.'

'This is everyone's business. I can't be expected to hold my tongue when a crime is being committed.'

'Calm down, *hijo*.'

The monsignor raised the index and middle fingers of his right hand as though exorcising Simón. 'There are things which, though they may seem like crimes, are actually simple justice. You need to understand. The momentary pain of one man, one sinner, can save the lives of hundreds of innocent people. Try to think of it that way.'

'The question is not one of quantity, Monsignor. As far as I am concerned to torture a single human being is the same as torturing all of them. As I've heard it said in the parish church in my town: when they crucified Christ, they crucified all humanity.'

'You cannot compare the two. There was only one Christ. He was God made flesh.'

'True, but two thousand years ago, nobody knew that.'

Emilia's breathing was ragged and she was beginning to sweat. She looked as though she might faint. Everyone turned and she felt embarrassed to be the centre of attention.

'I'm sorry,' she said, getting to her feet, 'I don't know what's wrong with me. I'm feeling a little dizzy.'

'Simón, take her up to her room,' the father commanded. 'Give us a moment to compose ourselves.'

'It's probably the champagne,' said Emilia. 'I don't drink. I'm not used to it.'

The mother too got up from the table, looking nervous.

'I'll just go and see what's happening.'

The president's wife smiled, dismissing the episode lightly.

'Perhaps she's expecting. Perhaps her little dizzy spell might be considered a godsend—'

'Don't be ridiculous,' Dupuy interrupted, embarrassed. 'Neither she nor her husband are ready to start a family. I've said as much to both of them and they agree.'

'Babies come without being called,' the monsignor said. 'We must respect the will of the Almighty.'

From that point, the dinner began to go downhill and by the time the mother came back with the good news that Emilia was much better and had fallen asleep, there was nothing more to say. Dupuy was left with the unpleasant feeling that the president blamed him for the pall cast by his son-in-law over the evening.

As he was leaving, the monsignor asked Dupuy in confidence whether he had had Simón's background thoroughly vetted. 'He's a member of your family, Doctor, so he can't be a Commie, though – God forgive me – he talks like one.'

More than once, Dupuy had noticed that his son-in-law made no attempt to keep his irresponsible thoughts to himself. He would have to bring the boy to heel. With things as they were, there was no place for dissidence, for argument. How could Simón not understand that in saving the country from toppling into the abyss, any and all means were acceptable? If it was necessary to torture people to purge the country, then there was nothing to be done but torture them. The sacrificial sufferings of Joan of Arc and of Miguel Servet had served only to make the Church stronger. True, good men sometimes paid for sinners, but such things were inevitable in wartime. The junta could not publicly admit to the summary trials and executions since this would simply allow the enemy to launch into an endless, disruptive debate. The only thing to be done was exterminate the subversives quickly and quietly. If a military leader preferred to take them prisoner and use them as slave labour, so be it, provided he did so in secret. This priest with the glass eye had had the gall to raise the case of a disappeared Christian with the president. Let him bring up the subject as often as he liked. No one would listen to him. Right-thinking people were sick to death of violence. What they wanted was peace and order. The spirit of Argentina which Dupuy wrote about so often in *La República* had risen from the dead, it was sanctified. *Dios, Patria, Hogar* – God, Country, Family – were words which Dupuy believed should be inscribed on the white band of the national flag beneath the Sun of May. He would suggest as much in his next editorial for the magazine. Using the Socratic method which was by now his trademark, he would say: 'If the Brazilians have forged their democracy with the motto *Ordem e Progresso*, which is emblazoned on their flag, and the United States have the words *In God We Trust* engraved on their banknotes beneath their own protective emblem, why should Argentina not publicly declare that it is founded on three hallowed words: God, Country, Family?' It would be a timeless lesson which would forestall any onslaught by totalitarian subversives. They do not believe in God, nor in the family, and the country for which they are fighting is Soviet or Castroist rather than Argentinian: a strange country, a Communist country.

Simón disappeared in Tucumán at the beginning of July. The days were mild and the nights frosty. He and Emilia had been sent to Tucumán by the Automobile Club on an easy mission, virtually a holiday. They were to map a ten-kilometre stretch of an invisible route – nothing more than a dotted line on the map – to the south of the province. 'It's changed a lot, that province,' Dupuy told them. 'Until recently, it was a brutal, feudal place. The subversives had the gall to declare it a free American territory. Can you imagine? Now, it's a wealthy, peaceful province: there are no more terrorist attacks, no more kidnappings. The kerbs are painted blue and white; everywhere you go, there is order. In less than four months, the military government has worked miracles.'

At Tucumán airport, there was an Automobile Club rental jeep waiting for them. They spent the night at a hotel in the centre of town and at 5 a.m. they started driving south. The early hour, the brittle air, the emptiness of the streets: all these details which seemed so trivial were the first things Emilia would later remember. The shimmer of dew on the fields of sugar cane. The shadows of dogs moving under the street lamps. The tobacco leaves lying lazily in thick mats. Every few kilometres there was a military checkpoint and at every one they had to present their papers and explain why they were going where they were going. They were stopped in Famaillá, Santa Lucía, Monteros, Aguilares, Villa Alberdi. At the check-point at La Cocha, a sergeant emerged from the toilets, trousers halfway round his ankles, and barked at his men to check the jeep again. 'Check under the seats,' he told the guards. 'These fucking subversives hide their weapons in a false bottom under the seats.' 'We're cartographers, we're with the Automobile Club,' Simón explained. 'We make maps.' This made matters worse. They were hustled into a storeroom and subjected to a barrage of meaningless questions. 'How do we know your papers aren't forgeries? Why did you rent a jeep instead of a car like anyone else?' In the corners of the storeroom were piles of corn cobs and rats. They were huge, grey, menacing. To allay the doubts of the guards, Simón sketched the route they were to map, from Los Altos to the banks of the Río El

Abra. He explained that most maps omitted landmarks and that the course of Ruta 67 was not accurately mapped. He and his wife were here to rectify these mistakes. 'There was a plane overflying the area yesterday,' the sergeant said. 'It came by twice, flying very low. I suspect they were taking photos. Right now I'm thinking maybe they had something to do with you. That's how they plan terrorist attacks, spying missions, people who pretend they're just passing through. Cardologists, natologists, everyone pretending to be something they're not. Cartologists like you.'

'Cartographers,' Emilia said. 'Why don't you check our credentials?'

'All right, I'll let you go through,' the sergeant conceded. 'But just remember, we've got our eyes on you. You still need to get past the checkpoint at Huacra. If they turn you back, I wouldn't like to be in your shoes.'

The military checkpoint at Huacra seemed deserted. The stifling silence, the empty, almost surreal sentry boxes felt strangely jarring. The checkpoint marked the border between two provinces and was usually patrolled by at least twenty soldiers yet they could not see a living soul. The first red rays of dawn rose up on the left. A bitter cold leached through the canvas sides of the jeep. They drove on as far as the Río El Abra, or what they assumed was the river – a dry gorge with a crude concrete bridge they could just make out in the distance. Simón left the engine running and they waited for it to be light before beginning preliminary sketches for the map. 'Have you checked the scale?' Emilia asked. 'See that embankment next to the bridge, we need to choose a symbol. Don't fall asleep on me, Simón.'

Her husband lit a cigarette to keep himself awake but

stubbed it out almost immediately. 'There's a terrible smell,' he said. It was true. The stench was everywhere, spread across the landscape like a sheet. 'Maybe it's the vegetation,' Emilia said. 'Sometimes the trees are covered with fungus and bird droppings.' 'But it's winter,' her husband said. 'The trees are bare, the whole place is a wasteland.' 'Then it must be putre-faction from the river,' she said.

Rats, she remembered, abandoned their young under bridges when they went foraging for food. Who knew how many starving animals were under the bridge devouring each other? But the smell shifted and changed; sometimes it was like blood, at other times like breath flecked with spittle from a toothless mouth.

Smells are supposed to thrive in the heat, but the stench that morning seemed to draw its power from the chill air: it was a miasma which, instead of dissipating, seemed to become more dense, more tangible. Ice crystals formed on the windows of the jeep and Emilia's joints began to ache. The air was slowly freezing and she wished that the smell, too, would freeze into flakes of mica. The wasteland was so monstrous, so absolute, that in the grey light of dawn things seemed to disappear, to vanish leaving only desolation: infinite placentas of abandon-ment, wounds that gaped beneath the jeep. 'We're going to get nowhere,' said Emilia. 'That's because we're already nowhere,' said Simón.

When, finally, it was light enough to see, they could make out shadows moving towards the jeep, crawling along, scat-tering the loose gravel of the dirt road. Emilia had no time for horror movies or fantastical stories about supernatural creatures, but the creatures that morning reeked of sulphur and crackled like a cauldron of cicadas, a sound that came from the dawn of time, the sound of the wilderness spawning its poison.

'Stay calm. There are people out there,' Simón whispered, checking the doors to the jeep to make sure they were locked. As he did so, someone outside started jerking one of the door handles furiously.

The dawn came slowly. For a long time, it was merely a distant violet glow. Wind whipped sand against the jeep. A new, more piercing sound split the air. This moan, this whimper – whatever it was – grew louder; there were three, four voices coming from all directions, raucous and piercing. Suddenly they stopped, but only so the voices could come together in a shrill chorus like a needle that drilled into their eardrums.

'There are people circling,' Simón said again.

He took out the barbecue knife he always carried with him and climbed out of the jeep. The half-light of dawn was darker than the night had been and Emilia turned on the headlights. A woman dressed in rags and tatters was standing on the side of the road, rubbing her arms to keep warm. Next to her, two arthritic old women cradled a bundle wrapped in newspapers. Behind them, a woman with a mane of hair was trying to rouse a man sprawled on the ground with gutteral shrieks. A man stumbled along the dirt road towards the jeep wearing a threadbare raincoat that served little purpose since he was naked underneath. Behind him, another man pushing himself along on his hands and knees. Under the bridge were others, urinating, defecating. There were no fires, no shelter to keep them warm, nothing but the rage of that stench which was deeper than the night itself.

When the creatures saw Simón walking towards them, they

howled piteous, meaningless words. The skin of the man in the raincoat was black with filth and grime. From a distance, he did not seem human. Emilia, recognising that they were as sick with dread as she was, got out of the jeep, throwing a blanket around her shoulders. As she approached the two old women, she heard a feeble wail and realised that wrapped in the bundle of newspapers was a baby. She offered them the blanket without a moment's hesitation. As she walked the scant hundred metres from the jeep to where they stood, day had finally broken. The sun now rose at a dizzying speed as if to compensate for the delay. An icy wind whistled, whipping up the sand.

In the distance, the strange creatures went on howling the same words over and over, the tone, the volume shifting. *The guy with the frizzy hair jus' shitted hi'self.* Or: *'ey, you, gi's some money for a drink. Can' you see 'm dyin' of thirst?* And in unison. *We're all Raya morada here, that's why they rounded us with nets like stray dogs. Raya morada, Raya morada.* Even more incomprehensible was the strange behaviour of the men, who threatened each other, bared their toothless gums or sobbed as though some terrible memory had crawled up their noses. Pressing a finger to one nostril they blew their noses then stopped to see whether the snot had landed on the gravel or their clothes. When they had calmed down, the woman with the shock of hair, who was easily the most articulate, explained to Simón and Emilia that they had been picked up in military raids shortly before midnight from the doorways and the church porches where they slept.

There were some eighteen or twenty of them and they had been living on charity. Some pretended to be mad, making people laugh playing guitars that were nothing more than broom handles or writing poems on pieces of newspaper. Others were genuinely mad. The man in the threadbare raincoat believed he had been transported back from the Last Judgement to a time when there was no God, since there was no need of God now. He believed he was surrounded by angels through whom he could communicate with the dead and he was never bored because he spent his time talking to them about family secrets and mysterious diseases.

They had been shipped out to Tucumán in trucks used by dog-catchers and dumped in the bleak wasteland here in Catamarca, under the El Abra Bridge, between piles of hospital waste – bloody bandages, cotton pads smeared with pus, vesicles, appendixes, pieces of stomach, ulcerated intestines, kidneys with tumours and the other insults visited by disease on the human body. Even on the bitterest nights, clouds of blowflies laid their eggs in the waste and flocks of carrion hawks fought viciously for scraps of human detritus. The feverish stench drove out all oxygen and clung to the bodies of these beggars with a tenacity that would last forever.

Simón offered to drive them in groups to the military checkpoint at Huacra. He was prepared to put off starting work on the map until the afternoon and spend the morning making as many trips as necessary, but they told him that two of the men had already made the trip during the night only to arrive, their feet bloody and raw, and be bundled into an army truck and brought straight back out into the desert. Simón suggested it might be better to go for help to a village called Bañado de Ovanta, twenty kilometres east. 'I'll go with you,' said Emilia. 'We need to bring back bread, coffee and blankets for these people before they die.'

The journey was very different. The blazing sun now

obliterated everything; they could barely make out the blots of Ñandubay trees and cacti. Clearly, there were mistakes on their map because they wound up not in Bañado de Ovanta, but back at Huacra. Later, Emilia would often wonder whether they had got lost by accident or whether someone had switched the signposts. They had been driving for twenty minutes when in a ravine on the right-hand side of the road they saw the two dogs they had noticed as they left Huacra. Everyone knows that images, when they reappear inverted, herald disaster.

Disaster occurred almost immediately. They found themselves surrounded by a hundred uniformed soldiers who forced them out of the jeep at gunpoint. The buttons on the soldiers' jackets strained from the pressure of paunches bloated by beer and noodles. The checkpoint, which had earlier been clearly deserted, was now teeming with soldiers going in and out of a corrugated-iron shack at the rear of a large courtyard.

The pot-bellied soldiers hustled them into a shack that served as a guardhouse. None of them wore badges indicating their rank, though from their ages they could only be corporals or sergeants. There might have been a captain; checkpoints usually had a captain in charge. Emilia tried to catch Simón's eye but he would not look at her. He seemed lost, his eyes blankly staring, bewildered, unable to believe what was happening to them. Many years later, she thought that this was the moment when her husband began to disappear from the world.

A clerk with a toad-like double chin and breath that stank of beer asked them for their papers and laboriously copied down the details, sucking his pen after every letter. Emilia, accustomed to the inertia of bureaucracies, watched his sluggish routine calmly. Simón hugged his knees like an abandoned child.

The interview turned nasty as soon as they brought up El Abra. At the mere mention of the name, the clerk swallowed his words and trailed off into silence. Their attempted explanations about maps and scales only served to make things worse. What were you doing at El Abra? What were you doing waiting for dawn in open country? Who were you meeting? What were they bringing? When? Emilia and Simón had nothing to tell but the truth and explained again that they were working on a map for the Automobile Club. They had told the same account, used the same words at every checkpoint and had nothing more to add. But still the officer was not satisfied. He demanded they repeat it over and over. Why? What for? How many of you are there? He was determined to find out why anyone would travel two hundred kilometres from Buenos Aires to map nothing. 'Since when did the Automobile Club start wasting money on such bullshit?' 'It's the truth,' Simón insisted. 'Besides, it wasn't our idea.'

'What are you, Cardoso, a Communist? A *Montero*? A Bolshevik?'

'I'm none of those things.'

'You know what Communism is?'

'I think so . . . It's what they have in Russia, in Poland, in East Germany.'

'Exactly. Godless countries where everything belongs to everyone. Even wives and children belong to the state. There's no such thing as private property. Anyone can take anything belonging to someone else.'

'Is it really that simple?'

'I ask the questions here. Yes, it's that simple. Where there's no God, there's no decency. You like the idea of some thug coming in off the street and fucking your wife up the arse just because he can?'

'No, I don't.'

'The Communist state gives everyone the right to do things like that. You could just as easily go to his house and return the favour, fuck his wife.'

'I've never heard anything like that.'

'Well, take my word for it. In Russia, even kids at school know this stuff, they're used to it, they don't know any better. Here, we teach people respect. God first of all. Then country, then family. It's the Argentinian holy trinity.'

'If you say so, I believe you.'

'That's better, Cardoso. Believe me. Where did you make contact with the subversives?'

'I already told you, we didn't see anyone. Only the homeless people.'

'And you're telling me they just suddenly appeared out of nowhere?'

'We didn't know there was anyone out there.'

'That's right, be a wise guy. Who are you trying to kid? Either you give me a straight answer right now or we'll interrogate your wife while I fuck her right in front of you. Maybe I can make her come.'

'I've told you everything. My wife and I don't know any subversives.'

'You can't answer for her. Do you know any subversives, Dupuy?'

'No, no one,' said Emilia.

'How would you recognise a subversive? This fucker you

came with is a subversive, a dangerous subversive. We've got a file on him.'

'He's my husband. You can check, ask anyone. You're making a terrible mistake.'

'You're the one who made the mistake when you married this Commie fucker. You had a meeting somewhere round here, didn't you, Cardoso? The *moishe* you were supposed to be meeting gave you up. Just tell me where you stashed the maps and the weapons you brought. Tell me, and you can go. You can both go. Don't waste my time.'

'I'm not going to lie to you. We didn't come here to meet anyone. We were sent to map the area. I explained all this to the officers at the last checkpoint. As soon as we finish, we're leaving. Two hours, maybe three. Nobody told us we couldn't.'

'You think I'm some fuckwit? In the last week, we've caught five Trotskyites armed to the teeth. They were carrying a whole library of maps. They told us everything. Terrorists use maps to prepare their attacks, to get in and get the fuck out quickly, am I wrong?'

Emilia bowed her head, hopeless. What was happening was a farce, something that had no place in the real world. She tried to reframe things, to return to a sensible, safe place. She said: 'I am the daughter of Dr Orestes Dupuy. You have no right to treat us like this.'

'You think so, *puta*? We don't give a shit about some Dupín here. This is a war, you get that? I can kill you right here, right now, give any excuse I like. I can say you were trying to escape, that you tried to take my gun off me, I can say the first thing comes into my head. Out here, you have no name; you don't exist.'

Simón didn't know how to appease the toad. He was desperate for this nightmare to end, for them to leave him in peace. With the country in the state it was in, who cared about maps?

Another paunchy officer appeared in the doorway and asked the pencil-pusher if he needed any help.

'Help? With this little whore?' the toad said. 'Are you shitting me? I could fuck her three times over and still have dick to spare. See the Commie fucker who came in with her? He's already given up.'

Simón's head had slumped onto his chest. Lashed to a chair with the toad's belt, he could barely move. The clerk rolled up his sleeves and went back to sucking his pen. He was preparing himself for more questions. He took the pot of coffee heating on the stove and threw it in Simón's face.

'You going to tell who you brought those fucking maps for? What about the weapons we found in the jeep?'

Maddened by pain and fear, Simón hauled himself to his feet, still lashed to the chair, and struck out wildly. It was a senseless thing to do, he couldn't hope to achieve anything, he didn't even succeed in loosening the belt. He slumped onto the floor with the chair on top of him. The noise attracted the attention of the paunches outside. Two of them quickly hauled him to his feet and slammed him against the wall. Emilia watched her husband slide down in slow motion. It seemed unbelievable to her that life should play them such an ugly trick, just when they were beginning to be happy. A few insignificant lines on a map had brought them to this place by chance, and now chance was destroying them. The world refused to be mapped, and those who violated this principle paid their price in tears. She heard a crack like breaking bone.

Simón's nose was swollen, his lip split; a trickle of blood stained his shirt.

Two green Ford Falcons, engines running, were waiting for them at the perimeter fence of the checkpoint. Emilia was bundled into the first car next to a guard in plain clothes. The pot-bellied officers pushed and manhandled Simón towards the other, her husband shuffling along, his legs faltering and uncertain.

This was Emilia's last glimpse of him, the image that in future she would dream of so often. But in her dreams, Simón was never Simón, but one of the other men they had encountered that day. Or a city that rose and fell. Or a flickering candle flame.

On the drive back to Tucumán, the sky grew dark. Every few kilometres the weather shifted and changed. At times, a furious storm burst, bringing clouds of steam rising from the asphalt. Further along, the sun shimmered and the air shattered into slivers of ice. They came to a point where a convoy of carts hauling sugar cane blocked the road. The officer guarding Emilia got out of the car to try and deal with the obstruction only to come back shaking his head. 'There's no way through,' he said. 'Two mules dropped dead in the road and there's no one to move them. We'll just have to drive round.'

He turned on the two-way radio and informed the checkpoint that they would be making a detour. The cane fields were deserted; the horizon veered from purple to a deep, ominous yellow. They drove along a crude dirt track, the car constantly getting stuck in potholes. Emilia no longer cared where she was being taken or when they would get there. She cared only about Simón. Over and over, at seemingly endless intervals, she asked the guard about him, but the man stared out at the eddying dust and did not answer. Maybe it was pointless to resist, Emilia thought, after all everyone else in the country had already given up. The military were the aristocracy of the spirit of Argentina, and that aristocracy was once more trooping out of its barracks to save the country. How many times had she heard her father recite 'El discurso de Ayacucho', in the same antiquated bombastic tones as the national poet who had penned it? Written in 1924, it was a piece of rhetoric which every schoolchild was forced to learn by heart. Every word of it was burned into her brain and circled there still.

As night began to fall, they were forced to stop by a passing train. Slowly, clumsily, the train approached. On freight cars smooth as still water, corpses were being shipped as though they were merely cargo. Except for the three wagons behind the engine, the bodies were exposed to the elements, indifferent to the obscenity of death. The wagons at the front were shrouded in black plastic which billowed open in the wind to reveal a hand, a head, a leg. Ash from the stubble fields whirled around the freight cars in dark flecks: a host of dying butterflies.

It was almost dark when the first Ford Falcon arrived in the suburbs of Tucumán. The broad avenues were lit up; the facades of the houses gleamed as though freshly painted. In the freezing air, the city huddled in on itself. Cars moved slowly; people walked with heads bowed, hugging the walls. The stillness was so deliberate it seemed artificial. Across the boulevard that divided the north of the city from the south hung a banner showing a photograph of three strapping, dishevelled, thuggish young men and, underneath, the words: *We will not allow the extremists to destroy the country. Help us eliminate them.* A block further on was a poster with an illustration of a hard-working broom bearing the legend, in blue and white: *Order and Cleanliness. Death to Subversion.*

Order and Cleanliness was one of her father's propaganda slogans for the government Emilia remembered. How many other slogans had he penned that she was not aware of? *God, Country, Family* she knew was his, though it belonged to everyone now.

She was taken to the police station where they fingerprinted her and made her sign a piece of paper admitting that Simón had rented the jeep. 'Under instructions from the Automobile Club Argentina' Emilia explained in a note at the bottom. Flanked by two guards, she was led down into a vast basement lined on both sides with a row of cells from which there came not the slightest sound. Emilia was locked up in the furthest cell. As soon as the guards left her, she lost all track of time. It took a long while for her eyes to adjust to the darkness. She could make out a cot bed bolted to the floor; in the corner was a bucket from which came the stench of geological strata of urine. The wall opposite was dizzyingly high, at least eight metres, and converged with the wall behind her meaning the cell was shaped like a pyramid. At some point, a guard passed a jug of water through the bars and she gulped it down in one breathless swallow. Her throat was dry, filled with sand and fear.

Just as she was about to fall asleep, a ghostly glow jolted her awake again. On the high wall opposite, some invisible machine was projecting dreamlike images. The pictures came and went, disappearing like shooting stars. She thought for a moment that she was seeing things and remembered a line from Dante she had read at school: *Poi piovve dentro all'alta fantasia.* It was true: it was raining in her imagination, but raining so hard that the forms and shapes blurred and melted almost as soon as they appeared. She saw Simón rushing headlong into a fire, but that too was one of Dante's images. She saw a newborn baby being strangled with an electrical cord. The umbilical cord was still attached, and the baby's face was crumpled in a rictus of terrible pain. The image swelled as though about to encroach on the real world; it grew larger and larger before dissolving into a poster whose typeface reminded her of old cinema newsreels: *Baby butchered by subversive criminals.* She saw the three persons of the Holy Trinity devouring one another: the Father devouring the Son, and the resulting two-headed monster devouring the dove that was the Holy Spirit, then the dove taking flight and, using his beak as a scythe, beheading the other two. And then she saw herself watching these things, and it was only then that she realised the images were not inside her head, that somewhere there was a hidden projector, though she could not understand why. Who would spend money creating such images? Could anyone else see them?

Every so often the images were repeated, always in the same order, as though part of an infinite loop. At dawn – she assumed it must be dawn by now – they vanished like flotsam carried out on the tide. She tried to sleep, but a radio somewhere nearby kept repeating the lottery results over and over. 'Two thousand nine hundred and ninety-eight. Eight hundred thousand pesos,' the presenter announced. 'Two thousand nine hundred and ninety-eight. Eight hundred thousand pesos,' echoed the darkness at the end of the corridor. Reality retreated, becoming more and more remote, its place taken up by the only two senses Emilia trusted: smell and touch. But were these senses free or were they too prisoners of some alternative reality which moulded her imagination as it pleased?

She woke again just as someone pushed a mug of steaming *maté*, a hunk of bread and some fried pork strips through the bars. The litany of lottery numbers continued, but the images on the wall had disappeared. If she wanted to survive, she thought, she had to stay calm, to clear her mind completely, to dissociate herself from what was happening to her body. Difficult as it seemed, she needed to sink into a trance. This would give her the strength to face the worst, if the worst should come. If she allowed herself to feel any emotion, she would be lost. Finally, when she could feel nothing she decided she was safe.

On the third day, a warder ordered her to wash and brush her hair.

'You're free to go, kid,' he said. 'Round here, rich people always land on their feet. Your parents are waiting for you outside.'

She was blindfolded and someone took her by the arm and led her across what felt like a damp courtyard to a room that smelled of sweaty clothes. Before closing the door he ordered her to count to twenty before taking off the blindfold. When her eyes adjusted to the dim light that flattened everything, she could make out a small sofa, a wooden desk, a few chairs. On the walls hung coats of arms, a photo of the Eel, a portrait of General San Martín. For no apparent reason, a memory buzzed in her brain like a maddening bluebottle, a phrase she had heard for the first time in primary school: *the battle, the treaties, the obligatory hero*. All across the country obligatory heroes were multiplying like saints in the Catholic Church. For every battle never waged, a new hero was created; for every miracle never performed a new saint was venerated. *The battle, the saints, the obligatory hero.*

A door opened behind her letting in a sudden burst of light and her mother's bird-like voice.

'Emilia, *hija*! Just look at the terrible mess Simón has got you mixed up in.'

Reluctantly, she allowed herself to be hugged. She had always taken comfort in her mother's warmth but she was shocked by this accusation against her husband.

'It's not Simón's fault, he's as much a victim of this mess as me. Where is he? I want to see him.'

'You can't see him like that,' her mother said, 'you look a fright. Go and get yourself cleaned up. We brought you some clean clothes.'

In the bathroom, the shelves groaned under the weight of shaving equipment and imported perfumes. The blouse and the bra her parents had brought from Buenos Aires were her sister Chela's and a little too big for her. Her mother had been right, she did look a sight – her face was haggard, she had deep bags under her eyes, her hair was greasy and dishevelled. She did her best to make herself presentable, but there was not much she could do. In the room next door, a voice she didn't recognise was making abject apologies to her father.

'Two days, Dr Dupuy, yes, I know, it's unforgivable. Almost all our men were out on patrol and the officers here at headquarters are terribly ignorant. They work twenty hours straight. They're so exhausted they don't know good from bad when they see it. It was late at night when your daughter was brought in and there was no duty officer. If you want, we'll look into the matter, get to the bottom of this, doesn't matter whose head rolls.'

'Tell General Bissio I want to see him,' her father demanded.

The general too apologised profusely, though only by telephone. He was in the mountains trailing a band of guerrillas, he explained, and did not want to keep Dr Dupuy and his family waiting in this inhospitable barracks with thieves and whores. He ordered that Señora Cardoso be shown the prison register proving that Simón had been released two hours earlier, at 8 a.m.

The father patted his daughter's waist then moved away. It had been this way since her adolescence. The vague gesture of affection made Emilia feel tainted. She read the list of items that had been returned to Simón: a Citizen wristwatch; a wedding ring; a pack of Jockey Club cigarettes; a brown leather bag; 27,000 pesos in thousand-peso bills; an Automobile Club ID card; a 1:5,000 scale map of the southern section of the province.

Dr Dupuy had tickets for the four o'clock flight to Buenos Aires, but Emilia did not want to leave immediately. Simón, she insisted, was bound to turn up at any moment. Her father headed off to the airport where he would wait in the restaurant while she and her mother went to check whether the rented jeep had been returned. Yes, they were told, it had been returned the previous day by a soldier. Another soldier had picked up Simón's suitcase from the hotel where they had spent their one, brief, night together. The bill had been paid, though no one at the hotel could remember by whom. The concierge and the girls working on the reception desk were not the same. It felt as though the past was retreating, leaving no trace, as though life was suspended in a continuous present where things happened without cause and effect.

They got to the airport just in time for the four o'clock

flight. Simón was probably waiting for her in Buenos Aires, Emilia's mother told her, where else could he be? 'But then why doesn't he answer the phone?' asked Emilia, who had been calling the San Telmo apartment every fifteen minutes. 'He probably took the bus back,' her mother replied, 'it's a twenty-hour journey, he won't get there until tomorrow morning.' 'But without leaving a message, without asking after me? That's not like him,' said Emilia. 'Fear changes people, *hija*,' her father observed. 'If he's afraid, then by now he's running away from everything, even himself.' It was only as they boarded the plane that Emilia realised her father had not bought a fourth ticket. She thought it best to say nothing and spent the next two hours staring at the clouds through the window.

Years later, when Simón still had not reappeared, she read an article in *Gente* that said Argentinian husbands often disappeared suddenly, without giving any explanation. They suffer from Wakefield's syndrome, a psychoanalyst explained, an allusion to Nathaniel Hawthorne's short story in which an upstanding London gentleman leaves his wife one day for no reason, moving to a house one street away from where he watches her go about her day-to-day routine until he grows old. Emilia knew in her heart that Simón was not like that; he would come back to her as soon as he could.

At the time, thousands of people disappeared for no apparent reason. Ambassadors disappeared, the lovers of captains and admirals, the owners of businesses coveted by the *comandantes*. Workers disappeared from their factory gates; farmers from their fields, leaving tractors running; dead men from the graves in which they had been buried only the day before. Children disappeared from their mothers' wombs and mothers from the children's memories. The sick who arrived in hospital at midnight had disappeared by morning. Frantic mothers rushed out of supermarkets searching for children who had slipped through black holes between the shelves. Some turned up years later, but they were not the same. They had other names, other parents, a history that was no longer theirs. And it was not only people who disappeared; rivers, lakes, train stations, half-built cities vanished into the air as though they had never existed. The list of things that were no more and those that might have been was infinite.

In an interview with a Japanese journalist, the Eel was forced to address the question of this rash of disappearances. 'Firstly we would have to verify that what you say existed was where you say it was. Reality can be very treacherous. Lots of people are desperate for attention and they disappear just so people won't forget them.' Emilia watched the interview on television, listened as he articulated every syllable, slowly nodding his bald head.

'A *desaparecido* is a mystery, he has no substance, he is neither alive nor dead, he does not exist. He is a "disappeared".'

And as he said *he does not exist*, he rolled his eyes to heaven.

'Don't use that word again,' he went on, 'you have no basis for it. It is forbidden to publish it. Let it disappear and be forgotten.'

Emilia left Simón standing in the doorway of Trudy Tuesday and – not letting him out of her sight – crossed the road to pick up her silver Altima from the parking lot at Hammond Atlas. She was not afraid that he would leave again – after all these years it made no sense. 'I'll go pick up the car.' Emilia whispered to him. 'We'll go home.' She did not even need to wait for an answer. On the far side of Route 22 she turned to make sure he was still standing where her senses had left him. He wasn't there. She saw him walking north, a smudge of light, a haze raised by the afternoon sunshine.

'Simón!' she called, but he did not hear her. Perhaps he could not hear her over the constant stream of trucks from Newark. A taxi stopped on the corner and, without hesitating, Emilia jumped in and told the cab driver to follow her husband. Simón was crossing a bridge less than two hundred metres away and she quickly caught up with him. When she opened the taxi door he climbed in, smiling, as though nothing had happened. Still panicked, her heart in her mouth, Emilia stammered her Highland Park address and explained to the driver the quickest way to get there. The enthusiasm her husband had shown some minutes before as he chatted to the Scandinavians seemed to have completely drained away. Now he huddled in the back seat like a timid boy, stealing glances at Emilia. He was carrying the case she had given him thirty-one years before: a wide, soft brown leather bag, perfect for overnight trips: the same case that, according to the prison register, had been returned to him at the police station in Tucumán. Back then, Simón had three original maps on fine card in the case, the names already printed, and plastic Stabilene overlays on which to apply the geographical symbols. Emilia would have liked to ask him whether he kept the past, too, in the case, frozen, the prisoner of a time that would not go away. It had been years now since cartographers had used Stabilene overlays. Nowadays, maps were the creations of computer programs, metaphors that had no place in reality.

'I'm not going to leave your side,' she told him. 'I don't need to be back at work until Monday.' It was Friday.

Simón stared out at the soulless monotony of suburbia, the Taco Bells and the Dunkin' Donuts spilling fat, satisfied families onto the street, the Kinkos, the Pathmarks, the Toys R Us and the other endless, sprawling temples to consumerism. Emilia talked incessantly. 'Ever since I moved to this country, I've been amazed by the food, the huge perfect-looking tomatoes, the lettuces that never wilt, the shelves of fruit that call to you like sirens as soon as you step into a grocery store. Now I understand why Disney's Snow White was bewitched by her stepmother's apple. A tasteless apple that brings eternal sleep. Don't you feel that, Simón? None of the food here has any flavour to it. The stuff they sell here is a genetic fantasy, a breeding ground for every future disease.' Every now and then, the cab driver would turn and ask, 'Everything OK, lady? Did you say something?' 'No, everything's fine.'

For a long time her husband sat, saying nothing, staring out at the bleak expressway. I have to be careful, Emilia thought. I'm desperate to make up for lost time, but maybe he's not. I don't want to crowd him, to pressure him. Sooner or later we'll go back to being the people we used to be. And even if we don't, it doesn't matter. At least we'll be together. A day, two days, the rest of our lives. Once that fact sank in, they would talk, tell each other all the things they had not been able to share. There was so much to tell! I've got nothing to be ashamed of, she thought, I never gave him up for dead, not even when those three witnesses stood up in court and swore they had seen his body, tossed like garbage in some courtyard somewhere. I never stopped loving him, I was never unfaithful. All through the terrible years I knew he would come back, I searched for him, I waited, I knew . . . I'd almost say I won him back, but to talk about the man I love like that would be to diminish him; my Simón is not a trophy.

The sun is setting quickly; soon now the darkness will envelop them. Usually by the time Emilia leaves work at Hammond it is already dark; she has rarely had an opportunity to see the twilight, the crimson and yellow death throes of the autumn trees, the blurred shapes of the identical buildings along the expressway as they flash past. In a few moments, everything will disappear, the afternoon light, the falling leaves; everything but Simón, sitting here beside her.

Always as she leaves the offices at Hammond, even on the worst nights – when it rains and snows and when the ambulances wail incessantly – she is met by evangelical preachers chanting their litanies – O Lord, O Lord – as they wave collection boxes at passers-by. Their ominous chanting still plagues her as she lays her head on her pillow because the sounds of the day always return to her at night as though they had retreated and were waiting for this moment to spread through the smooth surfaces of her head: the sounds of this day and other distant days. She would like to rid herself of these futile memories, but she has had no choice but to carry them with her wherever she goes. Once she was unaware of them. Time has brought them back. As the years passed, the memories receded. Now, with Simón sitting next to her, she has nothing to fear.

'What a perfect day,' she says, not expecting him to reply.

And indeed he does not reply. Barely fifteen hours ago, she was sitting with Nancy Frears in her apartment on North 4th Avenue watching *The Ghost and Mrs Muir* on television – an old romantic comedy in which Gene Tierney, who is recently widowed, moves with her daughter into a haunted house by the sea and falls in love with the ghost. Nancy had left at about eleven o'clock and Emilia had read for a while, some poems by Gonzalo Rojas which moved her with their fierce eroticism: *Lowing, bellowing female my beautiful / love entering God, made animal / anointing the brain of her old man/ torrents running over him.* The words had inflamed her; she still has life enough in her to be aroused, to masturbate, to belong to herself as she has never wanted to belong to anyone else.

'I never stopped loving you, Emilia, not for a single day,' says Simón. The roar of the expressway drowns out his barely audible voice. 'I never stopped loving you either, *amor*. Not for a single day.' Her mind is racing, there is so much to think about before they get home. But perhaps it is better to stay calm, to wait, to see how they feel being together. They have said that they still love each other. It is not much, and yet it is everything. She is afraid that Simón will be disappointed when he sees her as she is, the crumpled scrap of paper adversity has made of her.

As they turn off Route 22 to the even more arid plain of the 287, lined on either side by hotels vast as cemeteries (who but a ghost would think to stay out here in the middle of nowhere?) some ten or twelve miles from her house, she realises that she smells, that she is dirty, that her hair is thick with sweat. She showered before leaving home that morning, shaved her armpits the night before, and yet she exudes smells that only a second shower can staunch. If all goes well, maybe she could ask her husband to take a bath with her? No. She glances at him, so placid, so quiet, and her embarrassment immediately disappears. She will ask him what he wants to do, hope that he will ask her to come to bed with him tonight. She will give herself to him, follow him wherever he wants to go just as he has followed her to this corner of New Jersey without her even asking. He seems familiar with his surroundings, he doesn't even seem surprised when she points out the shadows of Johnson Park where she jogs on Saturdays and Sundays. Two blocks from her place, Simón finally speaks: '*All yet seems well; and if it end so meet / The bitter past, more welcome is the sweet.*' 'Shakespeare, isn't it? Your English is very good. How did you learn?' 'Television,' he answers. 'Six hours a day.' And she says, 'I worked on mine listening to audio books. Solitude leaves you time for everything.'

Emilia's apartment is dark: a small balcony overlooking the street, a living room, bathroom, kitchen, bedroom. The dining table is strewn with maps. In the kitchen there are dirty dishes and smells that have been lingering, festering since morning. She has let things go, she didn't call the landlord to get him to fix the damp patches where the wallpaper is peeling. She watches her husband climbing the stairs behind her, reaches out her hand. 'Is it you, Simón? Is it really you?' She grips his hand, slender, weightless, soft as she remembers it. As she climbs the last stair, she is overcome by desire, the torrential desire that has been building in her belly ever since she first began to miss him; she wants to feel his body, to hold him, she cannot bear this passion inside her any longer. As though reading her thoughts, Simón's voice comes to her aid: 'Not for a single day did I stop loving you,' he says. 'Me neither,' Emilia replies, 'not for a single day.' And with her whole being she says the words again so even the threadbare walls can hear. 'Not for a single day, *amor.*'

2

In dream I seemed to see a lady, singing

'Purgatorio', XXVIII, 40

Like Emilia, I've lived in Highland Park since 1991, on the deserted slope of the hill overlooking the Raritan River. In the mid eighteenth century, the Raritan was a bustling thoroughfare. These days, it's a trickle of water, a nesting place for thousands of Canadian geese whose honking disrupts the peace of the little town. Although, in September 1999, the geese vanished for no apparent reason. The sky grew dark, all nature fell silent. Nobody was prepared for what happened next. That night, Hurricane Floyd swelled the waters of the Raritan, which rose so much in a few hours that the river burst its banks, flooding the whole of Johnson Park a hundred yards from where I live. The nests of the geese – heavy, rugged straw things – were swept away by the current. The basements of all the houses overlooking the park were flooded. Whole libraries and photographic studios were wiped out and the maps marking out the *eruv* so crucial to the Orthodox people in town were destroyed. The following morning, everyone turned out to see the damage. The sun was so glorious that morning that even those who had lost things in the storm treated it like a pleasant autumn stroll. After all, it was impossible to estimate the extent of the damage, most of which was irreparable. A week later, life in Highland Park was the same as it had ever been. The waters of the Raritan had retreated and once more skirted the periphery of the town. The geography department at the university drew up a new map for the mayor's office that included two small islands which had appeared in the oxbow when the water subsided. Space calmly resisted the onslaught of time. Little had changed. The boundaries of Highland Park still comprised the sixty blocks it had before the storm, including the park, eighteen places of worship and some fifteen thousand souls.

My best friend back then was Ziva Galili, head of Rutgers' history department and one of the foremost authorities I've ever met on the 1917 Russian Revolution – a field in which there's no shortage of authorities. Every year, Ziva spends at least three months unearthing new surprises from the files of the now defunct KGB. Whenever I go round to her house, I overhear her speaking half a dozen languages fluently, including Hebrew, the language of her parents and of the kibbutz where she grew up. She's still my best friend, though we don't see as much of each other these days because she was appointed acting dean of the School of Arts and Sciences in 2006, and so now she's rarely ever home. About a quarter of the residents of Highland Park are African immigrants, refugees lucky enough to have escaped the massacres in Rwanda and Sierra Leone. Another quarter is made up of the tenured professors – of whom I am one – who hail from various countries predictable and unpredictable: Czechs, Chinese, Indians, Burmese, Russians, Bulgarians, Belgians, Israelis, Mexicans, Brazilians, Argentinians. I don't need to go on. The rest, and by far the majority, is made up of observant Jews, many of whom are ultra-Orthodox. This is why anywhere you go in town there's always a synagogue nearby, and why one of the most respected rabbinical schools in New Jersey is just outside town on Woodbridge Avenue about two hundred yards from the flyover on Route 1. At dusk on Fridays and on Saturday mornings, streams of students can be seen walking down Woodbridge Avenue wearing their long black coats, winter and summer, with the white wool *tallit* underneath. In town, hundreds of young mothers bustle around the synagogues in formal dress, wearing hats copied from the British court and conspicuous wigs. They energetically push buggies carrying two or three children of various ages (they're often already pregnant with their next child), chatting happily and enthusiastically about the food they've prepared for Shabbat. Their husbands rarely accompany them, spending the holy day in prayer and the study of God's laws. They are a devout and gentle people who have found happiness in this town where nothing ever happens. The police in Highland Park are bored to death. Their sole occupation is chasing down those rare drivers who dare exceed the 25 mph speed limit (15 mph near schools), or those who forget to wear a seat belt. Friendships are made on the steps of churches and temples and cemented over lunches where everyone prays together. Catholics, evangelicals, Jews: the inhabitants of Highland Park are believers and faith is at the heart of their lives. Since I choose to live without God, I know no one and no one calls on me. It's hardly surprising then that it was some time before I heard about Emilia Dupuy – known to the regulars at Chris Nolan's beauty salon and Vijay Maktal's pharmacy as Millie since it is easier to pronounce than Emilia, whose Spanish vowels are a death trap for Anglo-Saxons.

I first encountered her at Stop & Shop back when it was called Food Town. Before we realised we were both from Argentina and began to greet each other with polite mistrust, my only thought was to avoid being in the same checkout line as her. Not only did Emilia, like most of the older women in town, take her own sweet time squeezing the tomatoes and smelling the peaches, she also drove the checkout girls to distraction with avalanches of vouchers and coupons. The cashier would be bagging up the broccoli and the low-fat ice cream and suddenly Emilia would produce a coupon offering a $2 discount. Usually, she'd try to get a 100 oz tub of ice cream with just one coupon, and when the cashier refused, she'd start to bicker and the war of words would usually end with a supervisor rushing over to sort things out. By which time, of course, everyone else in the line had scuttled off in search of calmer checkouts. Whenever I ran into Emilia at the supermarket, I always made sure to leave before her, even if I arrived after her. She didn't look like a woman in her mid-fifties. Anyone would have thought she was ten years younger. She was tall, thin, willowy, with that air common to so many Argentinian women of a teenage girl who refuses to grow up. She had a deep tan – the result of hours on a sunbed (there are seven tanning shops in town) and tried to hide her thinning hair with a brittle shell of hairspray. What I most noticed, though, were her eyes, a luminous, almost translucent blue, as with indefatigable curiosity she watched the slow pulse of the world – which in Highland Park moved as slowly as a tortoise. She had small breasts and a shapely ass which emphasised her long legs. She was an attractive woman, and she knew it.

I met her because I'm interested in cartographers, who are very much like novelists in their determination to modify reality. I got my first insight into labyrinths and old naval maps in the geography department at Rutgers, but since no one there produces historical or comparative maps – which were what most interested me – I was directed to the offices of Hammond on Progress Street in Union, before they moved to Springfield. That afternoon, I spotted Emilia Dupuy in one of the programmers' cubicles and I realised that she lived in the same town as I did, about half a mile from my house.

At work, she was a different person. The woman I was introduced to at Hammond Atlas was nothing like the exasperating fifty-something-year-old at Stop & Shop. She was almost the antithesis: calm, obliging, sweet. She wore a pleated skirt that showed off her magnificent legs, her hair was piled into a simple bun that emphasised the graceful curve of her neck. Later, when I knew her better, I dared to tell her that I had never seen her as beautiful as she was that day. I told her I thought she should dress like that all the time, simple clothes, but she was shocked. 'The woman you met in Union wasn't me,' she said. 'My God, I hadn't set foot in a beauty salon in nearly a week.' I didn't say so, but I've always thought that in the beauty salons that line Raritan Avenue – three to a block – women like Emilia allow their natural grace to be stripped away. I've seen women come out of these places with hairdos like towers, eyelashes drooping from the weight of mascara, false nails painted with garish designs, all of which – together with their brashly coloured shapeless dresses – would have earned them a role in a Fellini movie if Federico had ever met them.

Emilia invited me to tea at her apartment on North 4th on Saturday afternoon. I accepted without a second's thought for the simple reason that I wanted to see the plastic Stabilene sheets on which mapmakers marked out planimetric elements in the 1970s, and to talk to her about 'scribing', the process used in making large-scale maps back then.

The two-family houses I'd seen in Highland Park, rented by students or visiting professors, were invariably sparsely furnished: makeshift bookshelves made of planks and cement bricks, a kitchen table where the computer sat alongside yesterday's lunch plates, a few chairs, a television and a bed that would not have looked out of place in a monk's cell. Emilia's apartment, on the other hand, took up the whole top floor. Maps and plans were strewn everywhere, covering up the rugs and the ruched curtains. She had invited Nancy Frears too to avoid any malicious gossip among the neighbours. While Nancy was setting the table, Emilia excitedly gave me a tour of the apartment's three small rooms: a bedroom hung with calendars, thermometers and photos of her nieces and nephews sending their love from San Antonio, Texas; a dining room with a small bookcase, a pair of overstuffed armchairs and a drawing table; and a tiny room about six foot by six foot whose focal point was an exercise bike. Opposite the bike was a hi-fi system and a pair of Bose speakers. I spotted albums by León Gieco, Almendra and Charly García between Bach suites and the chamber music of Charles-Valentin Alkan. I could easily imagine Emilia spending hours here, sculpting her legs and toning her abs.

Before I could persuade Emilia to talk to me about the Stabilene film used in map-making thirty years ago, or allow me to run my fingers over samples of coloured Mylar sheets – orange, yellow, green, midnight blue – I first had to brave the thick tangle of gossip and family tragedy Nancy had amassed on the residents of Highland Park: the screaming matches between the Flemms – professors of electrical engineering – that spilled out onto the street, a juicy tale of adultery and ruinous stock market investments; the scandal provoked by the sermon in which Father Landowski denounced the secret abortions of two Catholic teenagers; the shock imprisonment – for only nine hours – of local policeman Tom Nizmar's eldest boy for stealing a CD from Barnes & Noble. There was nothing that Nancy did not know, including the exact time I came out onto the porch to pick up the *Times* and the fact that I was disappointed when it was delivered late on Sundays. I asked how she managed to know so much about people who lived miles away and she informed me that you had only to keep your ears open in any beauty salon to be able to predict – with a tiny margin of error – who was getting married, who having a baby and which businesses in Highland Park were about to go belly up.

It was Nancy who asked me if I'd ever seen Large Lenny on Main Street. I didn't know who she meant until she described him. 'Sure, I know him,' I said. 'I've seen him walking up and down at all hours like a madman.' Lenny, she told me, really was mad. He was six foot ten tall and weighed about 370 pounds. He'd burst into elementary-school classes and rail against abortion and euthanasia. 'I am the way, the truth and the life,' he'd say. 'The life that I give in heaven no one can take away on earth.' Now and again, the police would take him into custody for disorderly conduct, but he was always released within a couple of hours because his constant bellowing of verses from the Gospels terrified the local cops.

Large Lenny would follow the kids when they got out of school, proclaiming: 'Be not deceived, children, be not deceived. Many will come claiming to speak in the name of the Father, saying that the end of the world is nigh, but they are liars. Do not listen to them. Listen only to me.' After school, the kids would always have stale cookies and bits of chalk in their bags and would throw them at Lenny to try to get him to shut up, but Large Lenny would not leave the Scriptures in peace. Nothing could stop him. When night fell and people took refuge in their houses, they could still hear the giant's supplications over the noise of Passover celebrations, bar mitzvahs, over the din of the television. 'Come from your lairs, your burrows, and touch me,' he'd roar. 'I am not a spirit, because a spirit has no flesh, no bones, and I do, as you can see!' 'You'd have to be blind not to see you, lardass!' they would call from their houses. 'That's enough now. Go home to bed!'

Three or four times a month the mayor's office would get a petition asking that Large Lenny be committed to an asylum. Nothing ever happened, however, because it would be a drain on public funds and also because his meanderings along Main Street brought in tourists from Princeton and Metuchen. 'Large Lenny might not be in his right mind,' Nancy said to me, 'but he's gentle as a butterfly.'

I left before it got dark, just as Nancy was trying to convince me that, with a bit of patience, it was possible to win a fortune playing bingo and the lottery. By then, I had managed to persuade Emilia to lend me some Stabilene sheets and partially completed maps her husband had drawn.

As she showed me out, she asked if I would mind meeting up now and then for a chat. 'I can't remember the last time I heard an Argentinian voice,' she said. I promised to call her, almost out of a sense of guilt. A week later, I bumped into her outside the Bagel Dish Café opposite the pharmacy and, having nothing better to do, agreed to join her for coffee. Without Nancy Frears around, Emilia turned out to be exactly as I expected: an intelligent woman preoccupied by the misfortunes of the world. She had just read Philip Roth's novel about Charles Lindberg and offered to show me the house where the hero's son had been kidnapped in 1932. 'If you like,' she said, slipping into the familiar Spanish *tuteo*, 'I can introduce you to the nice old man who lives there now. He's convinced he's Lindberg's lost child – he certainly acts like a child.' 'What do you mean, a child?' I asked. 'Twenty months old,' she said, 'the age Lindberg's son was when he was taken.'

When Emilia began to tell me her life story, I was writing a novel set in Buenos Aires and the last thing I wanted was to hear anything that would put me off: other people's memories can stir up private memories which I find distracting. But it was impossible not to be captivated by the skill with which she wove the tangled web of her story; by the measured, confiding tone that implied this was something she would not tell anyone else in the world. Sometimes, if I closed my eyes and followed the story, like a sailboat going where the wind takes it, it was like being alone with a good book because, like Maugham (Emilia had at least ten volumes of Maugham in Penguin Classics), she was a master of concealing the essential in order to reveal it gradually.

She was an avid reader with a keen intelligence. She could appreciate the similarities between Kafka's early work and Flaubert's *Sentimental Education*, and gave a detailed account of Guillermo Sánchez Trujillo's study on the influence of *Crime and Punishment* on *The Trial*, which theorised that Dostoevsky's novel provided Kafka with a template that allowed him to recount the break-up of his engagement to Felice Bauer. Our conversation was a series of endless, aimless stories, but we didn't care because this was why we were here, to talk about things that would be meaningless to anyone else in the town. I contributed my own share of trivia, mentioning – though it had nothing to do with the conversation – Dante's influence on Borges' mature poetry, something that seemed self-evident to me. I was about to explain why when Emilia interrupted me and recited long passages from *Infierno* and *Purgatorio*, interweaving them seamlessly with verses from *El otro, el mismo* and *Elogio de la sombra*, collections which Borges published just before he turned seventy. I don't know which Spanish translation of Dante she was quoting, but I know that what she did was a revelation, it made them seem like the work of a single poet. 'In both of them,' she said to me, 'and contrary to what the romantics and the symbolists believe, the state of blessedness and joy can attain an intensity that is more moving than that of suffering.'

I felt so comfortable in the hour and a half I spent with her, so surprised by her erudition, by the enthusiasm with which she bounded from one subject to another, that I invited her to join me for coffee at Starbucks in New Brunswick the following Saturday. When I called her at the Hammond offices on Friday to confirm, she asked me to swing by and pick her up half an hour earlier. She had something she wanted to show me, she said, and a story she wanted to tell me.

When I arrived, she was standing waiting for me on the stoop wearing jeans and sneakers with her hair pinned up. Only in that morning light did I notice that her eyes looked tired, her eyelids heavy, as though one half of her was hidden beneath the waning moon of her face.

'You know Loews cinema on Route 1?' she asked me.

'Sure,' I said. 'Everyone does.'

'Then you'll know that there's a grave in the middle of the parking lot.'

I was surprised, because I didn't know, though I park there every time I go to the movies. Sometimes, on summer nights, I drive up to the hill overlooking Raritan and gaze down at the gently flowing river and the lights on the far shore where my house is.

'What grave?' I asked.

'Come on, I'll show you.'

The vast wasteland of concrete behind the cinema stretched out in front of us. I parked next to a squat brick wall with an iron railing running around the top, as unremarkable as the oblique, lukewarm mid-morning sunshine. I had driven past dozens of times assuming it was an electrical substation, or a vent for the cinema's air-conditioning system.

'This is where they buried Mary Ellis,' Emilia said. 'According to legend, beneath her ashes are the ashes of her horse. If you come closer you can see her gravestone.'

I'd vaguely heard of Mary Ellis at some teachers' meeting, but always assumed she was a fictional character, someone from some unfinished novel by one of the Brontë sisters. But the delicate marble bust depicted a real woman with a long nose and ringlets in her hair, and underneath, her dates, cut into the stone: 1773–1794.

'Mary Ellis's diary is in the Princeton manuscript library,' Emilia told me as we sat down in Starbucks on George Street with our cappuccinos. 'According to their records, nobody ever bothers to read it. The information about her child-hood I've managed to find in encyclopedias on New Jersey is not very reliable, but what Mary herself wrote – her story – is as moving as Cathy Earnshaw's confession in *Wuthering Heights*. Mary, as she herself says many times, *was* the man she loved. At eighteen, she became engaged to a young lieutenant called William Clay. Mary was an orphan, she had no dowry and lived with a paternal aunt in a house in New Brunswick. Once or twice a week she would ride down to the riverbank to meet with Clay alone. The townsfolk talked. When the pastor of the local Presbyterian church gave a sermon about couples who outraged decency and courted the wrath of God, a number of accusing faces turned to stare at her. But Mary didn't think the sermon referred to her. She was about to get married; she was happy. Two weeks before the wedding, Lieutenant Clay asked her to meet him urgently at their usual place by the river. There, he told her that he had been called up to quell a farmers' uprising in Pennsylvania and was due to ship out that night. "Within the month," he told her, "I will come back for you; I'll hoist a yellow shawl on the mainmast and announce my arrival with two shots from a harquebus. Then we shall be able to marry." As proof of his love, Clay gave her the magnificent black horse he had inherited from his father. A month passed, and then another. News eventually reached New Brunswick that the uprising had been quelled in a matter of hours without a shot being fired and the troops had been given leave. After she heard this Mary would saddle the black horse every afternoon and ride to the clifftop overlooking the Raritan. Her diary begins here, in the first week of her wait. She gives a detailed account of her daily two-mile ride, describes the countryside in rain or fog and her trepidation whenever a ship hove into view.'

'I don't know much about you,' I said, 'but I can't imagine why you find Mary Ellis so fascinating.'

'There's no need to imagine. We have one thing in common: neither of us ever saw the man we loved again. Two years later, Mary found out that Lieutenant Clay had married the heiress to a South Carolina plantation. Yet still she went every afternoon to the same place by the river for a meeting with no one. Her diary after this is confused. She was losing her mind. In the autumn of 1794, when the waters of the Raritan rose to record heights, Mary rode out to the clifftop and, with her horse, leaped into the torrent without even leaving a note.'

'She didn't need to.'

'When her body was found at Perth Amboy near the mouth of the Raritan, Mary was still clinging to her horse, her feet still in the stirrups. No cemetery was prepared to give her a Christian burial so devout hands buried her on the hilltop and her horse with her. The grave was constantly covered with flowers and became a place where young girls would go to tell their tales of lost love, so the governor of Jersey declared the plot of land sacrosanct. In the years that followed, the land around it was used as a pig farm, later a restaurant, then a flea market. Now it's a cinema, though lovers no longer come to visit the tomb. But every time someone stops in front of the grave, they see the image of a woman, scanning the horizon, waiting for her lover to return.'

'So this is the story you wanted to tell me,' I said.

'No. I wanted to show you Mary Ellis's grave, but the story I called you about is my own. You said you don't know very much about me. From that first time we talked in the Bagel Cafe I've been thinking I'd like to tell you something more about me. But I don't know if we'll have time right now. It's noon. You need to get back to the university.'

'I'm free until two o'clock.'

I invited her to split a salad at Toscana, a quiet, discreet restaurant nearby. I regretted the offer almost immediately. Words poured from Emilia in that frantic torrent of those who spend too much time alone. I was afraid I would be bored.

The wind had picked up; the only people walking along George Street were a few idle students and shop workers finishing their shift. I was overcome, as so often, by a feeling of melancholy at being so far from my own country, in this foreign suburb in which nothing ever happened.

Within ten minutes, Emilia had filled in the trivial details of her friendship with Nancy Frears, the emptiness of her weekends, her routine of bingo, Mass on Sundays, trips to the beauty salon. Books and films, she told me, had saved her life. She said sometimes she was terrified that, like Mary Ellis, she would lose her mind.

'More than once I've woken up in the middle of the night with the feeling that my husband is in the room.'

'There's nothing strange about that. It happens to all of us. We're dreaming and when we wake up the dream lingers for a while.'

'No, it's more real than that. I feel that Simón is standing by the door to my room, not daring to come in.'

'It's because you never saw his body. That's why.'

'Who knows? The courts declared him dead and I did everything I could to kill him inside me. Because he had no grave, I was his grave. Now he wants to leave it.'

'You should buy a cemetery plot for him, even if it's only symbolic. Bury everything you have of his somewhere.'

'I don't have any of his clothes or his things any more. All I've got is a photo and a wedding ring. I couldn't bring myself to bury them.'

'Maybe the time has come to let him go . . .'

'I've spent years doing everything I can to make him go. I came to Highland Park to escape from the past, and I almost succeeded. I didn't go back to Buenos Aires, I stopped talking to my parents. Whole days would go by when I didn't think of Simón once, didn't even dream about him. The next morning I would feel guilty, but I would also feel a thrill of victory. Since then, he's come back, little by little. If I just knew where his body was, I wouldn't have to go through this agony.'

We had ordered pumpkin soup and tuna salad, but we barely touched the food. Much later I realised that we were so cut off from the real world that it hardly mattered whether we were in Toscana or somewhere else. Emilia seemed desperate to tell her story, though just then she had more questions than answers, more wishes than questions. But her wishes could not be fulfilled, or perhaps they had already been fulfilled without her realising. Nothing is more terrible than to wish for something you believe you can never have.

'It's all in the past. Don't torment yourself.'

'I don't. That's the worst thing: I don't feel any pain any more. I've grown used to the absence of the only person I ever loved. What's strange is that I know I'm not the same person since I lost him and yet I carry on as though nothing happened. I feel despicable.'

'You've no reason to. Nancy told me you spent fifteen years searching for him.'

'Fifteen? I was searching for him even before I met him. Now I'm waiting for him to come searching for me. At Mass last Sunday Father Flannagan's sermon was about purgatory. The Catholic Church used to teach that purgatory was a necessary purification for imperfect souls before they could enter paradise, that accepting suffering as an act of love for God and all forms of penitence was purgatory. That's how things used to be. Not any more. The Church is more tolerant these days, Father Flannagan said. Now, purgatory is seen as a wait whose end we cannot know.'

All things come to an end, I told her, even eternity. It was a cliché and as I said it aloud it sounded even more clichéd.

She shook her head.

'Not Simón. Simón is still there at the door to my bedroom. I know it's him. He wants me to see him, to let him in. I don't know how to do it.'

'It's not Simón in the doorway. It's your love for him that won't leave you in peace.'

'Simón disappeared one morning in Tucumán. That was thirty years ago,' she said. 'For a while I lived out what seemed like a normal life in my parents' house.'

From time to time, Emilia got messages from people who claimed to have seen her husband dead in this place or that. She went on drawing maps as though nothing had happened. Nothing seemed strange to her. She herself could have sworn she saw Simón at the Country Show or among the visitors to the Buenos Aires Book Fair. He was her God and, like the God of the Church, he was omnipresent. Sooner or later he would return. She had only to be patient. But she could not stop herself worrying when she received these messages about the life he was living far from her. She would lie awake for days convinced that at any moment he would ring the doorbell and explain why he had disappeared without so much as a word. But he never did come, and over time the physical need she felt to hold him in her arms waned. She became resigned to solitude, to abandonment; she began to forget there had been a time when she felt neither alone nor abandoned.

I asked where she had looked for him – cities, beaches, bars, hospitals. As she told me, something inexplicable happened to me. It has no bearing on this story but if I don't mention it I'll feel as though nothing that happened that afternoon was real. And it was. We were a couple of blocks from the train station and every now and then we'd feel a blast of wind from a passing train. I looked out the window of the restaurant and, in place of the grey shapes of the buildings, the discount clothing store, the university bookshop, the branches of the major banks that had always been there, I saw the gently rolling pampas outside Buenos Aires, with cows lifting their heads to the sky and lowing as though they too were leaving with the train. Emilia went on talking – about the beaches of Brazil, the mountains of Venezuela, the flea markets of Mexico City – and still I saw the pampas there where it had no business being. In that moment I believed that Simón stood in the doorway of Emilia's bedroom on North 4th Avenue. I was prepared to believe whatever she told me. If I did not believe her, why was I listening?

'The first news of Simón that seemed genuine came from one of my father's sisters,' she went on.

She was no longer looking at me. I felt like one of her maps. On a map you can be whatever you want to be: the pampas, the Amazon rainforest, a ruined city, an imaginary island.

'My aunt said she'd seen Simón at the Ipanema Theatre in Rio de Janeiro where she was working as assistant set designer. She'd gone over to say hello but Simón had run off. As soon as I heard this, I decided I had to go there. I spent six months in Rio going from one theatre to another and then from one map company to another. Nobody had heard of him, the whole story was a sick joke.'

I asked her whether she had tackled her aunt about it.

'I sent her a letter. She never replied. My sister Chela thinks my father put her up to it, asked her to lie to me to get me out of Buenos Aires. The country was in chaos at the time and I think my father, who'd always been so sure of himself, was afraid that I might become a troublesome witness. The thousands of dead, the concentration camps, the unmarked graves left behind by the military junta were just beginning to come to light and my father had sanctioned every one of those crimes. It was more than that – he did not think of them as crimes. After what we now call *the dictatorship* took power, my father became a rich man, a very rich man. The junta advanced him loans he never repaid, gave him million-dollar commissions, subsidies for public works that had no useful purpose. For my father, it was constantly raining money. He bought land in some of the most fertile areas of the pampas, luxury flats in Paris, in New York, in Barcelona.'

'Maybe you could move into one of his palaces,' I said with a sarcasm I instantly regretted.

'I left Buenos Aires with only the clothes I stood up in and what money I'd saved from my job. Later, I found there was money in my accounts that wasn't mine and I spent it, but only so I could go on searching for Simón. My father owed him that. My father doesn't know where I am now or what

I'm doing. The only person who knows is Chela, but if she ever tells him, I'll lose my only sister forever.'

'Just now, when you said "what we now call *the dictatorship*", I thought you were a collaborator too. I'm sorry. Because what we went through *was* a dictatorship, the most vicious dictatorship Argentina ever suffered, and God knows we've suffered a few. But since you were a victim of it, why do you still refuse to accept they murdered Simón? More than one witness testified as much, it was established at a trial that no one disputes.'

'Because they didn't murder him. I didn't believe it when I left for Rio and I don't believe it now. Simón is alive. It's been thirty years and he is still alive. I know. I can feel him inside me. The witnesses saw what they wanted to see. If they blew his head off, as they say, how could the witnesses have recognised him? The only person who could have was me. But I didn't see him. Simón is alive. I know it. When he comes back, he'll explain why he left and everything will make sense. Shall I go on?'

'Sure, go ahead.'

'After the Malvinas War, the dictatorship collapsed. By then, Chela was living in Texas with her husband and I didn't want to leave my mother all alone in Buenos Aires. The air was thick with old grudges demanding retribution. My father had been one of the junta's most visible collaborators – though he had also been one of the first to sing the praises of democracy – and he was probably afraid that I would mention Simón.'

'Nobody could have blamed you. Your husband was one of the disappeared. You were a victim.'

'Nobody did blame me. I blamed myself for having been stupid and gullible, for having been a collaborator, in my own way. My conscience wouldn't leave me alone. My father wouldn't leave me alone. He would come and stand by my bedside, stroke my shoulder, my hair. He'd never been demonstrative but now suddenly, whenever we were alone, he was overly affectionate. In the end all I felt for him was disgust, pity and disgust. There was nothing left for me in Rio and I missed my mother. I wanted to go back to Buenos Aires to take care of her. I checked the bus timetables – back then it was a twenty-hour trip – and decided to leave as soon as possible when suddenly I got a phone call from Caracas. Some woman I didn't know asked if I was related to Simón Cardoso. I'm his wife, I told her. "I'm Nurse Coromoto at the Centro Médico La Trinidad," she said. "Your husband was brought into the emergency department two hours ago suffering from paroxysmal atrial fibrillation. We've already given him IV digoxin." "I don't understand a word you're saying," I interrupted her. "You don't understand? Simón Cardoso is suffering from serious cardiac arrhythmia. He needs intensive care but claims that he has no money. If no one is prepared to cover the cost of his treatment, we'll have to send him to a public hospital where he'll be lucky to be treated at all." The nurse's voice was clipped, harsh, urgent. I begged her to admit Simón for forty-eight hours. I would leave immediately, I told her, and I would pay for everything. I'd never even been to Caracas. And I had no money left and was not about to call my father.'

'You must have been desperate.'

'I was, and I couldn't think about anything except how to get there. By the time I hung up, I was crying. It had been seven years since Huacra and the empty hours and days were finally beginning to be filled, to have a purpose, a direction. I went to Galeão airport at five in the morning and asked at every counter for the quickest flight to Caracas. I found a flight leaving Rio at eleven and connecting in Bogotá and bought a ticket with a credit card I'd never used before and didn't know how I would pay off. As soon as the banks opened, I went to withdraw the last three hundred dollars I had in my account. I was told I had a balance of five thousand dollars. My father, again. Sooner or later I would have to pay the money back, but at that point I didn't care how.'

'So your father knew where you were?'

'No. He'd been putting money in my account for months, though I never asked him for anything. He just did it, like he always did. To him, I was just something that bought and spent. Caracas unsettled me. I felt strange, as though I'd just arrived in Luanda or Nauru. The city centre was teeming with hawkers and office workers speaking some sort of onomato-poeic language in which I could only make out scraps of Spanish. In travel agencies and cafes and countless discount shops I asked for directions to the Centro Médico and every time I was sent off in a different direction, to some remote area: Antímano, Boleíta, El Silencio, Propatria. I had so much trouble finding the place I began to wonder if it really existed. I mentioned La Trinidad to an assistant in a clothes shop and she said that she thought there was a big clinic out there that dealt with infectious diseases. I decided to take a chance. I hailed a cab and the driver refused to take me, as did the next four or five taxis. They said that it was too far, that they'd have to drive out through the dark hills. When I finally did manage to persuade a driver, I realised how dangerous it was. La Trinidad is about fifteen kilometres from the Plaza Bolívar, at the end of a tangle of winding streets perched on a cliff overlooking a ravine. The taxi's engine coughed and sputtered, but it kept going. By the time we arrived it was almost midnight. The duty nurse took pity on me; she checked the computer for patients recently admitted or discharged. No one named Simón Cardoso appeared on the list and she went back several years.'

'It was a hoax. Like Rio.'

'I didn't think so at the time. At the time I didn't even realise that Rio had been a set-up. I hadn't had anything to eat for hours and I fainted. When I came round, I asked for Nurse Coromoto. The only person by that name who worked at the clinic was in the accounts department. I assumed I'd come to the wrong hospital. It was the logical explanation. Why would anyone go to the trouble of phoning me from Caracas in the middle of the night to tell me the one lie that could persuade me to leave Rio. What difference did it make whether I was in Brazil or Venezuela?'

'Your father again. Do you know why he was doing it?'

'No. Maybe to torment me, to keep me away. He didn't trust me.'

Sitting in Toscana listening to Emilia it seemed to me she was three distinct women, first, the woman who was gravely telling me about her tragic past, dwarfed by her father's looming shadow but determined not to be cowed, not to allow this dark force to destroy her will to survive. Next, the woman who wore white-and-purple-patterned false nails that made her slender fingers look unspeakably vulgar. And a third, who complemented the other two – the first perhaps more than the second – an intelligent woman who would recite the poems of Gonzalo Rojas and John Ashbery, who recited Marianne Moore's zoological creatures drawing out the words until they became disconnected from reality, until they were no more than words: *we do not admire what we cannot understand: the bat . . . a tireless wolf under a tree.*

'It's easy to get lost in Caracas,' I said to her. 'When I lived there, there were lots of clinics and neighbourhoods called Trinidad: Lomas de la Trinidad, Hacienda de la Trinidad, Trinidad Santísima.'

'I found that out in the weeks that followed. I rented a cheap apartment in Chacaíto, the only part of the city with sidewalks and cafes. Every morning at seven o'clock I'd set off on my tour of hospitals and clinics looking for Simón. I didn't always manage to get help. It was just before Christmas and people were in no mood to hear about other people's misfortunes. I told my story to the nurses and the doctors, but they barely listened. Thousands of Argentinians had come to Caracas before me, all telling the same story. After a few weeks it occurred to me to print flyers with Simón's photo and stick them up in the kiosks around Sabana Grande in case someone recognised him. The few people who got in touch wanted me to give them money, wanted me to come alone. They were con artists pure and simple. I was taken in by some of them and frittered away the last of my savings.'

'You could have got a job. It was possible to get work back then.'

'I did, I applied to be a cartographer with the Venezuelan Oil Company and they gave me the curious job of naming the intricate network of roads carved into the hills around the city like an amphitheatre. I spent my mornings walking up endless flights of steps, losing myself in the winding lanes that led to barns or sawmills, to storehouses of cardboard, carefully noting down the nicknames given them by locals, mostly names related to local characters: Iván el Cobero, Paloma Mojada, Coño Verde, La Cangrejera, things like that. What had been a series of dotted lines, an undocumented circulatory system, I drew together with a skein of words. I divided my time between this hare-brained task and my trips to the hospitals. I could feel Simón slipping through my fingers, but at night, as soon as I fell asleep, he appeared in my dreams. I was reading a lot of Swedenborg at the time, and took to heart his idea that human beings are merely "cyphers", a vestige of the writings of God which allows us to be other, to be elsewhere, if God should decide that what He has written means something different. More than once I went to the Cinemateca de Caracas to see Hitchcock's *Vertigo*, with Kim Novak as a ghost so carnal that you accept her death precisely because it is an oxymoron. But the true corpse in the movie is obviously James Stewart, a man who loses the woman he loves not once but twice. I couldn't bear to be Stewart, I couldn't bear to lose Simón a second time. I would have been better off forgetting, but I realised that I would never be able to forget. I had grown used to being alone, to fending for myself, to ignoring the sexual innuendos of the men of Caracas who didn't seem to know the meaning of the word "no". Like I said, I lived only to find him.

'In the Cinemateca, a film critic came up to me on the pretext of talking about Hitchcock. He was the first man I'd found attractive since Simón, the only one I might have fallen in love with. When he looked at me, it was as though I was the only woman on the planet; he devoured me with his eyes, not sexually but with a genuine desire to discover who I was. He had that cinnamon-coloured skin so many Venezuelans have, and pale, piercing eyes. After the screening of *Vertigo* we went to the Ateneo de Caracas for coffee. He was careful and precise in his words. He pointed out to me the wealth of clues Hitchcock gives in the first scene that Scottie – James Stewart's character – is impotent: the way he uses his cane, the detail that he hasn't had a girlfriend for two years. We talked for over an hour. When we left, he invited me to go to the beach with him the following Sunday – something that in Caracas is part of a game that inevitably leads to sex – and I was on the point of accepting. In the end I told him I'd think about it and call him. When I got back to my apartment in Chacaíto, I realised I was about to make a mistake. I would have liked to be able to spend time with him, to feel less alone, but his advances would have become more persistent, in the end we would have quarrelled. There was nothing natural about my ascetic life, yet I felt completely at peace. I thought I was avoiding men for fear that Simón would reappear just as I was about to start a new relationship, but it wasn't that. The truth was that I wasn't available to anyone but him. Losing him had not only quenched my sexual desire, it had snuffed out *all* my desires. I would not be myself again until I found him. I didn't go back to the Cinemateca and for weeks I didn't answer my phone or go back to the beach. I don't know how this guy found out I worked for the state oil company, but he ended up leaving me a slew of messages. Over time, the fear I might run into him subsided and I took to going back to the beach though only to more remote beaches where I thought it was less likely that I would run into him. In Oricao or Osma, I roamed wild untamed paths with the singer Soledad Bravo, who would sing as the sun was sinking into the sea, in a voice as huge and golden as the papayas.'

'How long was it before you realised Simón wasn't in

Caracas? In your shoes, I would have given up within a year.'

'Five years, two months and twenty-one days. From December 15, 1983, until March 8, 1989. And if I left Venezuela, it wasn't because I chose to. It was chance.'

The waiter at Toscana reappeared and asked if we wanted anything else. We were the only people left in the restaurant. Outside on the street, usually busy in the afternoons, there was only the hum of traffic. It was after two o'clock but Emilia seemed unaware of the time and indeed the world. In the grey flashes of light from the street I saw her as, two centuries earlier, the villagers of New Brunswick must have seen Mary Ellis: standing alone on the banks of the Raritan waiting for a man who would never come.

'We should go,' I said.

'Please, can we just stay a few more minutes? Don't leave me in the middle of the chance event that forced me to leave Caracas. The story isn't very long. It begins with an anonymous letter. I've no idea how the postal system in Venezuela works these days, but back then mail was sporadic – all the more so after the Caracazo uprising. On the Saturday after the riots, the mood of the city was solemn. No one dared to go out for fear of another wave of violence. The post offices were all closed and yet, bizarrely, that Saturday, I received a registered letter from Buenos Aires with no return address. I opened the envelope warily. Inside, there was a cutting from a Mexican newspaper, *Uno más Uno*, an article by someone called Simón Cardoso. It could have been by anyone of that name, but the article – which was about the hunt for and the arrest of the head of the Mexican Petroleum Workers' Union, a man known as "la Quina" – was illustrated with a map of

Ciudad Madero on the Gulf Coast, and in the map I recognised the mistakes my husband always made with place names. I never did find out who sent me the cutting, or how they found out my address – Chela was the only person who knew it. By the time I got the letter, the article was two or three weeks old. I couldn't wait. By then, I was deputy head of the cartography department, I was taking home twelve hundred dollars a month and managing to save five hundred. What with the chaos that followed the riots, flights took off as and when they could. I spent days sleeping on the floor at the airport. At 6 a.m. on March 8, a voice on the tannoy announced a flight departing for Mexico City, via Panama. I wept, I screamed, I invented illnesses, deaths in the family, anything so they would give me a seat. That's how I arrived in Mexico City, as penniless as when I left Rio. With my savings suddenly worthless, I holed up in a hawkers' guest house near Zócalo and started looking for my love all over again, though I didn't hold out much hope. I spent more than two years chasing mirages – newspapers that had been shut down, scandal sheets that had never started up, prying into illegal agencies that created maps of Utopia for the dreamers who wanted to cross the border into the United States. I risked my life in brightly lit rooms where, with state-of-the-art computers, the finest cartographers in the world helped drug traffickers find little-travelled routes between their laboratories and their secret airstrips. I helped them out as much to boost my earnings as to gain the protection of the drug bosses who, through their contacts at immigration, could find out who entered and left Mexico.'

'You could have stayed there.'

'I could. But then, one morning, I woke up convinced that

I would never find Simón. He was alive but he couldn't see me. I had to stop looking for him so that he could look for me. It was a revelation. He had to come back the way he had left. I felt that that was how things were, how they had always been, and they could never be otherwise. I'd spent years and years chasing a chimera. I'd allowed myself to be led by signs dangled before me by other people rather than being led by what I felt inside. It was too late to get back the time I'd lost. But at least I could help make sure Simón could see me, draw him to me, position myself within the same orbit. Maps,' she said. 'If I can put myself on the same map as him, sooner or later we're bound to meet. When I say it out loud, it sounds silly, but to me it seems self-evident. If time is the fourth dimension, who knows how many things exist that we cannot see in space–time, how many invisible realities. Maps are almost infinite, and at the same time they're unfinished. The maps of Highland Park, for example, don't include the *eruv*, they don't include those residents who will be born tomorrow. In order to be able to see Simón, I needed to drop off – or rise above – a map, if possible every map. I was still based in Mexico City at the time. I got up, I went to Sanborns restaurant in the Casa de los Azulejos, and I started sending letters to every mapping company in the US and Canada. I wanted to get as far away as I could. If I'd been offered a job in Hawaii or Alaska, I would have taken it. Two weeks later, I got a reply from Hammond. They had a vacancy for an assistant in Maplewood, New Jersey.'

'It's getting late,' I said. 'I'm sorry.' I was exhausted by the conversation and I still had no idea what she was trying to tell me.

'Let's go,' she agreed. 'I'm sorry for keeping you.'

I drove her back in silence. The streets of Highland Park were hung with banners advertising hot-air balloon flights, fireworks and free ice cream in Donaldson Park. The town was about to celebrate its 102nd birthday.

As we pulled into North 4th Avenue, we saw Large Lenny weaving from one sidewalk to the other carrying thick red candles that were burning his hands as they melted. He seemed insensible to the pain, staring at some fixed point in the middle distance. But however disconnected he was from the world, something had made him cry. Tears spilled silently from his eyes and followed a roundabout course to drip from his jaw. A gang of kids was following him, firing pebbles at him with elastic bands. Emilia couldn't bear it.

'Leave him alone,' she shouted. 'Can't you see he's crying?'

'I'm not crying,' the giant corrected her. 'I forgive them, for they know not what they do.'

'Are you OK, Lenny?' Emilia comforted him. 'You want me to take you home?'

The question was ridiculous, no one knew where Large Lenny lived. Everyone assumed one of the local synagogues gave him shelter, but it was impossible to know which since he visited all of them.

'I thirst,' he answered.

We had arrived at the door to Emilia's house and she went upstairs to her apartment to get him a bottle of cold water. A couple of neighbours were peering out of their windows. In the distance, I heard the announcer's voice from the sports field. Some high-school students were playing a match.

'Blow out those candles, Lenny,' I said. 'You're burning your hands.'

'They have to be lit. For the res'rection.'

When Emilia brought the water, the giant set the candles down on the porch and drank straight from the bottle, the water coursing noisily down his cavernous throat.

'Large Lenny thinks someone's come back to life,' the downstairs neighbour informed Emilia. The guy gave a little laugh, and from some nearby balconies came a chorus of jeers.

'Who's the dead guy? Him?'

'I am no longer of this world,' said the giant. 'Someone who was lost is coming back to the world and if these candles don't show him the light he won't find his way.'

'Where is this person?' Emilia asked, going along with his train of thought. 'So we can help them . . .'

'You don't need to, that's what I'm saying. You should know that better than me.'

Large Lenny handed back the empty bottle and headed off towards Main Street still shouting verses from the Gospel according to Luke, but I was no longer listening. I went home.

When they got back from their honeymoon, Simón and Emilia thought they were Parmenides' 'One Being, eternal', a being that would never move from itself into the past or towards anything else; things are never as we expect them to be, things are not even as they appear.

The taxi driver who picked them up at the airport told them that Ringo Bonavena had been murdered outside a brothel in Reno, Nevada, the week before. The flat-footed boxer with the rippling muscles and a voice like a little girl's had been killed by a single shot to the chest. Ringo would never again sing 'Pajarito pío pío'. 'He was killed by a gangster,' the driver told them. 'Imagine it: the eighteen-stone brick shithouse who KO'd Ron Hicks in the first minute, the guy who held out fifteen rounds against Cassius Clay, died because of some dumb argument with a bodyguard in some two-bit whorehouse, excuse my language, señora. They flew his body back last Friday. You wouldn't believe the number of people lined up to see him. Yesterday there was thousands of guys standing in the rain.'

At 9.30 a.m. the air seemed dirty, thick with fog and smelling of disinfectant. The car inched down the avenida del Libertador towards the San Telmo apartment which was as unfamiliar, as impersonal to Emilia and Simón as a hotel room. They had been so taken with the apartment when they had viewed it, with the balconies overlooking the Parque Lezama, that Dr Dupuy had bought it for them as a wedding present, and insisted they should not move in until it had been completely redecorated and furnished. Emilia's mother picked the paint colours for the walls, the dining set, the bedroom curtains, the carpets, the crockery and the cutlery. Simón had insisted that they at least be allowed to bring the drawing tables, the encyclopedias and the cartography manuals they had had when they were still single, so some part of their identity would be preserved.

The redecoration had taken longer than expected, forcing them to spend a month in Punta del Este after their long cruise back from Recife. They arrived exhausted but excited. It was Sunday and there was something melancholy about the light in Buenos Aires. Ringo Bonavena's body had been flown home so that he might be added to the list of national saints, a pantheon which already included Gardel, Perón and Evita. The streets around the Plaza Roma were crowded with parked cars from the funeral cortège, all decked out in black crape and floral wreaths. As they passed Luna Park, they were overtaken

97

at top speed by a Mercedes-Benz with tinted windows which jumped the traffic lights. Emilia recognised it as her father's car and told the driver to park wherever he could find a space in the fleet of funeral cars. She wanted to surprise her father; what she could not know was that it was she who would be surprised, because Dr Dupuy stepped into Luna Park Stadium with his arm around the waist of a woman who – from behind at least – looked young and glitzy. Simón reluctantly got out of the car; he did not want their return in Buenos Aires ruined by an ugly scene between father and daughter, but, as she told the story thirty years later, Emilia had known exactly what she was doing. Nothing, she believed, not even shame, could perturb her father.

When the stadium doors were opened, all eyes turned to the catafalque which now occupied the area at the foot of the empty bleachers where the boxing ring had been. The coffin was lit by four church candles, the kind that stream wax, and by the red and green glow of garish spotlights. Bonavena's *mater dolorosa* gently stroked the face of the son who looked so much like her, as though touching her own death. In a timeless mirror, events continued to repeat themselves. A television presenter knelt before the mother, took her hands and kissed them. Hadn't they seen this scene before on *Telenoche* or *Videoshow*? Everything was the same and yet everything was different, as though events had been rewound to be played out again. So the crowds of onlookers lining the streets to watch Bonavena's cortège pass waited with the same impatience they had twenty-five years earlier when they had waited for Evita's coffin, but this time there could be no miracle: though the events were the same, in shifting from one era to another they were recreated in a new form.

Dr Dupuy stood before the coffin for a moment and, turning, found himself face to face with his daughter. Emilia didn't recognise the woman on his arm, but Simón recognised her immediately. He had read an article in a doctor's waiting room describing her as a woman who collected powerful lovers, a writer of romantic novels that sold in their thousands though no one knew anyone who actually bought them.

'This is Nora Balmaceda,' Dr Dupuy introduced her. This, they knew, was the end of their honeymoon.

They didn't have time to say anything because just at that moment the undertakers set about sealing the zinc coffin with blowtorches and Ringo's mother fainted. 'That's the sixth time,' Emilia informed Señora Balmaceda; she had heard about the previous five fainting spells on the morning news. 'But I didn't tell her that until afterwards,' Emilia recalled in Highland Park, 'because the minute she saw that grieving lump of lard collapse, Nora Balmaceda rushed over to help her.' She managed to put her arms around her just as the paparazzi – at Dr Dupuy's signal – froze the scene with their cameras. The picture made the front page of the late editions, printed as big as the photo of the cortège at the intersection of the avenida de Mayo and the Nueve de Julio. Even the caption – 'A mother and a writer united in grief' – had been dictated by Dupuy.

Back then, anything was possible. Propaganda manufactured illusions of happiness in the wasteland of misery. Every week, magazines published eyewitness accounts of astonished gauchos who had seen fleets of flying saucers in the night sky. Schoolchildren were taught the topography of Mars, Ananke, Titan, Enceladus and Ganymede with as much dedication as they had been forced to learn by heart the names of the rivers of Europe and Siberia during the Second World War. The emissaries from alien planets, they were told, came in peace, took a number of human specimens to study their emotions and after some years – twenty, a hundred, no one knew how many – returned them to earth or kept them permanently in specialised zoos. A government minister had personally seen two large saucers collecting human specimens in the barren wilderness of the Valle de la Luna. The alien crew, he said, were small creatures with large heads ringed with a halo of light that seemed to protect them from our oxygenated atmosphere. With benign expressions, they were herding some twenty people they had undoubtedly collected in the cities into their spaceships. They invited the minister to join the expedition but he explained that his governmental responsibilities made it impossible. This account, from such a solemn governmental source, dispelled the doubts of even the most sceptical. News items about flying saucers were everywhere. *Voluntad*, a monthly magazine, interviewed six pilots who had encountered alien fleets while at the controls. One pilot, who flew the route between Río Gallegos and Ushuaia – virtually the end of the world – had even managed to photograph two spherical objects with their spindly landing gear.

Over Christmas, Nora Balmaceda became one of the chosen. Even the hardest of hearts in the country were moved by her tale – a tale that proved infinitely more successful than her romantic novels. She had persuaded her husband, a pallid heir to ten thousand hectares in the Humid Pampa, to spend Christmas of 1976 in San Antonio de los Cobres, some four thousand metres above sea level, and then drive down to Salta to see in the new year. On 26 December, they set off in their jeep towards Las Cuevas, forty kilometres south-east, taking the steep, rocky course of Ruta 51 at a moderate speed. It took more than two hours to cover the first two-thirds of the journey. Arriving in the tiny village of Encrucijada they stopped to urinate. A milky glow of stars was stealing across the nine o'clock dusk. Not a thing was moving, not even an insect, and the silence – as Nora told the newspapers – was thick as syrup. Her husband went around the hood of the jeep while she went to pee in the shelter of the escarpment. They were heading back to their vehicle when, from nowhere, they were blinded by a dazzling light that spilled its sulphurous breath over them. Nora managed, with some difficulty, to climb back into the jeep. Through the windshield she saw tiny hairless humanoid creatures floating in a firestorm of yellow flame. Suddenly, the light was snuffed out and she was left in an inexplicable state of torpor. Perhaps she fell asleep, though only for a minute or two. When she came to, she found herself several hours' drive away in Rosario de Lerma at the wheel of the jeep. Her husband had disappeared. The only possible explanation was that this light, by some preternatural magnetic force, had drawn him up into the heavens. Every TV channel showed the same footage: Nora, tearful, inconsolable, trans-figured as she described her visions of another world. 'There's nothing I wouldn't give to take my husband's place,' she said. 'He has found his Shangri-La, has entered the seventh circle of paradise, he has discovered the supreme wisdom of God.'

Nora was photographed in widow's weeds for *Gente*. The title of the article – in which Dr Dupuy's hand was evident – was borrowed from Quevedo: 'Love Constant Beyond Death'. Through her lawyers, Nora declared her intention to seek control and use of her husband's lands until he should return from space. After speedy proceedings, the courts ruled in her favour declaring the case 'Another close encounter of the third kind'.

Spielberg's film of the same title was causing a furore in cinemas at the time. Spielberg's aliens communicated by means of musical notes and – unlike those at Encrucijada or the Valle de la Luna – did not abduct objects or people. But whatever the form and the language of the alien visitors, in Argentina their existence was accepted as an article of faith. On the cover of the *Dimensión Desconocida*, the actor Fabio Zerpa formulated a question which the priest echoed in his Sunday sermon: 'Are we so vain as to believe we are the only children of God in the universe?'

The affair between Emilia's father and Balmaceda had been going on for about a year at the time Bonavena was murdered. The World Cup was coming up and women – with the exception of models and strippers – completely disappeared from the news. La Balmaceda was inconsolable at being suddenly eclipsed by virtue of being a widow and because of her lack of interest in the military junta. Her last novel had been published in 1974 and she was not writing another. Early in June, shortly before the start of the World Cup, she made another bid for fame, publishing an article in the *Somos* offering to 'motivate' – this was the word she used – the Argentinian players in the changing rooms and the gyms where they trained. The article, entitled 'Country Comes First' made her a laughing stock. Emilia's father felt so humiliated by his lover's blunder that he stopped taking her calls. Balmaceda wasted little time in replacing him with a tennis champion, posing with him next to his tennis trophies for the press, and later with a ship's captain who eventually ended up with the land that had belonged to the husband now lost in space.

She firmly resisted the mortifications of age. In photographs in *Gente*, day by day, month by month, it was possible to watch as her laughter lines, the bags under her eyes, the folds of her double chin, gradually disappeared; watch as her eyes became bigger, her lips fuller, as her tits and her ass defied the effects of gravity. Once the cycle was complete and she had recovered her lost youth, Nora stumbled on another profitable idea, one which once again sold thousands of books. In flights of mystical rapture she described a wrestling tournament between the angels: the seraphim who had six wings, and the cherubim who had only four. She wrote pages and pages of incomprehensible drivel (which people nonetheless reverently quoted by heart) which, she said, were dictated to her by beneficent angels lately returned from visiting God. Her greatest success came when she announced that she had witnessed an apparition of the Virgin Mary on the plains of Esteco, 1300 kilometres north-east of Buenos Aires. A prosperous city had been established there in the late sixteenth century, but by the time Nora Balmaceda drove past with a military escort in search of angels it was a barren wilderness. She had read somewhere that Esteco had been razed by the earthquake of 1692, and the winds of God's wrath had wiped out its heathen inhabitants. On the banks of the Río Pasaje, where a six-foot menhir marks the spot of the former settlement, Nora had met a goatherd, a little girl who was visited by the Mother of God at dawn every Wednesday. The little girl told Nora that the Virgin appeared as a form without a face, a gentle voice, enfolded in a mantle of light. These visions, wrote Nora, could only be of the Blessed Virgin. 'Our Lady has come back to this world to put an end to the brutality of atheist extremism and to redeem those who are prepared to repent.' In her conversations with the little shepherdess, the Virgin had asked that a maximum security basilica (a basilica, not a chapel, Nora insited) be built nearby where she would personally cleanse misguided souls and guide them to heaven. The magazine in which her article was published saw its circulation triple and before the place could be overrun with penitent pilgrims, the junta dispatched sick prisoners from jails and ordered them to dig the foundations of this new temple. Two months after first meeting the little goatherd, Nora wrote that the girl had watched, overjoyed, as the prisoners ascended into heaven on a carpet of light. On a local radio station the prophet was heard to say, 'Angels took them up to heaven.'

Nora Balmaceda basked for a little longer in her rapturous success, dealt with the avalanche of foreign publishers begging to translate her books. In the midst of this frenzied whirl of success, she committed suicide by taking cyanide. She left no letter, no explanation and no will. Before she lay down to die, she put on a white organza blouse and made herself up as though going to a ball. On the nightstand there were two other sodium cyanide tablets. Her faded beauty was intact. No one claimed her body. There had been no sightings of her husband since his abduction by aliens and no relatives appeared. Dr Dupuy gave one of his assistants the task of having her buried with modesty and discretion. Later, he called a bishop friend of his and asked that the Church take possession of all her worldly goods.

Stories that would chill the blood continued to circulate about the disappearances that took place during those years. In old bookshops in Buenos Aires, it is still possible to find copies of magazines telling the strange stories – written in the curious mixture of hypocrisy and collusion common to the period – of people who sailed out on the Río de la Plata only to vanish, leaving their abandoned boats adrift. Many, like Nora Balmaceda's lost husband, were landowners. Before they set out on their last journey, these people bequeathed their lands and factories to the military leaders who had been their friends and protectors. The courts were inundated by lawsuits from siblings and spouses left penniless, but none was successful since the bodies of those missing never appeared. Where there is nothing to see, no one existed, government spokesmen explained. Such doublespeak has since slipped into ordinary speech having been a staple of journalism. Where there is nothing to see, no one existed – these expressions were repeated over and over on the radio and on television. You can sometimes hear them still.

Other, less durable symbols of those times have vanished. The alien spaceships that once lit up the four corners of the heavens never returned. Of the Basilica to Our Lady of Esteco, not even the ruins have survived. All around lie the skeletons of disused trains. There are no villages, no warehouses on the old gravel road which connected the plains of Esteco with distant Buenos Aires. The trucks don't run any more, the villages have died out and the houses where no one lives are left to ghosts and rats. The one-horse town which, back in the 1970s, was the major market town in the area, was flooded when a dam was built. A number of elderly people refused to leave and took refuge in the church tower where they waited patiently for the waters to rise. A woman managed to climb onto the cross atop the steeple and huddle there. The fisher-men who ply the reservoir can still see the rusted cross rising above the glassy waters; there is nothing else.

While I was writing this page, I read an article about a

Patagonian lake that disappeared overnight. The lake was situated near the Témpano glacier at 50° south, it was three kilometres wide and five metres deep. Forest rangers last saw it two weeks ago. When they came back, they found only a dry bed with an enormous crack running up to twenty-five metres deep. Some believe the lake evaporated. It's the first lake ever to disappear into thin air, they said, forgetting that between 1977 and 1978 whole groups of lakes disappeared. This was how the lago de Sabón, the lago Pulgarcito and the lago Sin Regreso were lost, together, with other smaller lakes. At the time, military patrols witnessed them rise like hot-air balloons, shifted by the movement of geological plates, and spill into volcanoes in the Andes. They were erased from the maps and these lost zones were covered with the wavy blue lines that denote impenetrable snows. Foreign map-makers asked if they might have more information about these blank spaces and the Argentinian authorities invariably responded with Bishop Berkeley's observation: 'If it be not perceived, it exists not.'

Their first meeting after thirty years goes just as Emilia imagined so many times. Simón says the very words Emilia dreamed he would say; he moves as though his body has limits that he cannot go beyond. Aside from that, everything is calm, unsurprising. 'Is it you, Simón?' she asked him. 'Is it really you?' and as she climbed the stairs she reached back and took his hand. The hand seems frail, lighter than she remembers it, smoother too. She hears him say: 'I never stopped loving you, Emilia, not for a single day.' She replies, 'Me neither, *amor*. Not for a single day.' At that moment she decides she will ask him to stay. She desperately wants him to linger in the eternity of love she has prepared for him, wants him to undress her now, to satisfy this desire she has concealed from everyone so that he might be the first to know it. When he penetrates her, she wants the world to stop turning, the daylight to pale like the waning moon now rising, for the suffering to cease to suffer, the dead to put an end to death. This is what she wants, but will he want it too? She tells herself again that she should not want him so, with this selfish desire of those who have nothing, who can give nothing. She has searched for him until she was left without breath, without being, but who knows whether he searched for her with the same fervour, who knows what her husband expected to find? Thirty years have passed and they have many stories to tell each other. She wants to begin with the thing that worries her most.

'Sit down, Simón. Could you do me a favour and sit down for a minute, my love? I'm not the person I was when you left and it's important that you understand.'

'I didn't leave you,' he says, 'I'm here.'

He speaks as though age, which has spared his body, has taken refuge in his vocal cords, his voice is stripped of the authority it had when he was chatting with his European friends in Trudy Tuesday. It doesn't surprise her. Time is like water: when it ebbs in one place it flows somewhere else. This is precisely what she wants to talk to him about. Until a moment ago, all she wanted was to say nothing, to hold him. To lie down beside him and hold him. But the lost years fill her with doubts. She is afraid that if she tells him they are not the people they once where, she might sever the slender thread by which they are now connected. She doesn't want to hurt him, doesn't want to hurt herself, and this is precisely why she cannot control what she says.

'You're here because you pitied me because I searched for you so long. I combed every city where you were seen. I spent months in Rio de Janeiro, years in Caracas and in Mexico. I came here to this suburb because I couldn't keep searching any more.'

'I wasn't in any of those cities. You looked for me in places where I never was.'

'Then tell me where you were, tell me where I should have looked. What I want to say to you is that, all the while I was searching, I was growing old. I don't know how to make you see what I can't see myself. I'm the same person I was when we fell in love, I feel the same passion, I'm still the same romantic, I still love flowers though no one gives me flowers any more, I love the same music I loved then, and when I go to the cinema, it feels as though you're sitting next to me, holding me, feeling what I feel.'

'But we're not the same people.'

'That's what I was coming to. I'm the same person I was, but my body is not the same. Life has made me younger, but my body has gone the way of every woman's body.'

She asks him if he would like tea. She puts water on to boil and takes down two cups and a tray. 'Lemon? Sugar?' This is how she likes her tea. As does he, she knows that already. The sky is heavy with clouds swollen with rain. Night is about to fall, as all things which belong to the natural order falls. Emilia will not see it fall because some days ago, tired of having the students next door peering in at her, she covered the windows with adhesive paper. She finds it unbearable to have to expose her failing, fading body to the eyes of heart-less strangers.

'If we'd lived together, you'd be used to the way I look and

I wouldn't feel the embarrassment I feel right now. You look the same as you always did. Me . . . well, you can see for your-self. I would have liked to be the woman I used to be, *amor*, but I grew old. You'll be disappointed. It's been seven years since I had my last period. When I get up in the morning I have bad breath. I stink in places where once I didn't smell at all: my armpits, though I shave them and wash them carefully. Sometimes I smell of pee. The lips of my vagina have withered and even when I masturbate they're dry. Are you surprised I still masturbate at my age?'

'Nothing surprises me. You're wet now.'

'Aren't you? It's desire. Can you tell? It's something I thought I'd never feel again. Every time I missed you, I felt a physical ache. I felt it many times down the long years. Loneliness fell on me like a penance. I felt it coming and I consoled myself with the illusion of sex, with the illusion that I still could.'

The telephone rings: three, four times. Whoever is calling is impatient. The phone cuts off then rings again.

'Don't answer it,' says Simón. 'Don't go.'

On the caller ID screen Emilia reads the number of the Hammond offices. It is 7.30 p.m. If they are calling her, it has to be an emergency that only she can deal with. She lifts the receiver. It's Sucker, the security guard, a gaunt old man who shuffles when he walks.

'Are you sure it's mine?' Emilia groans. 'It can't be mine.'

The voice on the other end of the line is shrill and irritated. In the fifteen years since she was hired to work at the Maplewood office, the security guard's routine has never been broken. Inertia keeps him at his post.

'It's your car, Ms Dupuy.'

Dipthongs confound him. He pronounces it Dew-pew-y like a kid in nursery school.

'That's strange. When I left the office, I drove home in my car. Hang on a minute. I'll just go and check that it's parked where it usually is. I'll call you right back.'

'It's your car, Ms Dupuy. A 1999 silver Altima. I checked the licence plate. If I wasn't sure, I wouldn't have bothered you.'

'Maybe it was stolen. I've got no idea. But if it is my car, I can't come and pick it up. It's Friday night. I've got people coming round. Can't it wait?'

'No, I'm sorry, but it can't. You need to pick it up tonight or first thing tomorrow morning. There are trucks coming to pick up the school atlases from the warehouse at seven o'clock on the dot and your Altima is blocking the doors.'

That morning, when she arrived just before 9 a.m., all the parking spots at Hammond had been full. There was nowhere on the street to park, and she had had to park the car in front of the warehouse. When she clocked in she left a message with the security guard to let her know if she needed to move it. She had been nervous; Simón was waiting for her on the other side of Route 22. She hasn't forgotten the ride back to Highland Park. Nor what happened since. She is not dreaming, she can't be, Simón is still sitting in front of her, raising the cup of tea to his lips. This is her reality, the only reality. She has not strayed into a map drawn by lunatics. Nothing now can stop her from being happy.

There is smoked salmon in the freezer, and it's time to make dinner for her husband. There are some endives and the bottle of Sauvignon Blanc she bought two weeks ago at Pino's. She can put it in the freezer while she sets the table.

'I'll put some music on,' she says. 'Mozart? Jarrett? I haven't listened to Jarrett for ages.'

'Whatever you like. I'm going to touch you.'

'Touch me,' Emilia encourages him. And he comes towards her.

Her husband unbuttons her blouse; his fingertips gently brush her nipples. Her breasts sag and her once erect nipples are flaccid and wrinkled. They blossom again under Simón's touch. Slowly, he slips his hand under her skirt, strokes her thighs, slips down her panties. Without knowing how she got there, Emilia finds herself naked, lying on the bed with him – he too is naked, hovering above her tremulous body. Everything happens exactly as she would have wanted. The lips of her vagina part, suddenly engorged and proud. Simón is erect. And it looks as though he has grown in the years he was away; he looks thinner too. He mounts her with a skill Emilia has only ever seen in her father's pure-bred stallions as they desperately straddle the mare's back. She feels him deep within her, feels the constant pressure on her clitoris from his careful, measured rhythm. She is so happy to have him inside her, she wants him to go even deeper, but she shudders, lets out a triumphant howl and lies there breathless and quivering. 'Don't stop,' he begs her, 'let's keep going.' 'If it were up to me, we'd go on forever,' she says. She feels moved. She had expected their lovemaking to be the way it used to be, but it is better now, it is the wild, tender lovemaking of two teenagers. In the first months of their marriage, they struggled desperately to come at the same time as though each time were the last, but when their embrace was over they felt they needed to start again, to make it better. They both constantly felt it was possible to go a little further only to stop, awkwardly, at some barrier which the other would not allow them to cross. Now she knows that she was the one afraid of falling over the edge: he would have done anything. How much can a body take? Emilia wonders. How much can my body take?

She realised that love could be different the afternoon they arrived in Tucumán, before the absurd incident in Huacra. They feverishly undressed the moment they got to their hotel room, the sort of shabby, ill-kept room their bosses invariably reserved for them. The bed was uncomfortable, with a hollow in the middle of the mattress where the springs had worn out, but they threw themselves onto it, one on top of the other, heedless of everything, licking each other, devouring each other, urged on by the animal scent of their sex. It had happened only once and yet the memory has stayed with her, vivid and intense, everywhere, tormenting her. Now she does not need it any more. She half sits up on the bed and extinguishes the memory like a bedside lamp.

Simón gets up, goes over to the stereo. In the tower of CDs he finds Keith Jarrett's *Köln Concert*, a record which they used to listen to in the apartment in San Telmo.

'Are we going to listen to that?' she says. 'They play Part Two all the time in the office. They've played it to death, it's become like background music. Right there – next to your hand – is the *Carnegie Hall Concert*. It came out last year – I think you'll like it.'

'I know it. It's magnificent, but it's not the same thing. The Jarrett of *The Köln Concert* is still who we used to be.'

He comes back to the bed. The gentle rain of notes drips onto their bodies. Emilia lets the night slip past and all that passes is the night. From time to time, she gazes, incredulous, at her sleeping husband: the mole beneath his left eye is the colour of ripe figs, there are tiny, almost imperceptible lines at the corners of his mouth, and it amazes her to think this body belongs to her, anyone would think it obscene that a sixty-year-old woman should be hopelessly in love with this boy of thirty-three. It is an unexpected gift from fate and, now she thinks about it, perhaps it is fate's reward for all her years of waiting. She would rather have this wild, insatiable love than the life she would have had if everything had gone according to plan: a marriage held together by convention, moved by the rhythm of family celebrations, of talk shows, of late-night films. Her phantom widowhood immersed her in the stupor of so many TV soap operas that she cannot remember what she was in the middle of watching when Simón disappeared. *Rosa de lejos*? No, that came later. Maybe it was *Pablo en nuestra piel*, where she cried inconsolably at the scene where Mariquita Valenzuela and Arturo Puig say goodbye at the airport and, with tears in his eyes, he recites: *I want everyone to know I love you / leave your hand, love, upon my hand.* When she wakes, she considers telling him about that scene. Back then, people let themselves be numbed by sentimentality to forget the death that was all around them. The flying saucers, the soap operas, football, patriotism: she will tell him about all the straws she too clutched at, poor deluded shipwrecked fool.

She gets up at five o'clock so she can catch the 5.35 express from New Brunswick. She doesn't turn the light on but slips away silently, hurriedly scribbling a note that she leaves on the pillow next to Simón. 'I'll be back in time for breakfast. Get some sleep. I love you.' As she crosses the bridge over the Raritan and stares out at the ocean, she can just make out a purple glow appearing over the horizon and she imagines herself, like Mary Ellis, staring out through the window at nothing. She feels a slight twinge in a tooth she had filled a few weeks ago and remembers she needs to make another appointment to see her dentist. She'll do it on Monday. Monday without fail.

Monday, she thinks again. Suddenly, the week is hurtling towards her with the terrible weight of reality. Every time she moves away from the present, time fills up with half-finished images that need to be completed and the responsibility fills her with dread. There are no cars, no trucks on the road, all the lights are out in the buildings and dawn creeping over the horizon is enough for the weight of time to torment her. Monday, she says once more. Monday. When she met Simón in Trudy Tuesday, the weekend seemed to stretch out endlessly, but now in the early hours of Saturday morning, every second seems fleeting. She wishes she could stop time, chain it to the wall in shackles. She has not even thought about whether her husband needs to be at work too. She doesn't know what mapping company he works for, didn't think to ask him for an address, a phone number. Only now does she realise how fragile her happiness is, how slender the thread by which her life hangs.

The station is deserted and the train, as always, arrives on time. A fine mist hangs over the trees. Although the leaves are turning yellow and orange as they do every autumn, squalls, sudden thaws, and brusque heatwaves presage further storms and hurricanes. Natural disasters hold a mirror up to this country which has sown so much hatred, so many wars, thinks Emilia. In the past six years, the culture of the United States has rolled back half a century to the shadows of Senator Joe McCarthy and Tricky Dicky Nixon. It's not worth living here any more.

There are two elderly women and a young black man in her carriage. Barely have they leaned their heads against the window than they fall asleep. Emilia, however, is determined to face every second of the day with her eyes wide open, gazing at the sweetness of her life. As the trains rolls through Elizabeth, she watches the church steeples carving out a space in the greyish light of morning and although she has never taken the train at such an early hour she feels as if she has lived this scene before. It is as if the sleeping boy, the sleeping women have been here in this shadowy nook forever, as though everything that has happened in the sixty years she has lived has been a preparation for this inconsequential moment. Perhaps I am already dead, Emilia thinks, and what I am seeing is my hell or my purgatory. Every human being, she thinks, is condemned to linger forever in a sliver of time from which he can never escape. Her fragment of eternity, then, is here with three sleeping strangers on this suburban commuter train at 5.50 a.m.

The feeling fades as they draw into Newark station. She needs to hurry if she is to catch the number 70 bus out to Livingston Mall in Springfield. She has not made this fifteen-minute journey often. The sordid suburban scene depresses her, the sadness of people at dawn, the loneliness of the trees, the certainty that nothing will ever happen here because – she thinks – there are places so devoid of meaning that even the most insignificant events cannot blossom there. The last straw is that, when she finally arrives at the office, there is a hearse blocking the Altima. She rings the bell for Hammond but no one answers. It is a quarter to seven and the security guard is not answering. How inconsiderate. It's Saturday and she could be lying in bed with her husband but for the unexpected call the night before. She arrives punctually as requested, rings the bell insistently. When she turns, she sees a giant of a man in a heavy coat appear from nowhere and come slowly across the parking lot to the limousine.

'Morning,' he says.

'Good morning,' she replies. 'It's about time.'

The giant starts up the hearse and drives off without a word. Emilia would have liked to ask him what he was doing here but didn't dare. As a child, she shrank from undertakers and they still terrify her. All that matters is that her car is now free and she can take Route 22 back. The autumn sun rises quickly. She remembers leaving the bottle of Sauvignon Blanc in the freezer last night, the endives and the smoked salmon on the table. Dinner was ruined, but she doesn't care. The happiness she feels is venal, simoniacal, yet it compensates for all her losses. In buying heaven she has sold hell. But she needs to come back to earth if she is not to go on losing. So delirious with love is she that she even forgot to ask her husband what he wanted for breakfast. She is sure that, like her, he will want black coffee and toast.

In her North 4th Avenue apartment, the silence is abysmal, unbroken even by the startling hiss of the lights as she turns them on.

'Are you awake, *amor*?'

Simón is not in the bedroom or in the kitchen. Perhaps when he woke he didn't realise where he was and left. What if he's forgotten her? She sometimes forgets things she did only yesterday while still remembering her childhood. She knows this happens to people as they grow older and Emilia is now on the slippery slope – very soon she'll be eligible for a senior's discount on the train and at the cinema – but Simón is barely thirty-three and his memory is unscathed.

116

A streak of light appears under the bathroom door. It comes from the window that overlooks the house next door. Timidly she calls out: 'Are you in there, Simón?' Her husband immediately replies: 'Yeah, I'm here. I was wondering where you'd got to.'

He is wearing the pyjamas he wore on their trip to Tucumán. He must have kept them in his case all these years. Maybe he'd like to go with her to Menlo Park and buy some new clothes. She hums the opening bars of *The Köln Concert* as she makes coffee. She feels a rapturous joy flow through her body, the same electrical trill she felt the day they were married. When Simón opens the bathroom door, she rushes over to kiss him.

'I left my car over at Hammond,' she tells him, 'the security guard was right. It's a beautiful morning. Let's go somewhere, *amor*, somewhere far from this world.'

Simón concentrates on his rye-bread toast and his coffee. He reaches over and strokes Emilia's hand as it hovers in the air.

'Have you heard of the eternal noon?' he asks.

'Once, a long time ago,' says Emilia. 'I've forgotten what it means.'

'I learned about it in the old folks' home.'

'You were in an old folks' home?'

'Seven years. I worked there. I'll tell you about it some other time.'

For Simón to talk about some other day, about a future with her, assuages her anxiety at the mention of the retirement home. Ever since they put her mother in one, the most expensive they could find, she has never been able to forget the experience of that spectral kingdom where no one spoke or dreamed or existed.

'A retirement home,' she echoes. 'Seven years. I can't believe you were a resident.'

'I worked there, I told you. I'm too young to be a resident.'

'And that's where someone told you about the eternal noon.'

'It was a writer; he used to pace up and down the courtyard with a slate. He'd published novels and books of short stories, he'd been famous in his day, at least that's what he said. He showed me a drawing of a circumference touched by a tangent that extended off the edges of the slate. When the other patients were sunning themselves in the courtyard, the man with the slate would say: come with me now to the eternal noon. He explained that the circle was time, constantly revolving and the point of contact with the tangent represented the unmoving present. Our gaze tends to focus on that which moves, but if for a moment we were to stop and contemplate the present, noon would be eternal. The scenery changes and the seasons pass, the writer used to say, but the window that frames the scene is always the same.'

'I think I read something like that somewhere, in Schopenhauer or Nietzsche: *The sun itself burns without intermission, an eternal noon.*

'I don't know it. I stayed there in the courtyard, looking after the guy with the slate until the sun set. Night fell and we didn't notice. For us, it was still noon.'

'You didn't move?'

'We couldn't move. If we moved, time would move too.'

'Wasn't it torture,' Emilia says, 'that stasis?'

'Quite the opposite. The stasis was life. Even eternal noon comes to an end, just as waiting does in purgatory. You linger there for eternity, but on the far side of eternity is paradise.'

'If something ends, it's not eternal.'

'It's all a question of geometry. The guy with the slate and me, we literally escaped along the tangent. While the wheel of time kept turning, we were outside. As Zeno writes: *What moves does not move in the place in which it is or in the place in which it is not.* We were motionless in the present and yet moving forward. Towards what, we didn't know, and that was the best thing about it: the freedom to be suspended, not waiting for anything or anyone. You see where I'm heading?'

'Where?'

'To you. It was a return. We could die now and it would be all right.'

'Why? I don't want to die any more.'

3

Flame that follows fire as it changes

'Purgatorio', XXV, 124

Though Simón has changed in subtle ways, imperceptible to those who don't know him, Emilia loves the man he was and the man he is now equally. It is both men's lips that kiss her, both men's breath which, having kissed her, heave a gentle sigh. Her husband moves with the wariness of a cat, as though expecting one of the two bodies to overtake the other.

Sometimes, both are one, as they were the night before when he made love to her with a new urgency, or this morning when he told her the story of the writer and his slate. But then, he lapses into silence, watching her, smiling at her with an unfamiliar face as though he had to bring the smile from some faraway place. At such times she does not know what to do with the love she feels for both men, nor which of them she should go to first. She realises that after thirty years her husband is not the same. But it worries her that the man he was before has retreated into this other creature she hasn't been able to get to know. The Simón who disconcerts her can predict her desires, knows her thoughts before she does, understands the tensions of her body much better than the first. One is the obverse of the other, or the other way round, and she does not want to choose. Chance has bestowed on her unexpected gifts and she has no reason to scorn those that are to come. She deserves every possible gift as recompense for what she has suffered. And more than anything, she deserves the love of her former husband and the pleasures she has discovered with the present husband lately arrived. I'm lucky, she thinks. She does not dare to say the words aloud because happiness attracts envy and hard on the heels of envy comes misfortune.

She leaves Simón skipping from one piece of music to another, from Mozart's sublime Mass in C Minor to that stupid song by Frankie Valli they heard every day during their honeymoon, 'Can't Take My Eyes Off You', and goes to take a shower. At dawn, as she drove the Altima back from the Hammond offices, she remembered that on both sides of the Delaware are little towns full of antique shops where they could lunch al fresco.

She puts on a pair of jeans, a polo-neck sweater and the jacket she wears on days out. She comes up behind her husband, wraps her arms around him and kisses the back of his neck which smells of the cheap aftershave he used to wear when they were dating. His clothes are the ones he was wearing yesterday. And, apart from his long sideburns, there's not a trace of stubble on his face. She takes his hand and leads him downstairs.

'*Amor*, I'd like to show you the little town where we're going to live.'

The weather forecast on the radio claims the temperature is going to remain mild until nightfall. The sky is cloudless, the humidity low. On Saturday mornings, couples stream along

Main Street towards the synagogues, never moving outside the limits of the *eruv*. The heathens of the town make the most of their day off to go shopping at the supermarket and take their laundry to the Korean dry-cleaner. 'What will we do if we run into Nancy Frears?' Emilia asks. She has told her husband about this suffocating friendship which she is thinking of breaking.

'We go over and say hello, surely. I'm bound to meet her sooner or later. Life goes on.'

Raritan Avenue is deserted. The doors of Jerusalem Pizza and Moshe Food are closed – no one ever believes that Highland Park has stores with such names, but anyone can check – they've pulled down the shutters of Shanghai Kosher and Sushi Kosher. The place that sells Israeli gifts and the stores that sells bridal gowns (there are two, both thriving) show no signs of life either. It is Saturday morning and the devout inhabitants never cease to magnify the Lord. Emilia is surprised, however, that there are no cars, since Main Street is usually bumper-to-bumper. She does not even see anyone at their window. From time to time, a delivery truck stops at the traffic lights. It's 10 a.m., the sun is shining, but there's nobody to realise it. Only the squirrels coming and going among the trees, gathering up the last nuts of the fall.

'We're going to New Hope,' says Emilia. 'I parked the Altima on Denison Street a couple of blocks from here.'

Simón does not answer. Why would he say anything, if he simply wants what she wants?

They get to the Delaware Bridge just before noon. On the western bank, in Lambertville, there is a short street of antique shops. People are buying ramshackle chairs, ornate mirrors with faded paint moulding, umbrellas with wooden handles, cradles decorated with angels blowing trumpets. There is a cluster of curious onlookers in front of a shop window displaying replicas of an imaginary *Mayflower* and other heroic ships in bottles sealed with wax. They cross the bridge on foot. On the eastern bank of the river, New Hope, its twin, shares the same illusions as Lambertville. The brick mansions on the corners are proud to have weathered two centuries: 1805, proclaims the foundation stone on the post office; 1784 is carved on Benjamin Parry's house. In the window of a store selling mirrors, Emilia contemplates her reflection in the bevelled-glass door.

The reflection in the glass makes her conscious of her age, the heavy, slightly hunched shoulders, the broad matronly hips that refuse to be tamed by hours in the gym. She would like to go on standing here next to Simón and freeze this moment forever. But she does not have the courage to face the image of herself as an old woman, which is why she decided at the last minute not to bring a camera.

In the Italian restaurant overlooking the river, she has reserved a table by the window. They take their seats; she orders a bottle of coarse house Chianti and a single plate of pasta. The glimpse of her reflection, slightly overweight, has convinced her to go back on the diet she gave up three weeks ago, vowing this time to be strict with herself. Simón cannot tear his eyes from the river. The sun, shining full on him, blurs its contours. Moves over his body like a huge eraser.

She too gazes at the current moving languidly towards the same blind space which waits ahead for her, folding itself into something that does not know whether it is darkness or light, leaving the bank where everything happens.

★ ★ ★

Shortly after Simón's disappearance, Emilia's mother, in her own way, also disappeared. Waking one morning she saw the doctor knotting his tie in the mirror and did not recognise him. She asked him who he was, told him to get out of her room.

'Ethel, *querida*, I'm your husband,' Dupuy told her. 'What's the matter?'

'Surely you can see I am still in my nightdress, señor? Could you please leave? I'm a married woman.'

Her father called Emilia at the Automobile Club and ordered her to come back to the house immediately. He did not know what to do with his wife and it seemed to him that, before he called the doctor, it would be prudent to wait for the symptoms to manifest themselves more clearly.

'Emilia is going to come and take care of you, Ethel,' he told his wife, kissing her forehead. 'I've got meetings all morning.'

'Thank you, señor. I don't need anyone to take care of me. As soon as you've gone, I'll get up.'

When Emilia arrived, her mother was still in bed. She did not recognise her daughter either, but she easily accepted Emilia's offer to bring her a glass of milk and some biscuits from the kitchen. Seeing her return with the tray, her mother reacted oddly, greeting her again as though she had just arrived.

'Who am I, *Mamá*?' Emilia asked, giving her the answer.

'You're Rita my sister. Who else would you be?'

Rita had died ten years earlier. Emilia quickly realised that, for her mother, time had stopped in a happy eternity.

She was taken to the clinic opposite the house where they tested her reflexes and pointlessly asked her questions about her age, the city and the street where she lived. In the afternoon, she was still submerged in the same forgetful torpor. At times, Emilia thought she was almost her old self. At others, she was disheartened to hear her talk like a complete stranger, words that seemed to come from someone else's throat. One of the nurses said something that made her think: I've known patients who wanted to drift away, people who are weary of themselves. Some of them recover by staying in that state of nothingness only to get sick again if they're forced to come back. Emilia had read something similar in Proust: *The most humiliating suffering is to feel that one no longer suffers.*

The doctors asked how long she had been suffering these symptoms. No one knew; no one had been paying attention.

'She's been very distracted lately,' the father said, 'but then she was always that way.'

'A few weeks ago, she got it into her head that there were men spying on her,' Chela told them. 'Since then, she's been staying in her room with the curtains closed. She'll walk into the kitchen or the bathroom and forget why she's there.'

'That's strange,' the father said, 'I hadn't noticed.'

'And you don't know that she drops her trousers in the middle of the kitchen and pees in front of the servants.'

'You shouldn't talk about such things, they're private.'

'Any little detail is helpful,' the doctors said. 'You'll need to keep an eye on her for a while. When we have a clear diagnosis, we'll know how best to help her.'

'She'll be better cared for here in the clinic than she will anywhere else. Make sure she has a nurse with her day and night,' the father decided.

'That would be a mistake,' one of the doctors said. 'She has a better chance of improving in her own home. Nothing can take the place of the care and affection of her loved ones.'

'It's not that simple,' Dupuy countered. 'I'm out at work all day. I have important responsibilities I cannot simply give up. How are we supposed to deal with her if she's getting worse?'

'She is a very tranquil person,' said the same doctor. 'The best thing is to be gentle and patient with her.'

'Do you have any idea how long this might last?' the father asked. 'I need to be able to relax too.'

'If it bothers you, put her in another room,' the doctor said impatiently. 'Keep her company when you have the time. And leave the television on. That might help her.'

They brought Señora Ethel home. Emilia made up a room with two beds far from her father's bedroom and suggested she stay for a while to look after her. At dinner time, she turned on the television. There was a variety show on called *La noche de Andrés*. The host sang (very badly), danced, told inane stories, introduced other singers (who were even worse) and promised each new act would reveal the secret of happiness. Every fifteen or twenty seconds there was a roar of applause, a burst of canned laughter. Emilia noticed that her mother was weeping, her face expressionless. Tears trickled down her face, soaking her nightgown.

'Are you in pain?' Emilia asked. 'Do you want me to call the doctor?'

'This programme is really sad,' her mother replied. 'Just look at what these people have to do to get attention.'

'I don't understand what you're saying.'

'Can't you see they're prisoners. They're in jail and in order to get out they have to draw a car on the wall.'

'What car?'

'Any car. Can't you see them? They draw it with chalk, open the car door and disappear.'

The Eel found out about Ethel's illness that afternoon and on Sunday after Mass came to visit the Dupuy family.

'Ethel will recognise me,' he said to his wife with the swollen legs. They arrived at the mansion on the calle Arenales with a military escort. The priest's sermon at Mass had proposed a riddle with no solution. It had something to do with the Gospel passage about salt losing its saltiness. The priest had glared down from the pulpit: *Christ would know what to do with such salt. But what of us? Wherewith will we season it?*

'Why would anyone want to season something that doesn't exist?' he asked his wife.

'What do I know?' she replied. 'It seems obvious to me – you just buy some more salt.'

She said the sermon had depressed her and she no longer had the energy to visit sick people. The president did not feel like it either, but duty had to come before everything. He did his best to seem touched when Dupuy came out to meet him. And yet he could not suppress the tics that had been annoying him for months now: sudden, violent electrical discharges flashing through his face. He was wearing a twill suit and the same heavily Brylcreemed hairstyle he wore when he gave speeches. Dupuy went with him to the bedroom.

'Señor Presidente.'

To refresh the sick woman's memory, one of the daughters announced his name as he went in while she stared into space with an expression of bliss.

'Come on now, Ethel, who am I?' asked the Eel, bringing his perfumed face close to hers.

'Good day to you, señor. Thank you for coming.'

There was one of the silences which carried her off to

another place, then she went on in the same tone, though her voice was different.

'Come on then, out with it, you little coward. You went to Conti and told him everything. Get out, go on, fuck off.'

The president's aide-de-camp had the military escort leave the room.

'She's got you confused with Tito, señor,' Dupuy explained. 'Her twin brother, he used to play with her. Don't pay any attention. You'll have to forgive her, she's not herself.'

'Tito *puto*, go get yourself fucked by some germs. I hope they germinate you good and fuck you till you're fucked.'

The voice became more and more shrill as though sharpened with a sabre. Emilia rushed into the room and hugged her mother.

'*Papá*, leave her alone, please. All these people just confuse her. Poor *Mamá*, poor thing.'

Disappointed, the president shook his head, took Dr Dupuy's arm and went out into the corridor.

'I'm sorry, Dupuy. I had no idea she was so bad. Her expression is completely blank.'

'I'm the one who's sorry, señor. I don't know where she came up with language like that. I look after her as best I can. I don't let anyone see her. I'm not about to admit defeat over some minor setback.'

'You get more clear-sighted every day, Dupuy. I can tell as much from your editorials. Congratulations. I admire the pieces you've written about the Jews who are trying to stay in Patagonia. You brilliantly unmasked them and put an end to their little game. We have to show them that they don't rule the world.'

The mother sat up in bed. Emilia had the impression that

she had heard what was being said. Every word seemed to trigger a memory in her, and each memory triggered another word. A thin wail like the bleating of a lamb came from her mother. Then, with no transition, she began to sing in a tuneless voice: *L'shana haba'a b'Yerushalayim*.

'What's that?' asked the president, alarmed. 'Is she speaking Jewish?'

'No, señor,' said Dupuy. 'I think she's singing "Next Year in Jerusalem". It's Hebrew. She must have heard it when she was a little girl: a Jewish family lived next door. Her childhood is about the only thing she does remember now. My daughters and I have to treat her like she's five years old again.'

Emilia stayed in the house for several months looking after her mother. Even when she slept, she was alert to any changes in her mother's breathing, to her timid cat-like mewling. She would get up in the night several times to take her temperature or take her to the bathroom. Every time, her mother would treat her as though she were someone new, a character from the stories she read in *Maribel* and *Vosotras*, or a playmate.

'Oh, how lovely, I haven't seen you for ages,' her mother said whenever Emilia came into the room, even if she had only been gone a moment. She was clearly kept entertained because new characters were constantly appearing.

The following Sunday, the Eel's wife brought her a gift, a medal of St Dymphna, the patron saint of mental illness. The priest had brought it back from the Vatican together with a collection of colourful prints. The Supreme Pontiff particularly recommended the saint, whose miracles in Belgium and Africa had been well documented. 'Dymphna can be of great succour to those who have hallucinations,' the priest had said, choking on the consonants. 'Very few of the faithful are familiar with her because the illnesses she cured were little known before the advent of psychoanalysis. The Pope himself suggested that a candle be lit every night and ten Hail Marys offered up to St Dymphna so that she might smile on the sick person and bless her from her place in paradise.'

Summer passed, then autumn and still her mother did not come back to reality. Emilia did not move from the bed next to her. She could not bear the television being on constantly, but the doctors were convinced that it helped bring the outside world to her mother, helped stimulate her. Together they put up with seven to ten toxic hours of programming a day: lunches with Mirtha Legrand, the bucolic idyll of *Little House on the Prairie*, the exploits of Wonder Woman and the Bionic Woman. The evening news regurgitating speeches by the Eel surrounded by his uniformed acolytes. In chorus they explained that Argentina was waging a pitiless war against the enemies of the Christian West and that God would defend the blue-and-white flag of Argentina against the blood-red rag of Communism. After that came a warning, or rather an order: 'People of Argentina, we shall conquer!'

'Having to watch television day and night is frying my brain,' Emilia told the doctors. 'I'm not sleeping properly. I'm having hallucinations.' They prescribed a sedative for her. Emilia began to think that all these prayers to St Dymphna could have side effects, the way some medicines did. Every morning, she found it harder to get up, she felt her body opening up like a plant with spiders crossing from branch to branch on greasy strands of web. When her mother slept, memories of Simón would come to her, but Emilia never went beyond the boundaries of her body; as though her body were a house condemned, she would go to the door only to retreat. She tried to capture the memories, jotting them down in the little notebook she always had to hand: 'Thinking about S, my throat hurts, my chest hurts, my womb hurts. If I saw him dead, I would kill myself.' It seemed to her that she would never escape this plane in which few things happened and those that did were all the same.

Early one morning, after taking her mother to the bathroom, she saw the toilet was full of blood and there was a trail of drops leading away from it. The cook said that her mother had eaten a salad of beetroot and hard-boiled eggs and that beetroot always turned urine red. But the bleeding continued and Emilia, terrified, asked the family doctor for help. Shortly afterwards an ambulance arrived and took Ethel to a clinic in Belgrano. Dr Dupuy was on an official visit to Los Angeles and his daughter had no idea how to get in touch with him. It was 6 a.m. in Buenos Aires and everyone in Los Angeles would be in bed. Against her better judgement, she asked the Eel for help. He called her father at 6.30 a.m. and Emilia falteringly told him what had happened. 'And you thought it was worth bothering me for something as trivial as that?' Dupuy was indignant. 'I travel ten thousand miles and even here I can't be left in peace to get on with my work. Your mother has everything she needs, I don't see there's any reason to worry.' He was furious, however, to hear that two strangers had been in the house without anyone keeping an eye on them. 'What if they were subversives in disguise who intended to plant a bomb under my bed? What if they demanded a ransom for the nurse? I go away for a couple of days and the whole world falls apart.' This carelessness, this negligence infuriated him. Emilia decided to remain calm while her father fulminated down the phone; she could almost see the veins bulging in his temples.

'Can you find out what's happening with *Mamá* and call me back in half an hour, please?'

'You think it's as easy as that to call?' Dupuy retorted, even more furious. 'The phone system in the country is a disaster. The language in this country is a disaster.'

Señora Ethel was resting in the clinic, well looked after. Emilia spent hours in the emergency room waiting for a diagnosis. Eventually, a young man, his white coat unbuttoned, came out into the hallway, quickly taking off his surgical mask and his latex gloves. He told her that, for the moment, all he could find was a severe case of haemorrhoids. He asked whether the patient often complained.

'You may have noticed that my mother is not herself,' Emilia answered. 'She never complains about anything.'

'We're going to have to do a sigmoidoscopy and a complete blood analysis. It might be nothing more than anaemia. Right now, there's no need for you to worry.'

'A sigmoidoscopy. I've never heard of that.'

'We need to make sure she doesn't have cancer in her sigmoid colon.'

'I'd like to see her.'

'Not just yet. We'll let her rest for a while.'

It made Emilia nervous, the doctor's habit of speaking in the first-person plural, as though all of humanity were ill or convalescing.

She took a cigarette out of her handbag. An assistant rushing past with an IV drip dodged round her, irritated. She gestured to the large wooden crucifix next to the exit, and the sign above the cross that read: *Christ is always watching you.*

Shortly before noon, Chela came to relieve her. Emilia realised that her sister's mind was on other things. She had got engaged to a business consultant with the looks of a tennis pro and they were planning to get married in April or May the following year. Their mother's lunatic state made it impossible to hold the wedding reception at the bride's home and the major dilemma in her sister's life was where to host the four hundred people on the guest list which Chela made and unmade every day.

She arrived at the clinic complaining that the rain was getting worse. She fetched a chair so she could sit down for a minute, and when another nurse came and told them that the results of the pathologist's tests would be ready in an hour asked whether she could leave yet.

'What are the tests for?' she asked anxiously.

'To see whether *Mamá* has cancer,' Emilia told her. 'She probably doesn't.'

'What kind of cancer? What happens if she's got it?'

'There's no point getting worried ahead of time. I told you, just take it easy.'

'How am I supposed to take it easy? Can't you see she's trying to ruin my wedding? She's been like this for months, playing at being ill and swearing like a trooper.'

'Well then, you just do what you have to do. I'll look after her, I don't mind.'

Two days later, when Dr Dupuy came back from his trip, the tests had revealed a tumour in the sigmoid colon. There was a silver lining, according to the doctors, because there were no signs of metastases. The mother's bony, emaciated body barely swelled the sheets. She had cannulas in her nose, and the usual intravenous feeding tube in her arm. After midnight, the rain stopped and the air began to move sluggishly between the buzzing of the blowflies and the death throes of the foul-smelling flowers. The corridor was covered by a slick, humid film and Emilia could clearly see the prints left by the nurses. Her father talked with the doctors for about half an hour and then shut himself up in a phone booth. He emerged having already made a decision.

He did not inform his daughters of his decision until the following day. He called them into his study, a place they were only admitted to on special occasions. He closed the curtains and made sure the door was locked. Chela, as unsettled as Emilia, perched on the edge of her seat as though she wanted to escape. The study had always been gloomy, but now it was worse. The walls which were free of books were hung with the diplomas and citations from his years of service to his country. The doctor addressed his daughters in a voice so subdued, so secretive, it seemed to dissolve into the air. Ever since they were little, the daughters had known that everything their father did and said was a secret and did not even discuss it with each other. It made no sense to ask them to be discreet, but this is what Dupuy did. He went further: he forced them to swear that they would never repeat what he might say that day or in the difficult days ahead to anyone, anyone, he repeated, not even to your fiancé, Chela, or your husband when he's your husband, not even to the priest in the confessional. Emilia feared the worst. She feared – though she did not dare to formulate the thought – that her father had decided to kill their mother, out of compassion or for some other reason, and was going to ask them to be complicit in his crime. In the thin small voice that was all she could manage, she asked: 'You're not going to confess a sin, are you,

Papá? Because if it's a sin, we have to confess it.' 'How could you think such a thing?' her father answered. 'I'm a Catholic, I abide by God's commandments, I would never do anything to make you lose His sanctifying grace.'

He moved his chair over to the desk and went on talking, his face turned towards the window as though even there, even out there in the garden, his enemies might be listening. Emilia never really knew who these enemies were her father talked about, because one day it would be the Montoneros, then it was the People's Revolutionary Army and later, when they had all been exterminated, it was a brigade led by some admiral who was plotting against the Eel, or an envoy of the American government, or Pinochet threatening to invade the islands on the Beagle channel, or corrupt intermediaries paralysing the nuclear power plants. When one group retreated, another advanced, and sometimes none of them retreated.

'Last night I stopped them operating on Ethel,' he told them. 'It would have been butchery. I called Dr Erich Schroeder and he proposed an excellent solution. I'm going to take Ethel out of the clinic and have Schroeder take over her treatment.'

'I'm sorry, but I don't see how that will be better for *Mamá*. Who is this Schroeder?' asked Emilia. 'I've never heard of him.'

'He's a world-renowned specialist. You've never heard of him because he treats only a very few select patients and he has a 100 per cent success rate. He's been living in Argentina for twenty years in absolute secrecy. He has built a machine that captures gamma rays from space and focuses them on the patient's body. In one or two treatments, they're cured.'

'At the clinic, they recommended she have surgery, and I thought that was the best option. It's more reliable. *Mamá*'s heart is strong, she'll have no problem with the anaesthesia. If you have such confidence in Schroeder, why don't you ask him to operate?'

'If he'd offered to operate, I would have accepted without question. But he's against the idea. Schroeder's rays can only work if the patient has not had an operation. He explained to me in a cancer as aggressive as your mother's, when the scalpel touches the tumour, there's a danger that abnormal cells will quickly move through the circulatory system.'

'I'd like to find out a bit more,' said Emilia.

'I don't understand what the two of you are talking about,' said Chela. 'Whatever *Papá* decides will be for the best. Do I have to listen to any more? Can I go now? Marcelo is going to come by and pick me up soon.' Marcelo Echarri, the fiancé. Dr Dupuy had not told them everything, and what was left unsaid was the heart of the secret that the sisters had sworn to keep. Chela would never know it because she left as soon as her father opened the door and Emilia would have preferred not to find out what it was. Years later, when she thought about the episode, she was not sure that it was not a wild dream in which they had all become entangled, or whether St Dymphna's influence had also harmed their father. The name Erich Schroeder would one day be famous, but not for his gamma ray machine. In 1984, it was discovered that in Auschwitz and Dwory he had developed a system for using energy from space to kill prisoners and he was convicted as a war criminal. When Dr Dupuy knew him, he had been living under his real name on the outskirts of Buenos Aires and no one had bothered him for years. His gamma ray machine attracted the attention of the intelligence agencies and quickly became the focus of a cold war between the three governmental forces. Each of them wanted control of the machine, but Schroeder had no respect for any of them. He respected only Dupuy.

'Schroeder,' Emilia's father told her, 'is the only person in the world who knows how this machine works. He has not shared that knowledge with anyone, has not written down his formulae for posterity, and when he dies all that we will be left with will be a pile of useless metal which can say nothing, which will mean nothing. I've seen what this machine can do, but its inner workings, the way in which the treatments take place, is a mystery that may rely on creatures that are nothing like us, creatures that are pure energy, who move effortlessly between realities, between the future and the present.'

Emilia listened, astonished and incredulous, and wondered if this lunatic who talked like a character out of Lovecraft or Poe was the same father who believed that even God (especially God) was governed by the laws of reason.

The remainder of the tale was even more unexpected.

'The machine draws its power from Ganymede,' said her father, imperturbable.

Emilia did not understand, or did not want to understand. She knew that Ganymede, one of Jupiter's inner moons, was the largest satellite in the solar system; chains of craters had been seen on its surface and it had its own magnetosphere, but it gave off no gasses and was not protected by saints like Dymphna. Her father seemed to believe, moreover, that there were intelligent beings living beneath the crust of ice and silica, something for which there was not the least evidence. Words continued to pour out of him, there was no other way to describe it. 'Gamma rays cure illnesses that cannot be detected; they are also capable of causing them. If we can absorb them, we must be able to emit them. I've watched Schroeder use them. He places the head of the patient in a device that looks like the hairdryers they use in salons and connects an antenna which picks up the body's signals. The antenna draws a graph which the gamma rays read. This information makes it possible for them to surround the cancerous cells and send them to Ganymede where they are examined and archived. The rays are like a flock and an untrained shepherd would madden them. The only person who knows how to guide them is Dr Schroeder.'

Her father's story went on flowing, in tributaries, estuaries, streams, deltas. One story ran into another and this into a third, sometimes moving away, sometimes circling back to the beginning. When he finished a sentence he fell silent and reminded Emilia of her solemn promise to say nothing.

'Are you sure about this, *Papá*?' The daughter did not know what to think. Creatures from another world had always seemed to her to be the sort of madness designed to entertain the gullible. She took it for granted that if God had created Man in His image and likeness, there could be no beings in other worlds. Nor, obviously, other gods. Dupuy was prepared to counter this. A Polish theologian he had admired for some time, the Bishop of Krakow, had written that life as described in the Scriptures 'is universal'. At the Second Vatican Council, his mentor, Pope John XXIII, had preached: 'How small would God be if, having created this vast universe, He allowed only us to populate it.'

It was almost noon. When her father opened his study door, Chela was talking excitedly on the phone.

'Go to the clinic, Emilia, and pack up everything in your mother's room. We'll move her in about half an hour.'

An ambulance sent by Schroeder transported her mother. Dupuy and Emilia drove behind. The caravan made slow progress. As it crossed the avenida General Paz and ventured into the pallid suburbs of greater Buenos Aires, the ambulance took cross streets and began to head out into the countryside. The mood of the heavens, forgetting the violent storm of the night before, was tranquil, indifferent. A few fat clouds glided roundly over the cattle and the wind lay becalmed over the vast greenness waiting for nothing. After an hour, the plain began to sink and the road to climb above it, twisting like a vein. A few petrol stations dotted the barren landscape. In the distance, a long, flat building appeared, stretching out across the ravine. On the flagpoles flanking the gates fluttered a pair of flags: one was the flag of Argentina, its horizontal stripes emphasised with pale blue stitching; the other bore two black crescent moons connected by a cord against a white field. Behind them, set on a concrete pedestal, was a hemispheric dish cast in steel. It was huge and concave with a tall, transparent pistil.

'Schroeder's laboratory,' her father announced. 'The national flag. The labarum of Ganymede.'

The building was protected by a wire fence. She could clearly see the walnut trees, white cedars, the crouching dogs, the partridges, but what most caught Emilia's attention was the pistil in the steel hemisphere which intermittently showered sparks over the grounds.

'Those are the rays,' her father told her. 'On auspicious days, multitudes of rays stream down from Ganymede. Sometimes they hang, suspended in the sky, for weeks waiting for the moment to fall. Schroeder is forcing them to drop so we can see them. It's a privilege.'

'They're falling now,' Emilia observed.

'They fall into the antenna which filters them. A lot of the rays are of no use in the healing process. Those that collide with the asteroid belt are contaminated by the time they arrive, can you see? They bring a film of dust with them. Schroeder tested them on rats and on goats. He bathed the animals in the contaminated rays and left them to bloat and swell until they exploded.'

'My God, that's cruel.'

'That is how we save the human race. Cruelty is what saves us.'

The ambulance moved forward. From the gate, Emilia saw Schroeder (she was certain that it was Schroeder) walking towards them, arms spread wide. It was difficult to look him in the eye because his pupils constantly flicked like a pinball from side to side.

'Welcome. We've been lucky,' he said to them. 'The limpid air is favourable to the arriving rays. We will be able to see them.'

He had a harsh accent, pronouncing his Rs in such a way that they spilt his words, but his Spanish syntax was irreproachable. Every item in his laboratory occupied the one space it could occupy in the universe, the same methodical, ineluctable order that objects possessed in a painting by Vermeer. On which subject, if the painting hanging above Schroeder's desk to the right in the room as one entered was not a genuine Vermeer, it looked very much like one: it

143

depicted a young woman in Delft sitting before a window reading a piece of sheet music, her face bathed in the unmistakable light of the master.

'Is that what I think it is?' Emilia asked.

'A Vermeer? Yes, but it's not mine,' Schroeder explained. 'I risked my life for it when I left Germany. Some day its owner will come and collect it.'

Next to the office was a vast room completely filled with devices with flickering needles and coiled serpentine condensers that looked like something out of a Hollywood movie. 'Come and see the scanner,' said Schroeder, 'we've just started it up.' They had seated the mother in a high chair. One of the doctor's assistants took her temperature and her blood pressure. Another moved the hood and placed it ten centimetres from her head. The machine gave off blue flashes which lit up the whole room for seconds at a time. The mother's face registered neither surprise nor pain. It was frozen in a beatific smile.

'We will now begin the procedure, which is as much spiritual as it is physical,' said Schroeder. 'If you will allow me to focus.'

He stepped behind a screen next to the bathroom mumbling something that might have been a prayer in an incomprehensible language which seemed to borrow from Sanskrit, High Gothic, Armenian and some dialects of Anatolia, sounds that had been lodged in the human throat since the dawn of Indo-European language. Schroeder emerged euphoric. His pupils fluttered like moths around a flickering flame. 'It's done,' he said. 'Place the hood on her head.'

The assistant pressed the pedal and the hood was lowered to cover the mother's head down to the bridge of her nose. The needles flickered and the valves glowed with all the colours of the rainbow.

'Now, lean out the window and see the effect of the rays in the pool,' said Schroeder.

Outside, next to the house, was a rectangular pool of water with trampolines at either end. From the surface, liquid spikes rose fifteen to twenty metres into the air, never for a moment losing their narrow, needle-like shape. It was as though the water was rising and falling across a transparent surface. As it reached its upper limit, it became tinted with colour. Sometimes blue or purple, sometimes an intense green. Everything suddenly became calm and a silence descended on the room that seemed older than time itself. Schroeder triumphantly lifted up a tube containing a dark, viscous substance.

'The cancerous cells have surrendered,' he declared, standing on tiptoe. 'Here they are, encapsulated, the demons of her disease.'

'You mean the cancer's gone? Just like that, with no pain?' asked Emilia. 'Is that possible?'

Schoeder did not answer her. He took Dupuy's arm and led him out to the gallery which ran around the house.

'More than possible. It's real. On Ganymede, all reality has its obverse. Your wife is there and she is also here.'

'How will we know when Ethel is Ethel?'

'You'll never know,' Schroeder responded, imperturbable. 'Someone, on Ganymede, has divined in her a wisdom that warrants scientific study. I have no idea what Señora Dupuy will be like there. The Señora Dupuy who remains here will be just like the person who arrived with you: sweet, gentle, lost, with no memory. But healthy.'

'What wisdom could they possible have seen?' Dupuy asked sarcastically. 'There must be some mistake. Poor Ethel always was terribly ignorant. She could just about read and pray.'

'Make no mistake. Your wife is very precious, Dupuy, make no mistake. Look after her. She can go home with you now, all trace of her illness has been eliminated.'

'You take care too, Schroeder. Your connection to Ganymede is also very precious, more perhaps than you imagine.'

'I know. But I need take no precautions. I am protected by powers much greater than anything in this world.'

The afternoon is placid, even the Delaware does not seem to flow. The round, grey cloud that looks like a sheep still hovers. Everything persists in its essence, except Emilia. The memory of her mother has passed over her like a shadow and changed her. She has barely sipped the Chianti, barely touched the plate of pasta. All she wants is for Simón to talk to her. But Simón is still staring at the unmoving river, he does not speak. He seemed excited that morning when he told her the story of the writer with his slate, but then this expression returned, the indifferent expression that so reminds her of her sick mother. It's unfair, Emilia thinks again, she does not even know the storms he has weathered. Seven years in an old people's home. It is the sort of place she has only ever briefly visited, and even then, every time she left she found it difficult to shake off the feeling of anxiety. 'So where was the retirement home, Simón?' she asks. When he does not answer, she decides to tell him about the terrible dream she had two nights before she encountered him in Trudy Tuesday. She says:

'I saw myself turning the corner onto an empty street. You were striding along on the opposite pavement, head down.

"Simón!" I shouted. You crossed the street, came up to me, I gave you my hand. "What a pleasure to see you again, Señor Cardoso," I said with a formality that seemed natural in the dream. "I don't know whether you remember, but I was married to you." "Oh, really?" you said. "That's nice." "I was married to you." "I don't know what else to say on the subject, señora. The dead have no memory. Now, I'm afraid I have to go, I'm in rather a hurry." "Please remember," I begged you. "Remember me, Señor Cardoso." I made a gesture you didn't understand. The deserted street filled with voices, with people jostling for space. My parents, Chela, the cartographers at Hammond, Nancy, the people from the hills above Caracas, James Stewart's character from *Vertigo* and behind them a numberless, infinite multitude. All clamouring for my attention while I tried to stop you from leaving, but you had already left without saying goodbye. I've never been as surrounded by people as I was in that dream, and I didn't like it. When I woke up, it occurred to me that the most unbearable loneliness is not being able to be alone.'

Before the night draws in, they head back to Highland Park in the Altima. Emilia drives in silence. She does not know what to say to her mute husband. She has already told him that first thing on Monday she will go with him to pick up his papers, his social security card, his driver's licence if he has one. She should ask him where he left them, but not now. Now, as they cross the bridge over the Raritan, they see brightly lit stalls on the bank: tombolas, bingo, stalls selling crafts, a string of coloured Japanese lanterns swaying in the wind. 'What do you say we go down and look at the stalls later?' she asks. The only fair she is familiar with is the one they hold on Raritan Avenue on the Fourth of July. She never heard of one on the banks of the river, still less in November when the rains come unannounced. This has to be the first. If it fails, there won't be another one. 'Shall we go down and take a look?' 'Later,' Simón says, 'later.'

When they arrive at the apartment on North 4th Avenue, however, he shows no sign of wanting to go out again. He takes off his shoes, reheats the coffee from breakfast and toasts himself a slice of rye bread. As he sits down at the table, he looks as though he is about to speak. He reaches a hand out towards Emilia and strokes her. He says:

'The writer with the slate who used to pace the corridors of the old folks' home also told me a dream. It wasn't a dream exactly, it was the memory of a recurring dream. A huge black dog was jumping on him and licking him. Inside the dog were all the things that had never existed and even those that no one even imagined could exist. "What does not exist is constantly seeking a father," said the dog, "someone to give it consciousness." "A god?" asked the writer. "No, it is searching for any father," answered the dog. "The things that do not exist are much more numerous than those that manage to exist. That which will never exist is infinite. The seeds that do not find soil and water and do not become plants, the lives that go unborn, the characters that remain unwritten." "The rocks that have crumbled to dust?" "No, those rocks once were. I am speaking only of what might have been but never was," said the dog. "The brother that never was because you existed in his place. If you had been conceived seconds before or seconds after, you would not be who you are, you would not know that your existence vanished into nowhere without you even realising. That which will never be knows that it might have been. This is why novels are written: to make amends in this world for the perpetual absence of what never existed." The dog vanished into the air and the writer woke up.'

Without Emilia asking him, he tells her where he has been all these years. She listens to the sentences fall as though she knows them, sentences that form stories that seem to be projected on a screen. It is the same deceptive impression she had as images rained upon her in her cell in Tucumán.

'I don't know how I ended up in the retirement home, and I don't think it matters. The manager was expecting me. The building was surrounded by iron railings. Above the wooden door I saw an opaque glass canopy. All the rooms had high ceilings, beds without headboards and various crucifixes. All the rooms looked out onto courtyards with palms and ipe trees where the patients took the air and the sun. The courtyard I was to look after had large mosaics with ornate patterns and edging tiles. The men were separated from the women, and in the seven years I spent there, there was never any communication between the sexes. The men did not talk much, we played checkers, watched television. I saw you on the news once, you and your father.'

Emilia is surprised. 'On the news? It can't have been me.'

'It was you,' Simón insists. 'It was during one of the World Cup matches, the first or the last. Your father was seated on the main stand behind the *comandantes*, who kept turning round to talk to him. You were on the grandstand opposite yawning. You were wearing a blue-and-white scarf and a white wool cap. You were yawning and laughing.'

'It was me? How embarrassing.'

'It was you.'

'No, during those months I had stopped being me. I started

to lose myself when you left. Or, what is worse, I became someone I didn't want to be. It's too late, Simón. I'm sixty years old. You've already given me more than I deserve, you have made me happy. You can go now, you can save yourself. I'm not worth anything. I don't even matter to me.'

'That's not true. If it were true, I wouldn't have come back. You started to lose yourself, as you rightly say: that's a different matter. You lost a part of yourself. With what remains, you can start again. Don't undervalue yourself. I love you.'

'I love you too, I love you so much, so much. I don't know what to do with myself.'

'What to do? The life you're living has diminished you. I've seen the pile of useless coupons you collect to buy things you'll never eat: money-off vouchers for pickles, Campbell's soup, chocolate puddings. And the bingo cards. And the false nails. And the friends you've chosen. Instead of being your mirror, they are your humiliation. What have you done with your life, Emilia?'

'Nothing, that's the worst of it. I've done nothing with it. It is my life that has done everything to me.'

Some weeks after the visit to Dr Schroeder, no trace of the mother's tumour remained. The doctors who had recommended surgery performed two further sigmoidoscopies and incredulously admitted that the tissue now appeared to be healthy. In all other ways, she had got worse. She still did not recognise anyone, she confused the past and the present, her memories were muddled and she was doubly incontinent. Emilia had to go back to her job at the Automobile Club and could not continue caring for her. At the nursing home, she had met two excellent nurses, who were fond of her mother and agreed to care for her in alternating shifts. But Dr Dupuy had had enough. He considered that he had done more than was necessary to respect his wife's unshakeable will to live and that it was now time to shut her away in a home to be cared for by professionals. Had Ethel decided to be immortal, there she would be able to enjoy a perfect eternity, with no memory, no world. She greeted all displays of affection with the same indifference. When Chela kissed her forehead her expression was exactly the same as when the Eel's wife stroked her hands. She greeted everything with a beatific, meaningless smile. What difference did it make, then, whether she was cared for by her daughters or by nurses who were strangers to her? The nurses, at least, would clean her up more promptly. Chela insisted that a nursing home was the best place for her. Her friends knew nursing homes where patients were like guests in five-star hotels. Emilia, on the other hand, had heard horror stories about such places: old people left to God's tender mercies, ill-fed, their sheets and mattresses never washed or aired, human beings tossed onto the scrapheap and left to die. 'You're both exaggerating,' Dr Dupuy insisted. 'I will make sure that Ethel is in the best facility in Buenos Aires. Chelita is getting married soon and what are we supposed to do with her on the wedding day, how do we protect her from the commotion, the telephone, the guests? I always know what's for the best,' said Dupuy. It was a phrase Chela loved to repeat: 'You know me – whatever *Papá* decides is for the best.'

In a country that had been many years divided, Dupuy had long since learned to predict the winning side and distance himself in time from those about to lose. When he confined his wife in the institution in Parque Chacabuco he was proud that he had never yet been mistaken. He had succeeded in persuading Marcelito Echarri to propose to his daughter Chela (he could hardly claim the boy was in love) and agree to marry her. Even her father could not deceive Chela. She was impulsive, thoughtless and at the least effort declared herself exhausted. Marcelito, on the other hand, had graduated from Wharton with honours and had the makings of a first-class son-in-law. He had worked as a financial adviser in Miami but wanted to move back to Buenos Aires. When Dupuy discovered this, he immediately hired him to write a financial column for *La República*. In his first article, Echarri advised state-run companies to take advantage of easy foreign lines of credit which offered advantageous rates of interest. Now was the time to take a gamble, was his advice. And he was right. The companies secured loans at no risk to themselves since the Central Bank acted as guarantor. They made fortunes and gave Dupuy unlimited access to the private jets and the villas in Europe. 'The respect I enjoy now is fully deserved,' Dupuy told Echarri. 'After so many years without one false step, people finally respect and fear me.'

There was only one mistake for which he reproached himself, but he never spoke of it to anyone. It had happened when, against his better judgement, he had allowed his eldest daughter to marry an insignificant cartographer whose background seemed so disreputable that he did not even bother to have it checked out. This was a serious mistake. The young man had been a student leader in the geography department, a member of the youth wing of the Montoneros and a left-wing idealist so arrogant he had dared to expound on his ideas at family gatherings. Out of force of habit, he initiated an investigation, but the files with the relevant information arrived too late, after the wedding Mass, when it was no longer possible for man to put asunder what God had joined together.

All his life, Dupuy had remained true to his Christian principles and he was convinced that this was why God was showering him with blessings. He expected surprises from Emilia, from his lunatic wife, but not from Chela. And yet it was she who put his faith to the test.

A few months before the date set for the wedding, she began waking up with dark circles under her eyes, she would wander around the house not bothering to get dressed until late in the afternoon, lock herself in the bathroom for hours at a time, she did not even bother to answer the telephone, which rang at all hours of the day and night. The telephone had been her passion, there was nothing she enjoyed more than talking to her girlfriends about the details of her trousseau, about what to wear on the beach, how many pairs of sandals to take, whether Bahía or Ipanema was the more romantic place for a honeymoon. The wedding day was drawing near and still Chela sat staring at the television, watching soap operas all afternoon, as though she had decided to retreat from the world. There was little difference between her and a nun. She only got to her feet when Marcelo Echarri arrived, as he did punctually every day after work at *La República*. She would shut herself away with him in her room, which smelled of damp and dirty laundry, and they would talk and talk for hours. Emilia was intrigued to know what kept them so occupied and finally resolved to ask her sister with whom she had not exchanged a word for several months.

'I don't know what sort of reaction you're waiting for,' she said. 'Whatever is going on can't be so serious that you have to lie around in bed all day as though you were dying. If you're not in love with Marcelo any more, that's easily fixed. Postpone the wedding, or cancel it. A mistake like this is something you'll end up paying for your whole life. He's strong, he's intelligent, he'll get over it—'

'You don't understand,' Chela interrupted her. 'It's serious, it's really serious. I can't get married. I'd be a laughing stock. I'm pregnant. If you look hard, I'm already showing. I've been wearing loose dresses – luckily, the peasant style is in fashion right now, ruffles and flounces and overskirts, but this fucking bump just keeps growing.' She sobbed inconsolably. 'Who's the father?' Emilia asked, alarmed. 'Who do you think it is?' Chela shouted. 'It's Marcelo. What do you take me for, a whore?' 'So, what's the problem then? He doesn't want to marry you any more? He doesn't want the baby, doesn't want you?' 'No, no, God, it's so difficult trying to explain things to you. It's hard to believe we're sisters. I'm the one who doesn't want the baby. I want to have an abortion before it's too late. My last period was three months ago. I can't get married like this, I don't want four hundred people watching me walk down the aisle with a big belly. Can you imagine the gossip, the whispering? Just like you a minute ago, people will wonder whether Marcelo is the father, whether *Papá* is forcing him to marry me. Can you see me walking down the aisle in a white dress seven months pregnant? It would be in all the magazines, I'd look like a fool.' 'No one will dare publish a thing,' said Emilia. '*Papá* will quash any rumours. You need to get a grip. Children are not something to be hidden or aborted. You need to tell *Papá* before your gynaecologist does.'

That night, Emilia talked to her father. She began by minimising the problem. She told him it was their duty as a family to support Chela. 'Marcelo?' Dupuy sounded surprised. 'I can't believe he betrayed me.' 'What he did is only natural, *Papá*, it's not a betrayal. *Mamá* was ill and we left Chelita on her own all the time. One thing led to another.' 'What are they going to do now?' 'Chela wants to have an abortion to avoid the shame, but I've already managed to get that idea out of her head.' 'How could she even think of such a thing? Abortion is a mortal sin, it's worse than murder, and I won't have hell coming into this house.' 'What if we brought the wedding forward?' Emilia suggested. 'I don't know,' her father replied. 'The monsignor wants to perform the ceremony himself. The date has already been set, and who knows what other commitments he has. How far along is the little fool?' 'Not far, but the wedding needs to take place as soon as possible.'

'I'll ask for an audience with the monsignor, though as you know he's terribly busy with good works – things no one but a saint would do. Every day, he visits the prisons, takes confession, comforts the prisoners, gives them the last rites. But I'm sure he'll make time for me. You will both come with me. Chela needs to take responsibility for her actions, and I don't want you leaving her on her own.'

The monsignor received them in the palace which the government had recently put at his disposal. The armchairs in the great hall where they were asked to wait were large and upholstered in maroon velvet. Young priests and seminarians in soutanes came and went carrying heavy files. The monsignor was wearing a business suit. When they entered, he extended his hand bearing the Episcopal ring. Emilia and Chela bowed and kissed it.

'What a pleasure to have you all here, what a privilege,' the monsignor sighed. Emilia, who had not seen him since the dinner with the Eel, noticed he had grown fatter and balder. His bald head glittered.

A seminarian came over and whispered something in his ear.

'Tell them I'm busy. They may wait for me if they wish. They must wait their turn like everyone else. Put the files on my desk under the others.'

'May we speak in private, Monsignor?' Dupuy asked. 'We have come on a rather confidential matter.'

'Very well, come with me into the library. If it is confidential, then I shall treat the matter as though administering the Sacrament.'

He led them into a room filled with scrolls and handsomely bound books. A spiral staircase carved from a single block of wood rose to the gallery above. He put his embroidered stole about his shoulders, kissed it. '*Reconciliatio et Paenitentia*,' he intoned. 'I trust you have truly searched you consciences.' Dr Dupuy interrupted him: 'We won't take up much of your time, Monsignor. We need to bring forward the date of Chela's wedding. You offered to perform the ceremony. We were hoping you might give us a date that suited you.'

'What has happened, my child?'

Chela started to cry. 'Why is this happening to me, Monsignor? You can't imagine how much I was looking forward to getting married.' After her fashion, she told him what had happened. Her tale was interrupted with sobbing, and it was difficult to understand what she was saying. Emilia took her sister's hands in her own and finished explaining.

'What does Marcelo think?' asked the monsignor.

'He wants to get married as soon as possible,' said Dupuy.

'In that case, I can't see the problem.'

Chela again started to talk about the shame she would feel appearing before her guests, the rumours that would hound her and her unborn child for the rest of their lives.

'Have you repented of your sins?' the monsignor wanted to know.

'Of course I have. I confessed and I said ten rosaries as a penance.'

'Well, my child, there's no need to make so much out of such a little thing. I know some nuns who will make you a wedding dress finer than anything in Paris. I've seen them. They can hide a pregnancy, however advanced it is, and what's more they use the latest fashions. Dry your tears, now, and don't worry your head about it. Your *papá* and I will set a date.'

He commanded Chela to kneel and gave her his benediction. *Ego te absolvo in nomine Patris et Filii et Spiritus Sancti.*

'Amen,' father and daughters replied as one. Dupuy made to get to his feet, but the monsignor stopped him. He wanted to ask him what the *comandantes* thought of his work in the military prisons.

'They think it is invaluable, Monsignor.'

'Perhaps, but this is merely the tip of the iceberg,' said the monsignor. 'I need reinforcements. From morning to night, I listen to extremists and to their families, I tell them to make a clean breast of things, to confess everything they know. In doing so, I do no harm to anyone, quite the reverse.'

There was a knock at the door and a seminarian popped his head round. The monsignor, clearly irritated, waved his hand. It was enough. The terrified messenger fled. 'Don't they understand orders? Can't they leave me in peace?' He gestured to a pile of abandoned files next to the spiral staircase. 'The priests here are mere novices, they do not know how to offer succour to so much human misery. Now, if you'll forgive me, Doctor. You can rely on me to marry that silly girl Chelita as soon as you wish, in the Basílica de Santísimo, the Iglesia del Pilar, El Socorro, in the cathedral, wherever you choose. It can wait another two or three weeks, don't you think? Might I suggest the newly-weds spend as little time as possible at the reception to avoid any prying eyes. They can simply greet the *comandantes* and leave. The *comandantes* will be attending, will they not?'

'I shall be inviting them, obviously.'

'Ah . . . well, when you do speak to them, don't forget to tell them that you've seen how overworked I am.'

Chela and Marcelo Echarri were married with all pageant that the bride had ever dreamed of. The security cordons operated without a hitch, Emilia did not leave her sister's side for a moment; stood in front of her whenever she noticed someone staring a little too insistently. Dupuy, for his part, banned magazines – even those loyal to him – from taking photographs. No one gave a thought to Señora Ethel's absence; there was a rumour that she was suffering from terminal cancer and had been sent to a clinic in Switzerland where the family visited her every month.

The honeymoon lasted three months. Chela had an uncomplicated labour in a clinic in Uruguay (a boy, eight pounds, eleven ounces). When she got back, she was bored to tears changing nappies and watching soap operas while Marcelo went to *La República* first thing and came back shattered when it was dark. Marriage was exactly what she had expected it to be: a routine from which there were no distractions and no reprieve, which snuffed out any spark of love before it appeared. As the months passed, her husband wrote less and less for the paper, allowing himself to be caught up in the new businesses now thriving in Argentina fuelled by cheap credit and a weak dollar. He began importing things as useless as they were baffling, selling them on calle Lavalle where people mindlessly lined up to buy them. His father-in-law was his guide. It was Dupuy who advised him, long before the announcement, that the government was going to abolish import duties to force Argentinian companies to learn to compete. Excitedly Marcelo started buying up watches from Hong Kong, screwdrivers from Malaysia, shirts from Taiwan, coats in fake fur and astrakhan from France. However outrageous the merchandise he imported, shopkeepers ripped them out of his hands, paying him in hard cash, determined to satisfy the greed of their insatiable customers. Though the son-in-law barely slept, he made sure not to forsake Dupuy. Every day he spent an hour in the offices of *La República*, dictating to various copyists optimistic predictions about the state of the economy which he insisted was now safe from speculators and prophets of doom. Industries were collapsing but nobody cared about their downfall. The secret of wealth consisted of leaving money with companies in the financial sector and waiting for it to multiply by itself, which is what Marcelito did, though this was something he did not mention in his articles, which recommended restraint and prudence and endlessly repeated the fable of the ant and the grasshopper, while he took the fortunes he was earning and invested them with the banks recommended by his father-in-law: those which paid 12 or 13 per cent interest monthly, sailing full steam ahead, secure in the knowledge they were protected by the state.

Chela found it difficult to accept this transformation in her husband. She too had changed. She was fat, she permanently carried around a box of chocolates and she would go for days without taking a bath, putting on make-up or even looking at herself in the mirror. She was still breastfeeding and her huge breasts spilled out of her nightdress. She was three years younger than Emilia but now she looked older; she even began to get grey hairs which she forgot to dye. At the height of her bitterness, she told Emilia that she spent nights lying awake, waiting for her husband, the baby in her arms, while he sat up, yoked to the calculator, the telephone and the tele-type machines.

'I take him to Mass with me on Sundays,' she told Emilia, 'and he rushes out of the church afterwards to find out the exchange rate of the dollar against the yen. I wear the baby-doll nightdress I couldn't wear while I was pregnant and he just goes to sleep, can you believe it? He doesn't even wake when the baby is squalling, never picks him up, and I don't think he's having an affair, because he doesn't even have time for that.'

In a few short months, the little bank which Marcelo Echarri bought blossomed, buying up agricultural coopera-tives, empty factories and shares in businesses that existed only as a letterhead: it was a lavish graveyard peopled with the dead that no one wanted. The Echarri empire – as the magazines called it – rose like the villages Potemkin built for the tsarina as she travelled through the Crimea only to vanish as soon as her carriage had passed.

Everything was happening too quickly. His wealth was colossal, but existed only on paper. To escape the firestorm would require an act of daring. He looked for short-term investors prepared to entrust their modest fortunes to banks that promised the best interest rates, and his were the highest. Inevitably, the moment came when he could not pay them.

The more people deposited the deeper he sank into this dirty business. Bankruptcy loomed, but still he was not prepared to give up. He had never failed and did not see why he should fail now. After a sleepless night plotting and scheming, he happened on what he thought was a providential solution. Rather than paying the monstrous interest rates demanded of them, his frontmen invested the reserves in banks which offered more realistic interest rates. He had two or three million pesos invested for a fixed term in Philadelphia, where he had lived during his carefree student days, but he had no intention of touching it. This money was his shield, his safeguard for the future. But the future was now moving away and rather than coming towards the present, as Bradley's Metaphysics proposed, it was disappearing. Whichever way he turned, Marcelo could see no future. The future, like the money, had run dry.

He could not sleep for worrying. 'If you carry on like this, you'll give yourself a heart attack,' Chela said to him. 'Why don't you talk to *Papá*?'

'No, your father gave me some advice. He said: "You've got to play this like a game of chess, Marcelo. Before you attack, think about how you're going to defend yourself. Nobody's going to sit in your seat and play the game for you."'

He had followed this advice and sunk ever deeper. He bought a second foundering bank and opened up branches in the provinces to attract new deposits. In every branch, he had a motto engraved in Latin which cashiers translated for customers: *Fac recte nil time*: Do right, fear nothing. For the first few weeks everything went well. Customers entrusted their savings to him because the word *bank* inspired confidence. But when they returned to withdraw their funds, they found the doors closed, or they were sent away by the security guards with implausible excuses: we're waiting for funds from another branch, it will all be sorted by 9 a.m. tomorrow morning, go home, don't worry, don't believe the rumours, your money is safer here than with the Pope in Rome. It sounded like mockery, because at the time, the Pope in Rome was on his deathbed and the Vatican Bank itself was foundering.

Marcelo had no lack of imagination, but now he lacked the funds to use it. He considered laundering money through the drug dealers who were beginning to flood in from Colombia and Mexico, but he knew that if he got into debt with them and did not pay up promptly he would be signing his own death warrant. 'I can't take the risk,' he said to Chela. 'I haven't got the guts to leave you a widow, all alone with the baby.' 'You need to talk to *Papá*,' his wife insisted. 'How many times do I have to tell you?' For several days, Marcelo hesitated, but finally decided to do so when thousands of furious investors staged a demonstration outside his bank, smashing windows and furniture, stealing telephones, forged paintings and typewriters. His debts amounted to more than two hundred million pesos.

He invited Dr Dupuy to the Jockey Club, where they were able to lunch away from indiscreet witnesses. In plain language he explained the hopeless situation he found himself in, employing all the rhetorical devices for compassion he knew while his father-in-law did not move a muscle.

Dupuy listened, impassive. He shot Marcelo a bleak look and sat for a moment in silence, devoting his attention to the shrimp cocktail the waiter had just brought.

Marcelo was about to take out a photograph of his son, Dupuy's only grandson, prepared himself to shed tears if necessary, but in the end he did not have to lower himself to such stratagems.

'How are we going to write up the story for *La República*, Marcelo? What possible explanation can we give, when there is none? How are my readers, the good men who have trusted me their whole lives, going to go on trusting me?' At no point did Dupuy raise his voice, yet his voice boomed as though it filled the heavens. 'They won't understand why I gave you a position of such responsibility at the paper when you're a piece of shit who couldn't even see what was coming. They'll ask why I didn't warn you. How can I tell them that I did warn you, that I gave you more time than anyone else had, and that you were stupid enough not to listen to me?'

Marcelo was trembling. This was no time to apologise; all the while he had felt he had not put a foot wrong, and now he discovered that his one mistake, the one which a whole lifetime would not suffice to excuse, was not to have heeded the infallible voice of his father-in-law.

'It's not just a few banks that are failing,' Dupuy said, 'the whole system is falling apart, foreign credit has dried up and now the country is being asked to pay its debts. Even if I wanted to – and I don't want to, I can't – how would it look if I asked for you to be thrown a lifeline when the *Titanic* is going down?'

Marcelo's voice faltered; he felt on the brink of tears. 'So what do you advise me to do?'

'Leave the country. And before you go, think about how to preserve your good name. Though it pains me to say so, it is my grandson's name too.'

'I've been thinking about that. I was going to ask for an audit, a financial inspection, but I don't have time to doctor the figures and delete the fraudulent transactions. As soon as the auditors look at it, they'll know my only way out is to get the state to cover my debts. I could speak to the *comandantes*, but if, as you say, the whole ship is going down, my hands are tied.'

'Tied? You'll be lucky not to have your hands cut off. The *comandantes* aren't going to put themselves on the line for anyone. They're gouging each other's eyes out as it is. Will the books stand up to a slightly underhand audit?'

'No. Anywhere they look there are papers implicating me.'

'Papers,' echoed Dupuy. He sat for a moment in silence. Marcelo feared his silences more than his poisonous tongue. 'Paper is a perishable material. Are these papers scattered around the place?'

'More so than I would like.'

'How long would it take you to get them all in one place? You need to gather them together as if they were the bones you're going to be confronted with at trial. There can't be a single scrap, a stamp, a file missing.'

'Twenty-four hours, thirty-six, I'm not sure. Maybe a little longer if the branches don't move quickly.'

'That's a long time. You need to get your press office to issue a statement today saying that you are going to get your files in order so that the government can see that you have acted with complete rectitude. You need to denounce the damage being done to your business by these unfounded rumours. And you need to promise that, as soon as the audit is complete, you'll pay back every last centavo. The statement needs to sound utterly sincere. Repeat that hypocritical Latin motto your bank uses: *Fac recte* . . . what's the rest of it?'

'I don't understand, Dr Dupuy.'

Marcelito Echarri, who, as a student in Wharton, had solved

the most complex theoretical equations, was completely at a loss. 'If I ask for an audit, they'll find enough evidence in half an hour to arrest me. I'd be better off leaving the country like you suggested. Chela and the baby will be fine, don't worry.'

'I'm not worried about them. I'm worried about me. You have dragged me and *La República* into this mess and you have to get us out. You can't do it on your own, because in the state you're in, you're worthless. I'll advise you. You and Chela and my grandson are going to disappear, but not yet.'

'What should I do, Doctor? I'll do whatever you say.'

'Get your managers to gather all the paperwork together by tomorrow after you've issued your statement to the newspapers. Then announce that, while the audit is taking place, you are going to take a holiday with your wife and son. Choose your destination wisely. You might not be coming back.'

'The papers will need to be handled by people we can trust. Don't worry, I won't forget anything.'

'The way you've been recently, it's impossible not to worry. Keep a close eye on the papers. I'll send official vans to pick them up and drop them off at your bank's head office. Nothing else is to be moved, not the furniture, not the paintings. When you lock up for the night, there will be an unforgettable fire.'

'An accident? No one will believe it.'

'It won't be an accident, it will be an deliberate act of sabotage. An attack against you, against me, against the *comandantes*. Another terrorist attack by subversives. There won't be anything left in the rubble.'

Two days later, on the radio from Miami, Marcelo Echarri declared that this atrocity (he used the word *atrocity*, everyone remembers that) had ruined him. All the money in the banks' safes had been burned, he said, millions in bearer bonds, a

Picasso harlequin, one of Francis Bacon's cardinals, priceless, irreplaceable treasures. He had no doubt that subversive elements were responsible for the conflagration. 'They have committed yet another crime against the country,' he said, 'against peaceful citizens and their savings.'

After this fleeting appearance, he vanished. The *comandantes* promised to mount an exhaustive investigation and track down the perpetrators wherever they were hiding. A few hours later, six suspects who had holed up in a warehouse on the docks were surprised by a naval patrol and died during the altercation. Marcelo moved with his family to the Bahamas, and when the last spark had died down, he moved to San Antonio, Texas, where he bought a luxury-car dealership and a house in the Dominion, the most expensive neighbourhood in the city. Chela phoned Emilia from Nassau to tell her she was pregnant again.

As usual on Saturday nights, Emilia does not feel like cooking and is preparing to order Japanese food from Sultan Wok or Megumi. Japanese food was an exotic concept back when she and Simón lived in Buenos Aires and she does not know whether he has tried it since, whether he likes it.

'Why do you ask?' her husband said. 'I like what you like.'

Just as Emilia goes over to make the call, the phone rings. It is Nancy, worried because she has not heard from her for several days. She has decided to give back the file of newspaper clippings her friend gave her to organise. 'I'll bring it over,' Nancy insists, 'it's all sorted.'

'No . . . you can't,' Emilia says, 'I'm going to be away for a couple of days.'

'What about the file?' Nancy is not about to give up.

'Hang on to it. And stop bugging me.' She doesn't care

when Nancy says she is offended. She'll be back, she always comes back, she is a loyal, meek little puppy.

Simón is sitting at the drawing table and is sketching the outline of a map, an island. 'I've been looking for this island for a long time,' he says. 'I find it, and when I try to pin down in space where it is, it slips through my fingers. Maybe that's my mistake, maybe there is no place in space for it. I try to draw it differently. I put it down on paper and turn away for a minute, and when I look at it again, the island is gone. It has vanished.'

'It must be situated in time, then,' Emilia says, 'and if it is, then sooner or later it will come back. Sooner and later are refuges in time.'

'We've spent our lives making maps,' says Simón, 'and I still don't know what they're for. Sometimes I wonder if they're not simply metaphors of the world. What do you think?'

'Not metaphors, but maybe metamorphoses, like words or like the shadows we project. By the time a map has circum-scribed reality, reality is already different. In the first geography lesson I ever took, the teacher told us that the principal purpose of maps is to stop people getting lost.'

'The opposite of what your father wanted,' says Simón. 'Maps to make people lose their way, so they don't know what day it is, what time it is, where those who still are, are. He would have liked you and me to draw maps in which people disappeared and became dust from nowhere.'

'Maybe that's what we did,' Emilia says. 'Maybe we were just figures on a map that he and the *comandantes* were drawing, and everyone on that map got lost. There's nothing more disorient-ing than falling into a map and not knowing where you are.'

'The writer with the slate who paced the corridors told us that twice he had disappeared inside a map. The first time was in Japan, he said, just after the war. He was supposed to be coming back from Nagasaki to Buenos Aires, he'd got his ticket, but he had barely any money. He was desperate. He spent his last yen on the taxi that took him to the airport. Bad luck always comes at the worst possible time, and that was what happened to him. There was torrential rain and all the flights were cancelled. If the writer didn't make it to Tokyo that night, he would miss the weekly connecting flight to Buenos Aires. He didn't speak a word of Japanese, didn't have a penny to his name, as I said, he had no idea how to ask for food or shelter. He was worse than a beggar, he was a man without a language. Someone working for the airline took pity on him and gave him a ticket to Hakata train station. In nearby Fukuoka he would be able to take a flight to Tokyo and all his problems would be over. Miming, he asked how many stops it was to Hakata. Six stops, the attendant told him. To confirm it, he held up six fingers. The writer got on the train, saw an empty seat and rushed over to take it. All around him were other passengers relaxing in comfortable berths. The conductor offered him a white dressing gown, but he refused, he was afraid he might have to pay for it. Everyone else had a dressing gown, and he felt ashamed to be the only one not wearing one. Before the first stop, he saw some of his fellow passengers eating balls of rice they dipped into a dark sauce. The writer was famished but to calm himself he tried to think about something else. As he fell asleep, he began to repeat the only word that mattered to him: Hakata. Hakata-ga? Hakata-wa? One of the other passengers scornfully held up five fingers. He felt reassured, since this confirmed that after the first stop, he had to wait five more stops. He leaned his head against the window and fell fast asleep. He woke up in the middle of the night. Rain was lashing at the windows, as though the skies had been ripped open. The mountains in the distance were framed by moonlight, and next to the trackers, peasants were harvesting rice. He could not imagine where he had strayed on the map. He didn't dare to think what would happen when the conductor forced him to get off the train. He resigned himself to spending the rest of his life in the paddy fields with people he would never understand. Eventually, the train stopped. He could not work out the name of the station, because the signs were all in Japanese ideograms. "Hakata?" he asked the neighbour who had previously held up five fingers. "Hakata-ga, Hakata-ka," the man replied. He unfolded a map and pointed to a huge icon which meant nothing to the writer. It looked like a box raised on a pair of legs. "Hakata," the passenger said again. He opened a secret door in the icon, winked at the writer and gestured for him to go in. The writer thanked him and entered. On the other side, it was daytime. A brilliant sun blazed in the sky. In front of him he saw a little station which looked just like the icon he had just come through. Two soldiers stopped him. They were talking to each other in a language that was not Japanese. It sounded more like Hebrew or Arabic. The writer spoke to them in English and, to his surprise, they understood. "Where am I?" he asked. "You are at the Mandelbaum Gate, on the border," they said. "If you want to cross, you have to show your passport." The writer had his passport with him, he also seemed to have his suitcase, his umbrella and the books he had brought with him. "Hakata?" he asked fearfully, showing them the passport. The soldiers stamped it and pointed to a long track. "*No-man's-land*," said one of them. "*Hakata no-man's-land*," the writer repeated, satisfied. He walked along the track between pebbles, twisted metal, rusted fences and the skeletal remains of useless tanks. In the distance, he could make out the minarets of a mosque, could hear the chanting of the muezzin. He didn't know which side of the border he was on, and he didn't care. "Hakata?" he said aloud to cheer himself. To the right of the path, unseen by anyone, on a ruined wall, was a huge map of the city of Jerusalem: the Jerusalem of Ptolemy, the centre of the world. Above the map was the Japanese ideogram he had never been able to understand. He was amazed and heard himself exclaim: "Hakata!" A door opened in the map and, unable to resist, he popped his head through to see whether it was night-time on the other side. He hoped that by going through the door he might find himself back on the train, get to Hakata and catch the plane to Buenos Aires. "In a sense, I was right," the writer said, "because I wound up in the old folks' home and now I can't leave here. Sometimes I try to draw the Japanese map on the slate. It never works, I end up drawing islands, countries even, I don't recognise." I asked him to show me the drawings,' says Simón, 'and he set me in front of the blank slate. I told him there wasn't a single mark on the slate and he told me that it was his finest drawing: an island that disappeared as soon as it found a place in space. That's what I'm trying to do too,' Simón goes on. 'I copy the island, carefully reproduce every line, every curve, but nothing happens. Sometimes I draw the sea around it, put a compass in the corner so it can find its place in space, and when I look again, the island is where it always was.'

'Your island is just a metaphor,' says Emilia. 'But the man with the slate, on the other hand, managed to make his maps a metamorphosis. In fact, now that I think of it, the man himself must have been a moving metamorphosis. He escaped along the tangent, allowed himself to be enveloped by his eternal noon. The man who left Nagasaki was not the same man who boarded the train to Hakata or the one who crossed the Mandelbaum Gate – which, as you know, doesn't exist any more, and hasn't since the Six Day War in 1967 – or the man you met in the old people's home. You were lucky to run into him there. It could have been anywhere, or nowhere. At least you met one person you could talk to about maps. I'm surrounded by cartographers and I've never had a conversation like the one you had that night.'

The doorbell rings insistently. Unhurriedly, Emilia goes downstairs and pays for the food. She sets the table and warms the sake. She reminds herself that she should barely pick at the food – the steam from the rice has already made her aroused and she does not want Simón to see her as an oversexed animal. 'What happened to you in the old people's home is like what happened to me in my dreams,' she says. 'I saw places that no longer exist, people who disappeared the moment I tried to slip inside them. I saw cities shift onto maps that had not yet been drawn. The seasons passed quickly in my dreams; winter at night was spring by morning, summer became autumn or west became south. Why don't we eat, *amor*?'

'Let's eat later, let's eat tomorrow,' says Simón. 'Right now, let's just go to bed.'

Emilia once more feels like the smitten girl who listened to 'Muchacha ojos de papel', who walked the streets of Buenos Aires with Simón's hand in hers; she feels a great tenderness burst inside her, a door opening in a Japanese ideogram; she says something that she did not believe herself capable of, in a voice that comes from some other body, some other memory: 'Fuck me, Simón. What are you waiting for? Fuck me.'

4

As one who believes and does not, saying:
'It is, it is not'

'Purgatorio', VII, 12

Every morning I glance through the online editions of the Argentinian papers. One day in autumn, before planning one of my classes, I was surprised to find myself reading that Dr Orestes Dupuy had died from a lung infection. He was eighty-six years old and had been in an intensive care unit for some time. I was convalescing from a serious illness myself but I wanted to go and see Emilia and offer her my insincere condolences. Neither she nor I would mourn Dupuy's passing.

I hadn't seen her since our conversation over lunch at Toscana. I still hadn't talked about the illness which had forced me to move away from Highland Park for a period and which I prefer not to dwell on. I had been seriously ill, I still don't know how the doctors managed to keep me alive. My body was completely ravaged and the list of doctors who helped me is long: Jerome Richie, a urologist; Anthony D'Amico and Jan Drappatz, both oncologists; Peter Black, a neurosurgeon; and, most importantly for me, José Halperín, an old friend, someone with whom I shared my exile and through whom I met the others. I'm sure they remember me, if only because I constantly pestered them, sending them my books.

Emilia sent a get-well card to the hospital and a Keith Jarrett CD, *The Melody at Night, With You*, which I loved. It's been months since then and I still haven't even called to thank her. I know she's still living in the same apartment on North 4th Avenue, that she's still working at Hammond. When I figured she would be home from work, at about 7 p.m., I called round. She opened the door, looking pale and wizened as though suddenly older than her years. I felt that she was genuinely pleased to see me, that, apart from Nancy Frears, she had no one she could talk to. I didn't want to stay long, and was about to refuse the tea and cookies she brought out almost as soon as we had sat down, but I accepted so as not to offend her. One of the Jewish communities in town had asked her to redraw the map demarcating the *eruv* which had been destroyed in the flood of 1999. She was about to show me the drafts she had been working on when suddenly she broke down and cried. The situation was awkward, I didn't know what to do. Had we been in Buenos Aires, I would have hugged her, but here in New Jersey, alone in her apartment, I had no idea how she would take it. She dried her eyes with a tissue, went to her bedroom for a minute, and when she reappeared she was calm once more. 'Sorry,' she said, 'I'm being silly. It's just that I miss him so much. I miss him more with every day.' She took it for granted I knew who she was talking about, but she explained anyway. 'I miss Simón,' she said. 'Now that I'm really an orphan, I find it reassuring to think I haven't lost Simón.'

From our conversation at Toscana, I'd assumed that her search for her husband was ancient history. Emilia had arrived in Highland Park, weary of following one false lead after another, of believing that he was waiting for her somewhere, hidden inside a map. She had laughed at that, it was nonsense, she said, a sort of private game she played, one of those comforts, like a pair of winter gloves, you keep and then forget, but now I realised that she was being serious, that she was still waiting for Simón. 'I hardly sleep,' she said. 'I wake up several times in the middle of the night. Sometimes, I see him leaning in the doorway, and when I turn the light on and he's not there, I go over and sniff the door frame, sniff the floor like a dog for some trace of a scent he's left behind. A car will park outside, someone will get out and I'll rush to the window to see if it's him. It's never him. The night *Papá* died, Chela called me from San Antonio. She asked if I wanted to go back to Buenos Aires with her, the funeral was going to be postponed for a couple of days. I told her I couldn't leave, that Simón was coming back at any moment. Chela asked me if I was feeling OK; she didn't insist. I called Hammond, left a message saying there had been a death in the family and that I wouldn't be in to work the next day. I really believed that, when he heard that my father was dead, Simón would come back. I stayed awake until dawn, watching two old Argentinian movies, *Tiempo de revancha* and *La fiesta de todos*. In the first, Buenos Aires is a sordid, crumbling city filled with the concrete pillars of half-constructed avenues. Watching it reminded me of the morning I saw those same ruins, saw the families left homeless in the wake of the demolitions. In *La fiesta de todos*, there's a brief shot of *Papá* on the VIP stand at River Plate Stadium on the day Argentina won the World Cup. Later there's a shot of me in profile, scanning the crowds. Hoping I might spot Simón in the stands somewhere, I watched the video over and over. It was a waste of time.'

I felt sorry that I couldn't talk frankly to Emilia, because, like the witnesses at the trial of the *comandantes*, I believed her husband had been murdered in Tucumán the same night he was arrested. A warrant officer had testified that he had witnessed the commanding officer personally kill Simón Cardoso, put a bullet in his forehead. Two others testified that they had seen him before he was taken out to the court-yard to be executed, shuffling along, his body broken from the torture. The human rights organisations investigating the case were convinced that Dupuy was behind the killing but could find no conclusive evidence. The body was never found. Details of the case were published in *Diario del Juicio*, Emilia had probably read them but did not believe. Even the flicker of a doubt would have destroyed her because, if her husband was dead, it meant her father was guilty, her mother was complicit; it meant that she was the daughter of two murderers. If that were true, she would rather she had never been born, rather she had been a foundling, a baby in a chil-dren's home, a piece of trash without a name. What I knew but could not bring myself to say created a yawning gap between us, a wordless, desolate no-man's-land like the borderland by the Mandelbaum Gate. It was something I regretted, because I had begun to think that she was very like me. We had both fought against death in our own ways, and neither of us was prepared to surrender. For me, the only way to go on living was to pretend that death would never happen, to embrace each happy new morning. Emilia, braver than me, refused to allow the tragedy of her past to destroy the present and so she carried on with her routine, hoping and believing that doing so brought her closer to the fateful day when he would finally come and find her. When she said 'I miss him so much', her voice sounded like a branch breaking. She was not the same person who had lunched with me at Toscana.

She was in complete denial. She had to know about the atrocities her father was alleged to have committed when the dictatorship began to fall apart after the Malvinas War. It was then that the dam burst and the horrors of the past were brought to light: the prisoners who had been tortured, blinded, tossed into rivers or into mass graves; the newborn babies kidnapped, the rapes, the struggle to the death against enemies that did not exist. Dupuy was in each and every circle of that hell: he helped make them possible, gave them his blessing, told Jimmy Carter's envoys that they were fictions dreamed up by subversives. In the final editorial he wrote for *La República*, he announced that the magazine was to cease publication because these days people would rather listen to the radio or watch television than read anything. He was a man of words, he said, and he did not care whether his speeches were printed or spoken so long as he had free speech. He admitted that, in the past, he had been guilty of serious sins of omission (he still talked in terms of sins), a fault, he said, he shared with millions of Argentinians. He apologised for paying more attention to the peso's flotation against the dollar than to the bodies floating in the Río de la Plata. 'I am responsible for those mistakes, as are thousands of my compatriots.' The editorial concluded with a sentence that was a model of abject cynicism: 'The dictatorship that we, the Argentinian people, endured was more criminal, more corrupt than any that has come before. It kept us in ignorance of the atrocities committed even as it allowed itself free rein to commit them. Thanks to God's great wisdom, the nightmare is finally coming to an end.'

He agreed to television interviews in which he sidestepped difficult questions and, now, stripped of his fascist conviction, extolled the virtues of democracy and tolerance, pronounced himself a Christian who was prepared to discuss even those ideas and beliefs he found distasteful, without explaining what these might be. Though he took great pains to upset no one, some of his actions were brought up during the trials. He was spared punishment, but not rejection. The director of an orphanage for girls declared that the doctor used to visit the inmates from time to time, choose one of the prettiest and take her for a drive in his car. None of them ever returned. They were young girls, little more than teenagers, learning to sew, to cook, to do accounts. They had no families to claim them, they lived in the orphanage isolated from all contact with the outside world. I read the woman's statement in the *Diario del Juicio*, and for days afterwards the horror of it made me feel physically sick, it made me feel ashamed to think what we had silently allowed to happen, to think of the depths to which the human race could sink. When I told my neighbour Ziva Galili about it, she said that Lavrentiy Beria, one of Stalin's butchers, had been accused of similar atrocities. Just before the Second World War, he had been the head of NKVD, the Soviet Union's internal security police. At the end of the day, he and his henchmen would go hunting for girls on the streets of Moscow, of Kokoschkino, of Noginsk, or whatever far-flung suburb his duties as a spy took him to. When he found a girl he liked, he ordered the car to follow her discreetly without attracting attention. Suddenly, he would attack. One of his henchmen would block the girl's path, throwing open the car door, while another bundled her inside where Beria would examine her more closely. If the examination proved satisfactory, he would take the girl to a secret house, gag her and tie her up. After the rape, the least submissive girls were thrown into the Moskva River, the others were sent to the army brothels in Siberia. I had read fragments of this chilling story in a book by Donald Rayfield about Stalin's 'hangmen' and their abuses. In the book, I had seen a disturbing photo of Beria when he was about forty in which he looked very like Dr Dupuy: the same broad forehead, the same lascivious mouth, a nose like the beak of a bird of prey. Democratic openness made it possible for a number of newspapers to mention other sordid stories about Dupuy, but they were quickly snuffed out by the avalanche of civil and criminal suits he filed to defend himself. Many of those who could have denounced him had been his accomplices and even the teachers at the orphanage were not prepared to identify him as the man who took away the girls.

In late 1977, Dupuy had been the adviser to whom the *comandantes* most often turned, the only one they were prepared to accept as a moderator in their power struggles. One November night he was summoned to the presidential palace. It was seven months before the start of the World Cup and everything had already been completed: the stadiums, the hotels for visiting journalists, the motorways, the TV station which would broadcast the games in colour. Dupuy assumed he had been summoned to mediate in another of the endless wranglings for power. He would be blunt, tell them to sort it out themselves. Or perhaps they would ask him to discreetly get rid of the annoying gaggle of women who gathered at the Pirámide de Mayo every Thursday afternoon right under the their noses, demanding the return of sons who were lost or dead. Whatever the mission entrusted to him by the *comandantes*, he would know how best to deal with it, which would make all three of them happy.

By the time he arrived for the meeting, it was almost midnight. The corridors of the presidential palace were deserted: Dupuy had negotiated these hallways many times and knew he had to move carefully. Every twenty or thirty metres, someone would step out of the shadows and demand that he produce his papers. As he walked, the air became hotter and hotter. He leaned for a moment on the balustrade of the gallery and looked down at the palm trees in the courtyard. The night swelled, the darkness swelled (there is no other way to explain the slow inflammation of reality), and pollen stained the floor tiles a cloying yellow. An aide-de-camp came to meet him and walked with him to the dining room where the *comandantes* were finishing their meal. They seemed nervous, upset. The table was littered with press clippings from foreign papers, cartoons, stark headlines about the secret concentration camps, the torture, the numbers of the disappeared. One of the cartoons depicted the Eel with a little moustache like Hitler's and the same lock of hair falling across his forehead. The artist had taken pains to make sure the hair looked shiny and stiff with hair cream. Dupuy had the impression that the commander-in-chief of the navy was amused by this display of rubbish. He was a strapping, muscular, arrogant man, the opposite of the Eel. He apologised to Dupuy for summoning him at such a late hour and asked him to take a seat.

'We don't want to take up too much of your time. I'm sure you've realised why we asked you to come. We need your help, your imagination.'

'A vicious campaign has been unleashed against us,' the

Eel interjected. 'It needs to be stopped as soon as possible. In a few months, the whole country will be on display for all the world to see. Our every move is going to be examined under a microscope.'

'I assume you've read my latest editorial in *La República* refuting this sleazy campaign.'

'"Rights and Humans"? It was a model of intelligence, Doctor, as your writing always is,' said the admiral. 'However, what you write unfortunately only influences opinion in this country. And the country needs no convincing. They realise that when they attack the government, they attack the nation. What we cannot control are the lies spread abroad—'

'The vicious campaign against Argentina,' interrupted the Eel. 'You've seen the cartoons attempting to ridicule me.'

'Your editorial has been translated and sent via our embassies to foreign newspapers,' said the admiral. 'We have offered a lot of money to have them published. Most of them replied saying they won't publish, not even as a paid advertisement.'

Dupuy felt embarrassed by the comment.

'It's not your fault, Doctor,' the Eel intervened. 'A number of extremists have escaped and have been making harmful statements about us. They've been travelling all over the world smearing our good name. They're tireless. Even the BBC in London has broadcast a documentary full of lies. We plan to sue them, but who knows whether it's wise to aggravate them, whether it will only give them more rope to hang us with.'

'To do nothing would be much worse. But how can I be of help, señores?' Dupuy asked. 'You know more about counter-intelligence strategy than I do.'

'We can't destabilise subversives by the book,' said the

admiral. 'What we need is a little imagination. That's why we've called you in. What are your thoughts?'

'Nothing, just at the moment. I'll give the situation careful consideration and come up with a quick, effective solution. Something that will silence the liars once and for all.'

'A lightning flash that will win over the sceptics. Another Star of Bethlehem,' said the Eel.

'A blinding flash, certainly, but something lasting,' Dupuy amended, 'something that will leave its mark on history. A century from now, any memories of us will be vague. To some in Argentina we will be heroes, not to others. But when they look on what we achieved, we will be remembered with respect, as the Borgias are in Florence, as Napoleon is in France. Of this sleazy campaign of lies against Argentina, on the other hand, no one will remember a thing. We will refute them now with something that will last forever. With a monument, but not one carved in marble. A monument that is imperishable. If you will excuse me, señores, I need to think.'

He did not sleep that night. The image of the Eel with the fringe and the Hitler moustache lay in wait like a starving cat. He reviewed the speeches Hitler had made when he carried all the world before him and wondered what his legacy to posterity would have been if history had not ruined it. He thought of the scale models of the Berlin Olympiad which the architect Speer had given Hitler for his birthday. He recalled the arresting opening scenes of Leni Riefenstahl's two classic documentaries and sensed that this was the key. The finished motorways and the stadiums for the World Cup were equal to the ambition of Speer's scale models. What was needed to complete the picture was a film like Riefenstahl's, an enduring work of art which would tour the world, singing the glories of Argentina, which would carry off the prizes at Cannes, at Venice, at the Oscars. It needed a great opening and a great director. He thought of the unforgettable opening images of *Olympia* depicting the ruins of the greatness of Greek civilisation; he imagined thousands of balloons and doves rising in the late-afternoon air as a providential plane crossed the sky, a reference to *Triumph of the Will* where the Führer's plane comes in to land at Nuremberg. The problem was the Eel did not have the gravitas of Hitler; he was scrawny, surly and the moment he opened his mouth he sounded like a barracks sergeant. This was something that could be dealt with later: using body doubles and long-distance shots. Right now he needed to think of a director capable of the same epic feat as Riefenstahl, someone who was already famous and respected.

He had met Orson Welles in the bullring in Toledo. He had only the vaguest idea of what Welles had done, but he knew that his first film, *Citizen Kane*, was considered by critics to be the finest in the history of cinema. That was enough for him. He didn't need to see *Citizen*, all he needed was to find out a little more about the man himself. He had been a prodigy and at the age of thirty had married Rita Hayworth. He was not egotistical – his failures had cured him of his pride. If Welles was prepared to follow his orders, this documentary about Argentina would go down in history as the bible of cinema. The more he thought about the project, the more convinced he was that it could not fail. The characters would be heroes like those in Greek mythology. And the plot, ah, the plot – he would have to fashion it carefully. It would depict battles of the stature of *War and Peace, Moby-Dick*, the *Iliad* but played out on the football field. He would have liked to call the film *Gods of the Stadium*, but this was the Spanish title of Riefenstahl's *Olympiad*.

The Welles he had met in Toledo was an educated man, more a jaded ox than a fighting bull. And, according to his informants, after Toledo, things had not gone well for him. He was constantly in need of money, constantly fighting with producers who mutilated his works of art.

That won't happen with me, thought Dupuy, I speak the same language as he does. He had first seen him before the bullfight which was Antonio Bienvenida's farewell to the bullring. He had been lying on a red velvet sofa, in a waiting room outside the matador's dressing room, wreathed in the smoke from his huge cigar. Dupuy had had no idea who he was. He had never seen him act, did not know the man was famous. These were things he realised only later. Taking him to be a bullfighting critic, he greeted him respectfully: 'Hail Mary, most pure.' Welles looked him up and down without answering. 'You're not Catholic?' the doctor said, surprised. A good Catholic would respond 'Conceived without sin'. Welles smiled haughtily. 'Please, don't talk about my private life, señor,' he said in impeccable Spanish. 'Are you or aren't you?' Dupuy insisted. 'I don't know. Let me put it another way: once a Catholic, always a Catholic.' 'I certainly believe so,' the doctor agreed. 'That is the catechism.'

Bienvenida emerged from the dressing room wearing the bullfighter's traditional 'suit of lights'. He was a gentleman of melancholy disposition and he was nervous. The bulls that afternoon were the last he would face in his life. 'I hope you get to see a good fight,' he said. 'By the grace of God,' Dupuy corrected him. Then he turned back to Welles who had looked up. 'Come now, *hombre*, say something. What are you waiting for? Wish the man luck.' Welles did not say a word, but held out his hand to Bienvenida and stubbed out his cigar.

Dupuy smiled as he remembered the encounter. He had no doubts now. He would provide Welles with whatever he wanted, vast multitudes, fake cities like those in Hollywood; he would allow him to bring his own crew and would ensure that they lacked for nothing. He, Dupuy, would choose the music for the soundtrack. He would persuade Welles that they needed military marches, exuberant music and, especially, tangos. He would take him to meet Piazzolla, who had spent the past months writing a suite about the World Cup. He would tell Piazzola he had written the music for *Last Tango in Paris*, that he was a Richard Strauss, a Nino Rota. Orson would get down on his knees and thank him.

The following day he presented his idea to the *comandantes*. He spoke to each of them individually, because when they were together they constantly competed for control. The solution, he could convince them, was magnificent, but immortal? It would be difficult for a film – any film – to rival the Great Wall of China, nor was it as symbolic as the Obelisk of Buenos Aires. Wouldn't it be possible to build another obelisk, they suggested to him, one twice as high with a football at the top? Dupuy wasted hours talking to them while they interrupted him, taking phone calls, signing decrees, consulting with the high command. The commander-in-chief of the navy said that he would agree to the idea if he could be filmed entering the stadium with Perón's widow. The widow was in jail and the scene would have to be shot in secret. The commander-in-chief of the air force wanted the film to open with a fly-past of fighter planes. The Eel demanded that, instead of balloons and doves, Welles could make a speech asking for God's blessing on Argentina. Dupuy said yes to all of them and suggested they let the director work in peace until it was finished. They were about to spend millions, he did not want to get embroiled in arguments before he had to. He phoned Welles's agents and, shortly afterwards, flew to Los Angeles to firm up the details of what he was already calling the *film of the century*.

Orson, he was told, travelled a lot and it was extremely rare to find him at his home in Beverly Hills. Sometimes he would take the overnight flight to Boston and, the next day, fly to some godforsaken town in Arizona. He was working tirelessly on the filming of *Othello*, adapting a short story by Isak Dinesen and writing a screenplay based on a novel by Graham Greene. One of the agents repeated to Dupuy Welles's comments when he was informed about the project. A film about Argentina? Flamenco and bullfights? I'm intrigued. Tell this man to come and see me. I've had Capone and Lucky Luciano and Costello hounding me to make films for them – I dealt with them and I'm still alive.

Welles was waiting for him on the terrace at the back of the house, next to a vast swimming pool shaped like a kidney. It was December, a strong breeze was blowing, whipping up eddies of yellow leaves. As in Toledo, the director was chewing on a fat cigar. There was no smoke this time. He chewed it and spat the dark tobacco fibres onto the ground. He was still physically imposing, but more bloated now and the fat around his belly fell in folds over his trousers. A liveried servant brought two whisky glasses and poured generous measures, though Welles did not seem to notice. He was engrossed in reading Dupuy's business card (his name, phone numbers and the logo of the newspaper), and every now and then he would glance through the papers and photographs piled on the table. Scripts, Dupuy supposed, and photographs of actors. He doesn't need to prove he's a busy man. I know he is. He realised Welles did not remember him. It is hardly surprising, we only met briefly one afternoon, he thought. It will come back to him when he hears my offer, an offer bigger than Hollywood, than Spain, an offer (Dupuy repeated to himself, excited now) as big as the world. He spoke to Welles in Spanish. The director replied in English.

'May I call you Orson?' Dupuy said. 'We met about ten years ago, in Antonio Bienvenida's dressing room.'

'Call me Orsten,' said Welles, giving no sign that he remembered Bienvenida. 'That's what Lucky Luciano called me, Orsten. I called him Charlie. Mind if I call you Charlie?'

'If you like. Let me explain my project to you.'

Dupuy had to make several attempts. Welles knew nothing about football, had never heard of the World Cup, and his impression of Argentina was a vast horizon of pampas. He vaguely remembered Buenos Aires – he had been awarded a prize there for *Citizen Kane* in 1942. 'I remember there was a fascist march protesting against my visit. Your country was sympathetic to fascism back then, wasn't it, Charlie?' The doctor said nothing, he did not want to get entangled in ideological explications. It was a potential quagmire. He, Dupuy, was a master of politics; Welles was barely a novice. On the other hand, it had been years since Dupuy had set foot in a cinema. 'I won't take up much of your time, Orsten. I've come to pitch a documentary with an unlimited budget, can you imagine? Obviously, the footage will be served to you on a plate, at least half the film would be taken up with the matches.' This, he knew, was not true; Riefenstahl had had to painstakingly craft her film, but he did not want to discourage Welles. 'It's just a documentary, child's play. We wouldn't need much from you at all, Orsten, just your voice and your vision. And your name, Orson. When you're done, you'll have more than enough money to complete all the projects you left half finished. You'll be able to go back to filming *Don Quixote*, *King Lear*, *The Magic Mountain*.' 'I've never been interested in *The Magic Mountain*,' Welles corrected him, 'and the things in my past will stay in my past.' 'Allow me to explain our documentary to you a little better,' Dupuy insisted, 'it will only take two minutes. What my government wants is for you to make a great film, something that will go down in history, a *Citizen Kane* of documentary film-making. Just imagine the opening for a moment, Orson. The blue sky, dappled clouds, thousands of birds, the excited voices of the crowds we cannot see yet. And a microphone descending from above, just like in *The Magnificent Ambersons*' – his advisers had recommended that he not forget this point: the microphone, the stentorian voice, the commanding ego – 'and then . . . and then, your voice as the screen opens up: "This is Orson Welles in Argentina. I wrote and directed this film." What do you think?'

Welles stared at him, incredulous. 'In the papers I have here it says that there are magicians in your country, Charlie, illusionists . . . is that true? As you know I am more of an illusionist than a director.' Dupuy had been advised that Welles had recently released a film about forgery and magic, *F for Fake*. He had a copy in the screening room at *La República*, but had not had time to watch it. 'You want to film magicians?' Dupuy was surprised. 'No problem,' he said, 'there are lots of them in

Argentina. I'll make sure you have everything you need.'
'Listen to me, Charlie, I read in here' – Welles once again placed his huge hand on the files piled on the table – 'the magicians in your government make people in the streets disappear.' Dupuy began to panic. 'Who told you that? They're lies. Argentina has been the victim of a vicious smear campaign, a tissue of lies put about by subversive terrorists. Nobody is disappearing. There would be no need for you to address the matter in your film. We would prefer to show that ours is a peace-loving country and that our people are happy. We need to think positively, Orsten.' He did not like this turn of the conversation, it was going off-track, and the longer it went on, the more difficult it would be to rectify. He needed to stop it before he or Welles lost their patience. He had been about to ask Welles to name his price. He restrained himself. The director was more astute and more refined than the intelligence services.

'Maybe we can come to a deal, Charlie,' said Welles. 'As you probably know, many years ago I caused a panic in this country with a radio programme. I convinced two million people that Martians were invading New Jersey. People rushed out into the streets, crazed with terror. Art is illusion, Charlie, reality is illusion. Things exist only when we see them; in fact, you might say they are created by your senses. But what happens when this thing that doesn't exist looks up and stares back at you? It ceases to be a something, it reveals its existence, rebels, it is a someone with density, with intensity. You cannot make that someone disappear because you might disappear too. Human beings are not illusions, Charlie. They are stories, memories, we are God's imaginings just as God is our imagining. Erase a single point on that infinite line and you erase the whole line and we might all tumble into that black hole. Be careful, Charlie.' Dupuy was confused, he couldn't see what Welles was driving at. If he didn't like the project, why didn't he just say? There was no need to beat about the bush.

An icy wind whipped across the terrace. The director had a large black cloak and a scarf next to him, but he did not even look at them. He seemed impervious to the wind, to the gathering darkness, to the rusty December leaves that went on falling. He called for another whisky. 'More than twenty years ago, I was asked to direct a documentary about Babe Ruth,' he said. 'You know who Babe Ruth was? A baseball legend the like of which has never been seen since. I didn't like baseball, I'd never seen Babe in his glory days, but people worshipped him and I was interested in recording that idolisation on film. I took on the project and went to work. We shot a few scenes with him. He was a very sick man by then, throat cancer, so obviously he couldn't talk much. I convinced the producers that we would invent Babe, that we would create a life for him. I wanted to show him shaking Roosevelt's hand, touching Marlene Dietrich's legs, playing dice with Gary Cooper. In cinema, you can create any reality you want, imagine things that don't yet exist, freeze some moment in the past and move to a point in the future; the football matches can be reflected in anything, Charlie, they're just smoke and air, the stadiums can be filled with crowds using special effects. Maybe we can come to some arrangement. Let's make this documentary of yours, but there is no World Cup, there are no players, no football matches. There's only magic. You stop seeing, you stop talking and everything disappears. It would be a great metaphor for your country.

'Charlie, take off your watch and give it to me for a minute,' said Welles. It was a $20,000 Patek Philippe. Welles held it in front of his eyes and told Dupuy to pay careful attention. Then he threw it on the ground and stamped on it. The inner workings of the watch went flying everywhere. The doctor was speechless. 'Don't worry, Charlie,' said Welles, 'you'll get it back. It will be identical to the watch you had before, but it won't be the same because we have to pluck it from the unreality where it is now. Stamping on the watch did it no damage, but in the seconds that have passed since you gave it to me, the watch has been transformed. Here you are, Charlie.' The director opened his fist and the Patek Philippe reappeared exactly as it had been before he threw it on the ground, or at least it seemed to be. Welles had recovered his good humour and Dupuy his hopes. He was not going to go back to Buenos Aires empty-handed, but now he was not sure that entrusting the documentary to Welles was a good idea. He felt that he was dealing with a madman.

'Orsten, could you explain a little more?' he said. 'Talk to me about the documentary. What do you think of the opening shots, the sky, the birds, the microphone?'

'Maybe,' said Welles. 'What's next?'

Dupuy unfolded the speech he had written during the long flight and began to read. 'In the film, it will be your voice, Orsten. It's in Spanish, but I'll have it translated for you. "My name is Orson Welles, I'm speaking from the River Plate Monumental Stadium in Buenos Aires, Argentina. We share the excitement of this righteous, humane country, one of whose greatest feats had been to organise and host the 1978 World Cup, defying the sceptics who said, 'They'll never succeed.' Here, stadiums, motorways and airports have been built in record time. Here, the people love life and live in peace." What do you think, Orsten?'

'It's not my style, Charlie, it's too eloquent. Get Robert Mitchum to read it. He has a more compelling voice.'

'Whatever you say, Orsten,' said Dupuy. 'We'll hire Mitchum, whatever it costs.'

'How much were you thinking of spending, Charlie?'

'Whatever we need to. The budget for the World Cup is four hundred million dollars. We could put fifty or sixty million towards the film, whatever you need.'

'Don't be so extravagant, Charlie. The documentary I have in mind is going to cost you two million tops. Most of the budget will be spent on tricks, special effects, editing. There's no need for stadiums, players, crowds. What we are going to create is illusion. Like in the radio play with the Martians. No political speeches, no patriotic eulogies, I don't do that kind of thing.'

Dupuy was more confused than ever by Welles. How was he planning to make a World Cup documentary without the World Cup taking place? The trick with the Patek Philippe proved that the director was a master of illusion, that he could confound millions as he had confounded Dupuy. But I'm a rational man, thought Dupuy, I'm not about to sell the *comandantes* hot air. I need something solid, I need to know what this necromancer is getting at. Maybe what he's thinking of is even more majestic than Albert Speer's imperial Berlin in *Olympia*, maybe he wants to make a film as ineffable as the Great Mass in C minor by Mozart, an intangible glory, pure sound, maybe we need to think in terms like that. 'Orsten,' he said, 'as you know, there can't be a World Cup without an audience. Millions of people in hundreds of countries watch the matches on television. We have to show the pitch, the stands, the fans cheering the goals. We can't have people screaming *gooooooal* if there are no goals. These are serious people. They're not actors.'

Welles's demeanour did not change. 'The more we talk the less you seem to understand, Charlie,' he said. 'The matches will be broadcast on television, but that doesn't mean there have to be any matches. People believe something happens when they are told that it's happening. Did you believe I broke your watch?'

'Of course, Orsten. I saw it with my own eyes.'

'But I didn't break it, Charlie. It was an illusion. It never left my hand. Cinema is that same magic raised to the highest power. In your country, Charlie, magic is possible: Martians, the apocalypse, prophets walking on water. Your people believe in all these things, even those that don't exist.'

'That's not how it is, Orsten. In Argentina, people want to hear El Gordo Muñoz commentating on the matches, cheering the goals. What is a sports commentator supposed to do if there are no matches, no goals?'

'Charlie, a truly great presenter can make and unmake reality as it suits him. Do you really think that this guy Muñoz has never imagined games, missed shots, fouls? He's seen thousands of football matches in his life. All he needs to do is take the best, the most exciting moments. And if he allows his imagination free rein, he could create unforgettable matches, games that no one could ever play. I'll make a deal with you, Charlie. I'll bring my magic to this documentary, you pay me with your magic.'

'I still don't understand, Orsten.'

'You don't understand, Charlie? I make the film for you for

free, with the best World Cup anyone's ever seen, and you and your generals will make the disappeared appear.'

Dupuy stalked out of the house indignantly. In the distance, the lights of Los Angeles looked like fireflies. Sullenly, he contemplated the tree-lined streets, the downtown skyscrapers, the glittering bars. In some dark corner of the city, he thought, Argentinian extremists were hiding. They had injected their poison into the files Welles had piled on his table and flicked through from time to time. It had to be them, he was sure of it, there were cockroaches scuttling everywhere. The World Cup would shut them up, it would wipe them forever from every map, condemn them to perpetual disappearance.

The following night he took the flight back to Buenos Aires. He was no longer interested in Welles now. He would make the documentary with another director and personally instil the spirit of Riefenstahl into whomever he chose. He would get someone like Mitchum on board, that would be easy. The trip had been useful if only for the fact that it had confirmed that reality is a creation of the senses, something men had known for centuries but constantly forgot. There are no disappeared in this country, the Eel would say, no one is disappearing, and under the spell of his insipid voice everyone denied the obvious; and the more people were disappeared into non-existent dungeons, the less their absence was noticed. I'll bombard the *comandantes*' offices with new ideas, thought Dupuy, I'll suggest they persuade the people to see the World Cup as something more than just football. They need to think of their team not just as eleven players against another eleven players, but to consider every match as a fight to the death between two countries, between the flag they worship and the flags of foreign countries. We'll need to come up with images, metaphors, he thought. That was what Welles had said, and though the director would not have liked the idea, in this they were in agreement.

In less than a month, it will be New Year. That would be an ideal opportunity to test the credulity of people, to see just how effective Orson Welles's illusions could be. He asked two like-minded journalists to meet him in his office and asked them if they could dress up as Joseph, a carpenter, and his wife, the Virgin Mary. The investigation would take them two days, writing it would take another two. No, *La República* would not publish the article: it would be circulated only among the elite. He would take charge of placing it with a magazine that sold hundreds of thousands of copies and ensure they were well paid. The fake Virgin Mary was to improvise the clothes they needed to wear and write dialogue for them. He would have to approve the text, it was a confidential matter. That night, the woman rang his doorbell. Her hair was covered by a blue shawl and she was wearing a loose white dress and crude sandals. She had padded herself and looked to be seven or eight months pregnant. Dupuy showed her into his study and offered her a glass of water or fruit juice. 'I'd prefer a whisky,' she said. She took off the shawl and draped it over an armchair. She showed him photographs of Joseph wearing coarse canvas trousers and a dark shirt and sandals. He was growing out his beard. 'This is what we're going to say: "I'm María, a housewife, and this is my husband José, he's a carpenter. We're expecting a baby on December the 24th. Joseph is unemployed. Could you help us?"' 'The beard is good,' said the doctor, 'but I think it would be better if you didn't wear the shawl. You need to be less obvious, to challenge reality, instil the symbolism in the minds of the readers, don't you think? The dialogue is good. And José can carry a carpenter's tool of some sort, a ruler, a saw so people don't think he's a tramp.' 'Don't worry, Doctor,' the woman said, and finished the glass of whisky before she left.

José came to see him a week later. 'We're exhausted,' he said. 'We've been to Victoria, to Carapachay, to the railway works in Remedios de Escalada, and having failed there, we tried our luck in Córdoba. We were turned away everywhere we went. The place where they treated us best was a filthy dive bar – they gave us food, rancid cheese and stale bread. There were two drunks in the bar who made fun of María. "So you're going to give birth on the 24th, on Christmas Eve? Who do you think you are, the Virgin? I could easily believe you're a virgin, you fat fuck. Get out of here." María, who's a devout Catholic, said, "God forgive you, how could you take me for Our Lady?" and that's when things went sour. I couldn't convince her to stay. I finished the article myself and have brought it to you, Doctor, just to fulfil our obligations.' 'Does the article explain everything exactly as it happened?' asked Dupuy. 'Word for word,' said José. 'Neither of you understands anything. Go back and write it again. Write about people being helpful, say they invited you to eat with them, offered you work, gave you clothes for the baby. I've already earmarked seven pages in the magazine for the piece. Just because you failed in reality doesn't mean I have to fail.'

One of the admiral's henchmen had infiltrated the Mothers of the Plaza de Mayo. It was at a meeting in the Church of Santa Cruz and as he left he kidnapped one of the mothers and two French nuns. The following day, the papers said that the Montoneros had claimed responsibility for the kidnappings and were demanding 'the release of 21 subversive delinquents' for the safe return of the hostages. It sounded like one of Dupuy's ruses, but the doctor was insulted that these copycats had been so sloppy in their work. He put in a furious call to the admiral. 'What idiot came up with the idea that the Montoneros would refer to their own comrades as delinquents?'

Did he have to do everything himself? Unless he was absolutely meticulous, even his best plans seemed foolish. In a speech he had not had the opportunity to read, the Eel rashly admitted that there were four thousand extremist prisoners. He spoke without thinking, that's far too many, thought Dupuy. He wrote the script for a fake documentary showing military operations against subversive troops who were launching attacks on the northern border using Soviet-issue missiles and mortars. In the film, they would be repelled by the military and mown down on the battlefield. National cinema had already created battles in *Savage Pampas* and *The Gaucho War* which people still remembered. It would cost nothing to breathe new life into epics like this and use them to justify the four thousand dead. He took the plan to the admiral, who was against the idea. 'Forget about the Montoneros, Doc. We don't need them any more. We need to show the people that Argentina has enemies with bigger firepower, ruthless despots determined to steal parts of the country from us.' 'Stroessner?' Dupuy ventured. 'How could you think such a thing?' said the admiral. 'The President of Paraguay is an ally. I was thinking of someone less cunning. A brute like Pinochet, for instance. The Argentine people don't like him, and the Chileans will be a pushover.'

Welles, thought Dupuy, had not been so wrong after all.

The people of Argentina will believe what they're told and the newspapers and the radio will say what they're told to say. Even an illiterate like Pol Pot has almost succeeded in creating the reverse situation in Cambodia: a Communist peasant society. What's stopping us from marching forward on our crusade (he loved the word *crusade*), doing the same thing, but under the banner of the one true God?

Welles had made a deeper impression on him than he had realised. His editorials in *La República* were no longer starchy analytical articles where military chiefs and businessmen could read between the lines. He now rarely quoted Descartes, Leibniz and St Augustine, preferring Eliphas Lévi and Madame Blavatsky. He did not mention Horangel's astrological predictions, though he read them. He talked about symbolism, about the influence of the stars, the relationship between numbers and letters, and, which was more astonishing, even the *comandantes* took his economic predictions seriously.

Alone in the house, Emilia wandered through the rooms where the things her mother had left behind were fading, the cane, the bed jacket she wore when she got up, the bedpan, the television with its still-flickering grey images. She visited her at the old people's home twice a week and every time she left her mother sitting out on the terrace with the other old people she was racked with guilt. As a teenager she had been fascinated by the things she didn't know and drew maps as though she were writing poems: maps of imaginary cities that existed only in books, or of countries wiped away by the dust of history. Now, none of this mattered: as an adult, she had moved from one disenchantment to the next. She spent her days between itinerant maps which disappeared even before they were fully formed.

When the nurses brought her mother out onto the terrace, Emilia would stroke her hair and tell her stories. She talked to her about the first time she had met Simón in the cellar bar where Almendra were playing songs that now sounded dated, sang the lyrics to her in a voice so soft the nurse could not hear, recounted the plots of movies they had watched together and of which Emilia remembered only fleeting images. She talked to her as she might to a doll, or to the daughter she had never had. And as she talked, she stroked her hands while her mother stared into the distance with her beatific Mona Lisa smile. Sometimes, she seemed to wake up, she would echo 'Ah yes, Simón, your Simón', but they were just sounds, like the first babblings of a baby. She was wasting away, if it were possible for an old woman who was already no more than a shadow of herself to waste away.

One of the doctors advised Emilia to take Ethel back to the family home from time to time. He explained that sleeping in their own bed, being in a familiar place surrounded by people who love them, could work miracles for people suffering from mental illness. 'There's no chance that she will ever be who she used to be,' said the doctor, 'the damage is irreversible, but if anything is going to help her, it's love.'

'*Baruch atah Adonai,*' muttered Ethel.

'Blessed is the Lord,' translated the doctor. 'Your mother is a very religious person. She repeats that prayer several times a day.'

'That's not the way she used to pray. Could she have converted?'

'How could she have? She's in no fit state. She calls on God the only way she knows how, the way she remembers.'

'Taking her home would create problems. We've given

away most of her clothes. My sister is about to get married. I'm out working all day and so is my father.'

'Think about it, discuss it among yourselves. Three days, maybe a week every now and then would be enough. And don't worry about the clothes, she doesn't need much.'

That night, Emilia raised the subject with her father and Chela who let out a scream. 'Who is this doctor? Is he crazy? Has everyone gone crazy? Didn't you tell him that I'm getting married and that if she's here it'll be a disaster?'

Her father considered the idea. He dropped by the sanatorium only rarely, claiming that it upset him to see the ruined shell that was the woman to whom he had given his name. He asked if they bathed her every day, whether they were feeding her properly, then he left. She had never heard him say a loving word. He loathed expressions of affection, or maybe (thought Emilia), he used them only when saying things he did not truly believe.

'I told the doctor everything,' Emilia said. '*Mamá* won't be coming back until after you're married. And she won't be coming back permanently. She just needs to come home from time to time for short periods. You won't even know she's here. I'll look after her, and if I'm not here, we'll bring in a nurse.'

She was still working as a cartographer for the Automobile Club. She earned a pittance but enough for her to live modestly without having to rely on her father. If she had known at the time that every month Dupuy deposited a sum equal to her salary into her account, she would have thrown it back in his face. When she was asked to work overtime, she gratefully accepted even though the money was pitiful. She was making plans to go out into the world to search for Simón. She would close her eyes and indicate a point on the map, telling herself that this was the place where her husband was hiding, the place from which he would return. She was hoping for a chance revelation, just as Bible readers hope to find illumination in the first line they happen on.

Contrary to what Emilia expected, Dupuy did not reject the doctor's recommendation out of hand. He said that he would think about it and make his decision the following evening. His daughter never knew who he spoke to during those hours, nor how he came to the conclusion she least expected. Her only thought was that, at a time marked by frequent social gatherings, single men were the subject of gossip. More than once, the Eel had said that though he sympathised with Dupuy over Ethel's illness, nobody understood why he didn't simply take his daughter to such parties. 'Emilita is a treasure, we've known her since she was a little girl, and she's a pleasure to talk to. Don't hide this precious jewel away from us, Doc,' the admiral agreed. 'Between us, we'll teach her to enjoy life.'

Dupuy did not believe his daughter worthy of quite so much attention unless it seemed she was basking in his reflected glory. However, it was not a bad idea to be seen at Mass with her, to take her to the theatre. The *comandantes* were right. Unaccompanied men aroused suspicion, and the Church would not give its blessing to him remarrying while Ethel was still alive. Emilia was a jewel, why not show her off?

He summoned both his daughters and told them that he would not object to their mother coming home to stay occasionally only if Emilia would agree to move back into the family home to look after her, and give up the fantasies that had her languishing in San Telmo and agree to be his escort when he asked her.

Chela became alarmed.

'Don't worry about anything. Your wedding comes first – after that we can think about bringing her home. As your sister says, there's no reason not to, it's only for a couple of days a month. I can't see why you would have a problem with it since you won't be living here.'

He turned to Emilia.

'But I don't want any problems either. While she's in this house, Ethel will have to stay in her room like the vegetable she is. If I see her or hear her, I'm sending her straight back to the home.'

'What about my job?' asked Emilia.

'You'll have to gradually give up working. Make up your mind: either you look after your mother, or we go back to the way things were.'

'But a nurse—' she managed to protest.

'I've thought about this carefully,' Dupuy interrupted her. 'I am not prepared to tolerate strangers in my house.'

What Emilia had not expected was the trap she had set for herself. Love and good intentions had forced her to trade one cell for another; this one, her father's, was the bitterest.

She would forget her troubles by burying herself in her work. She needed every penny she could make, needed it desperately so that one day she would be able to leave. She was a married woman, an adult. She had to throw off this yoke. She no longer even knew how to find her way around this city, a city she had once moved through heedlessly with Simón on her arm. What had been a street two years before was now fences and rubble; beneath the houses tunnels opened up, and in some places the Buenos Aires of the past seemed to have come back to life, watering troughs, horse-drawn carriages and hitching posts, things she believed had disappeared forever. Almost daily the Automobile Club redrew the maps of whole neighbourhoods, scarred by a network of motorways that was being built. She told them that she would have to take care of her mother and that soon she would only be able to work part-time. A number of areas needed to be remapped and she was lucky to be assigned Parque Chacabuco, where her mother's nursing home was. She would take her time, visit her every now and then, and gradually tell her the good news. '*Mamá*, we're going to be sleeping in the same room again, like we used to,' she would tell her, 'I'm going to take care of you again.' She had to make the most of these conversations about the world outside, which was changing so quickly.

Buenos Aires was different now: the newspapers called it progress, but the only progress Emilia could see was the steady advance of misery. The mayor had refugees forcibly evicted from the makeshift shanty towns. If they resisted, he had the electricity and water cut off. Tanks would burst through the walls of houses, rolling implacably over mattresses, stoves, half-cooked meals. She would not tell her about that, she would tell her simply that almost nothing was where it had been.

The area assigned to Emilia was a network of short streets and narrow tree-lined alleys: a corner of the city condemned to death. In a few short months, cartographers would have to draw their maps, fill in the blank spaces currently bounded by dotted lines. It was Monday. The heavy rains of the previous week had alleviated the sweltering January heat. Emilia got off the bus and walked across the park. She walked self-consciously, knowing that she was being watched but unable to tell from where. Perhaps from the porches, the balconies, the roofs of the houses. Her father always said that the best watchmen were those who never let themselves be seen, and she saw no one but she was certain she was being watched, she could feel eyes boring into the back of her neck. She stared at the little map she took from her bag. The alleys spread out in a fan on one side of the park: their names – Science, Good Order, Progress, Commerce – the last embers of positivism. She took out her drawing pad and prepared to makes notes. A sudden noise startled her. Behind her, a huge wrecking ball smashed through the wall of a nearby house, throwing up a cloud of dust and debris that settled on a family having lunch on a piece of rubble-strewn waste ground. The table was set: a chequered tablecloth, ruined *milanesas* covered with gravel and brick dust. The man sitting at the head of the table got up and eyed Emilia warily. 'Hey, señora, señorita,' he said, still chewing, his mouth enlivened by a single yellow tooth, 'are you here from the council about the census?' 'I don't know anything about that,' said Emilia. 'I'm making a map of the area.' 'Oh, you're from the land registry, it's the same thing. Could you find out for us when they're going to pay for the expropriation? They said they were going to send the money today, said there would be vans to take us to a new house, but nothing's happened, we've been waiting since first thing this morning. Our neighbours here left last week' – he threw his arms wide, gesturing to the waste ground – 'and those behind here have already been paid. You can see how we have to live. It's hell. Some people were lucky, they were given a month to leave. They tell me it could have been worse. An old woman in the Pasaje de las Garantías dropped dead when she saw the trucks rolling in. Fifty years she'd lived in the same place, cooked her meals in the same kitchen; she was the last to leave, she stayed behind to watch the collapsing roofs, the chicken coop, the plants in the garden.'

Emilia was due to map the Pasaje de las Garantías too, and went to see it. It was desolate, empty, grey as the surface of the moon and filled with craters. Maybe the motorway had scared the neighbours away. This was one of the few areas where work had been finished. At either end rose two prefabricated houses surrounded by dying gardens. One was little more than a cave which still stood in spite of the louring concrete pillars. Behind, beneath the sweeping cement curves, in a fantasy version of an old glasshouse, a few stubborn plants continued to compete for their share of oxygen and moisture under metal panels already beginning to rust. She thought she could see the glitter of freesias struggling up through the weeds. She bought a bunch of flowers from a stall on the avenue nearby. She felt a desperate desire to see her mother smile, for some small flame of happiness to spark in her life, a desire for Simón to suddenly descend from an alien sky, for people to dance on the pavements, for anything that would make her grief go away.

After Chela's wedding, Ethel spent a brief period in the family mansion on calle Arenales. Emilia shut herself up in the bedroom with her, soothed her with Schubert quartets and waltzes from the distant past when she had been courting; she changed her nightdress, put perfume on her, and at dusk she walked with her through the darkened corridors. She was just the same, or perhaps not, but the differences were imperceptible. She stared at her daughter with the same incomprehension, addressed her formally, called her by the names of friends now dead, muttered unintelligible words. When her daughter hugged her, the muscles beneath her fragile skin tensed as though she were a frightened tortoise. It seemed as if nothing mattered to her, as they stepped outside into the sunshine to take her back to the home.

Emilia paid the heavy price that Dupuy had demanded. She lived now in the family home as in another tomb, waiting for her mother's next visit: these fleeting bursts of happiness were her reward, her consolation. Leaving the apartment in San Telmo vacant was a waste, so she rented it for short-term lets to tourists. She left the furniture there so that she could go back whenever she needed or simply so she could shut herself up there and cry.

There were only a few weeks remaining before the World Cup began. One Sunday, her father insisted that she accompany him to rehearsals for the opening ceremony. 'We'll show the world how disciplined we are,' he said. 'They need to see us as we really are: tempered steel, a model of piety and order. Forty years ago in Berlin, German athletes had used their bodies to form the name of the fatherland and the swastika emblazoned on the flag. Now, the world will see that the young men of Argentina are every bit a match for those Gods of the Stadium. We shall do exactly as they did, hundreds of boys will spell out the hallowed word A-R-G-E-N-T-I-N-A. It will be a feat, since some of those letters are difficult. The G and the N require at least two somersaults.' Sometimes, Emilia thought, he talked to her like a dim-witted child, just as he had always spoken to her mother. 'Argentina, the name spelled out on the pitch with the grenadier marching band marking time. Magnificent, don't you think? We need to go. The *comandantes* and their wives will be there for the gymnastic displays, I can't be seen to be there alone, and they're fond of you, Emilia. They know about your mother. This is a celebration and women must be present.'

Dupuy had no interest in football but the World Cup, as he tirelessly repeated, was a patriotic crusade. He was already seated on the cloud of this imminent achievement and he had no intention of coming down. He would come home late with foreign magazines and newspapers he had furiously red-pencilled. He did not stay for dinner; his daughter barely saw him. 'Everywhere, there is an unjustified hatred of us,' he complained, 'a vicious campaign against Argentina. What the subversives failed to do with bombs they're trying to do with poisonous words.'

European magazines published cartoons showing a football surrounded by electrified fences like those in Auschwitz; ridiculed the Eel, dressing him up as Death carrying a scythe. 'Such disrespect is simply intolerable.' The doctor was indignant. He dreamed of having the authors of these abuses arrested and watching them being tortured to death. He resented the fact that they were out of reach of his justice. He paid 'the finest penmen in the country' to write eulogies for the papers about the peace and happiness that flourished in the country hosting the World Cup, articles intended to bury the calumnies of Julio Cortázar, Manuel Puig and the other Marxists who wrote for rags like *Le Monde*, *La Repubblica*, *Paris Match*, *L'Express* and *Il Manifesto*. He phoned the journalist who had unsuccessfully portrayed the Virgin Mary for him the previous Christmas and ordered her to visit the offices of the antagonistic magazines and discover what was at the root of this vicious hostility towards Argentina, who had paid these pen-pushers their thirty pieces of silver. 'In fact,' he said, 'ask them if they're basing this on confessions from subversives, tell them it's all lies, that before they print such garbage they should come and see for themselves that we live in peace and happiness; our doors are always open.'

He had thousands of postcards printed, the postage prepaid so that children in the schools could write a message he had devised to the footballers who would be visiting. The teachers would dictate the poignant reproachful words: 'Though you are far away, you dare to judge us. You are prepared to believe the words of criminal subversives who are destroying our country and not the patriotic soldiers risking their lives to preserve something this country is proud of: peace.' It was the responsibility of the teachers to ensure that the cards were sent and to inform on any pupils who refused to comply. 'In the new Argentina there is no place for those who stain our history,' wrote Dupuy in his editorial for *La República*. The more the World Cup approached, the more passionate his patriotism, his faith in the system, his conviction that the three hallowed words he dreamed of inscribing on the flag – God, Country, Family – were already engraved on what he called the spirit of the nation, or the soul of Argentina, it didn't matter.

Emilia was bored by the World Cup and it showed. A couple of years later, when Chela and Marcelito Echarri saw her in a brief shot from the film *La fiesta de todos*, they laughed at the fact that the camera had caught her in the middle of a yawn. She had flu and was coming down with a fever; she would have preferred to take her mother home and lie down next to her, but Dupuy wanted her to accompany him to the final at the River Plate Stadium and she could not refuse.

The match was due to start at 3 p.m.; the whole city was moving in slow motion and the driver from *La República* came to pick them up at 1.30 p.m. Crowds thronged the streets, blocking access to the stadium; vast human anthills swarmed, swathed in the Argentinian flag, wearing headbands, woolly hats emblazoned with the national coat of arms, wrapped up in blue-and-white scarves, all the trappings of patriotic fervour. Buenos Aires was affected by a madness of euphoria. Two policemen on motorcycles opened the way for them. Hundreds more were stationed around the grounds to look after VIPs. A number of fans jumped security barriers and applauded Dupuy when they recognised him. 'What a pleasure, what a privilege to have you here for the celebration, Doctor,' they shouted. Emilia's father succumbed to temptation, popping his head out the car window to shake hands with the fans. It was difficult to know who was who, they seemed fused like Siamese twins by their frenzy and fanaticism. A woman struggled through the wall and rushed over to him. 'Doctor, Doctor, you're my last hope,' she said, or rather shouted. 'My daughter was taken away from our house when she was six months pregnant. My grandson has probably been born by now who knows where. Make them give them back to me, Doctor, I can't go to my grave without seeing her again. Her name is Irene. Irene Cruz. You can do it, Doctor, you can.' She tried to stroke his hands, the words swallowed up by her sobs. Dupuy did not even look at her. His attention was fixed on the crowds clapping and cheering. The woman held out a card to him as the police lifted her bodily and dragged her off through the milling crowd. Emilia took the card and looked at it – a phone number, two names, an address in Villa Adelina. 'What are you going to do, *Papá*?' she asked. 'What do you want me to do?' said Dupuy and ordered the driver not to stop again. Inside the stadium, he took a seat behind the *comandantes*; Emilia sat with their wives on one of the stands nearby. She saw her father whisper something to the Eel. The woman's card trembled in her hand like a living thing and Emilia quickly tucked it into the waistband of her skirt.

Flares erupted around her; the whole stadium was jumping up and down, chanting *Argentina! Argentina!* She felt herself infected by this fervour, she felt it would be despicable to rush from the stadium to find Irene Cruz's mother and hug her. Who knew in what pit of hell her daughter and her unborn grandson lay buried while the crowds on the stand chanted *Argentina! Argentina!* Who knew whether simply approaching this woman might not condemn her to death. A few metres away, Dupuy was smiling, regaling the Eel with stories of intrigue in the high command even as he told the *comandantes* what they should do and even what they should say on the radio on the day of victory. Around Emilia, everyone in the crowd, even the most anaesthetised, were on their feet, shouting insults at the Dutch team, wrapping themselves in flags and painted bed sheets. '*Argentina, champions of the world!*' roared El Gordo Muñoz through transistor radios. '*Great and glorious, Argentina, Hear, mortals, the sacred cry!*' Emilia struggled from the arms embracing her, took Señora Cruz's card, tore it to shreds and tossed it into the air to join the rain of streamers and confetti darkening the five o'clock sky.

I was still trying to work out what exactly the *eruv* was when Emilia asked me to go and see her. Autumn lingered on, it was late November but it was not yet cold. Water was freezing in the lakes of Vietnam, the oases of Libya, but in Highland Park, where the first snows usually fall about this time of year, the defiant warmth of summer refused to leave and the neighbours went jogging in the park in T-shirts. The map of the *eruv* Emilia had drawn had now been posted on the Internet: Donaldson Park and the Raritan River were outside its boundaries. My friend Ziva pronounced it *eiruv*, or *ieruv*, as the Russians do. One of the rabbis in town took the trouble to explain to me that it was a symbolic wall separating public space from private. On the Sabbath, it is forbidden to move things from one to another. Some communities forbid women from wearing jewellery and even sunglasses unless they need to. He gave me an example: on Saturday – Shabbat – it is forbidden to build. To open an umbrella, he explained, is similar to erecting a tent. Consequently, on Saturdays, it is forbidden to move beyond the bounds of the *eruv* with an umbrella. Highland Park is less than five square kilometres and a large section of the black neighbourhood is inside the *eruv* because the Almighty belongs to everyone, even those unfortunate enough not to believe in Him.

When I rang her doorbell, Emilia had just recovered from a panic attack and seemed about to have another. I don't know how she made it down the stairs to open the door. I took her arm and helped her back into the hall. I find anything to do with mental illness distressing, I never know what to do to help. I'm terrified of saying the wrong thing and bringing down the whole fragile thing that is the mind. Emilia had turned on every light in the house. Her body was shaking as though her whole world had come crashing down. She wanted to tell me something but she was stammering so much I couldn't understand her. I suppose that, if anyone had seen it, my clumsy, frantic attempts to help her would have seemed ridiculous. I brought her a glass of water, asked her if she wanted me to call an ambulance. She drank the water and hysterically told me not to call an ambulance. She sat for a moment saying nothing, hugging her knees to her chest. I had always felt that she was three distinct women: the old woman who showered the cashiers at Stop & Shop with coupons, the woman who was in love with Simón, and the little girl Dr Dupuy had destroyed. All three were there in front of me and I didn't know which one to talk to. I waited until her breathing was calmer and asked her if she had any medication in the house that would help her sleep. I was going to give her some, stay with her until she fell asleep and see how she was the following day. She told me she had some pills in the bathroom cabinet she kept for emergencies and I went to look for them. There were about ten or twelve pill bottles containing the full panoply of pharmaceutical flora and fauna: Estradiol, a hormone replacement for women post menopause, Benadryl, Lexotanil, a sleeping pill from Argentina, Clonazepam and Vicodin, drugs used to calm anxiety and knock you out. Most of the drugs were dangerous, and there was more than enough for Emilia to commit suicide if she had a mind to. But she was not going to kill herself while she was still waiting for Simón.

Simón, once again, had been the reason for her call. 'Please, I'm begging you, go into my bedroom,' she said, 'see if he's hiding in there somewhere. I looked in the mirror and I didn't see myself, I saw him standing there instead. For days now I've been working on a map and I get up to go to the bathroom or make a cup of coffee and when I come back the map is full of mistakes, or it's been completely erased and I can't start over again.'

'Maybe you were distracted and you erased it yourself,' I said. 'Happens to the best of us. Maybe you made the mistakes yourself and didn't realise. You're not taking cocaine or LSD or something like that? You've got enough drugs in that bathroom cabinet to stun an elephant.'

'No, I've never been tempted by things like that,' she said. 'Maybe later, when I'm too old for anything else. Besides, I almost never make mistakes when I'm drawing maps. It never happens to me at work, why would it happen when I'm here? As soon as I come through the door, I feel like there's someone else here. Everything is exactly where I left it but nothing is the same. I don't know if my senses are playing tricks on me and I need to know what you see, what you hear, since your senses are fine.'

'I'll go and look at myself in the mirror,' I said. 'But don't put too much faith in me. My senses are shot, too. I think I'm losing my sense of touch, my hearing is going and so is my sight. I wrote a novel twenty years ago in which cats were stealing my character's senses; by the time he died, he had none left. Now it feels like he's come back for revenge.'

'I read that one,' she said. 'The character's name is Carmona.'

I was pleased she still remembered a book that few people had ever heard of. Besides, I was the least suitable person to bring her back to reality. I asked her whether she saw Simón or whether she thought she saw him.

'I don't understand the difference,' she said. 'I don't talk to him, I can't touch him, but I know he's there. Ever since I saw him standing in the doorway – that doorway' – she pointed to the door leading to the bedroom – 'he hasn't left, he doesn't want to leave. He's saying something to me, but I can't understand him.'

'I don't understand you either, Emilia,' I said. 'You need to be clearer in explaining what you remember. When you tell me things, there are blind spots, contradictions, things that couldn't have happened when you think they happened. I'm completely confused when you talk to me about your mother's visits to the house on the calle Arenales, about when you moved back from the San Telmo apartment, how many times Chela's wedding was postponed, about your father's machinations. Maybe my senses are as damaged as yours. You need to go and see a doctor. I can't help you. Just like you, I see things that aren't there, but it doesn't make me worry for my sanity. There are figures and feelings that are far removed from reality, or they're part of a reality different from ours. Have you ever been to the Jewish museum in Berlin?'

'No,' she said, 'I've never been to Germany.'

'I visited the museum in 2005, and I have no wish ever to go again.'

'Was it a painful experience?'

'It was painful in a sense, but that's not why. I experienced the same unreal sensations you're talking about. I heard voices, I sat down on a terrace next to my dead father, there were past lives inside me struggling to come out. I'd read somewhere that the museum is an architectural masterpiece, and it is. I can't explain why, there are lots of books about it. I don't want to overwhelm you talking about the angles, the weird vertical planes, the ceilings that seem to be falling in on you, the silences that open and close up as you walk through, but you quickly find yourself in a different reality, one that you feel you could be lost in forever. For years, you've lived in exile, moving from place to place, Emilia; you think you know what it is, but you couldn't begin to explain it, there are no stories, no words in this desolate terrain because everything within you remained outside the moment you crossed the threshold. You might say that at that moment you entered purgatory, if what came before was hell (and it wasn't, at least for me it wasn't), if after was paradise, which never came. And when the wandering is over, when you go back to the home you left behind, you think you're closing the circle, but visiting the museum you realise that the whole journey has been a one-way trip, always leaving. No one returns from exile. What you forsake, forsakes you. To the south of the museum is what's called the Garden of Exile, forty-nine columns that rise (no, they don't rise – every verb seems inadequate: rise, extend, stretch away?), forty-nine hollow columns of decreasing height; an oblique vision of life. Out of each column emerges a tree: you can't tell where the tree comes from, all you can see is the desperate struggle of the branches to reach the light, to meet the sky they once lost. Pity moves you to walk between the columns so the trees will not feel so alone. You walk. The ground is cobbled and sloping, an edge of the world towards which things slide until finally they fall. By the time you've taken two steps, you are nowhere, there are no columns, there are no trees, there is no sky, the compass that guided you has disappeared, your reason for existing has been wiped out, you are nothing and you have stopped in a place from which no one ever returns. Exile.'

I went over to the mirror and looked at myself. The photo of a young Simón smiled at the mirror from the nightstand. The room was a mess; it was strange that Emilia, usually so fastidious, allowed me to go in. Magazines lay open on the bed, the sort people read while they're queuing at the supermarket, featuring huge photos of Jennifer Lopez pregnant with twins, Britney Spears in her rehab clinic. I would never have imagined Emilia had such a morbid curiosity about the lives of others, though it made sense: the Emilia who collected coupons and played bingo belonged to that niche. It is impossible really to know another human being completely, and I had only ever seen Emilia on one side of the *eruv*, I never knew what became of her when she crossed over. I talked to her from where I stood, trying to reassure her. 'I'm standing in front of the mirror, Emilia. There's no one here. All I can see is the idiot standing here talking to you, I can see a shadow beside me, but it's the idiot's shadow. Try as I might, I'll never see Simón because the only reason for your Simón to exist is for you alone to see him.'

When did that happen? When was it that Emilia phoned me asking for help? When did I go round to her house and stand staring at myself in the mirror, and leave without recognising my own body, feeling that memories that were not mine had entered into my body and I could not shake them off, memories that insisted on staying inside me even though I ran out? I didn't make a note of it in my diary and recently the days have become confused. I haven't seen her since then. I tried calling her at Hammond to talk to her about the novel I'm writing but they told me that she'd stopped coming in. I went by her house a couple of times and was surprised not to see her beat-up silver Altima parked on North 4th Avenue or in the parking lot at Rite Aid where she sometimes left it.

More than once I was on the point of telling her something about my novel. But I held back, out of shyness, out of shame, for the nameless reason that drives all writers to hide what they are doing until it's finished. I said nothing because I was foundering in a swamp of first drafts I still haven't climbed out of. She is the character on which the story turns, she was even before I knew her, and now I'd rather not carry on with it until we have had a serious conversation. I'm not waiting for her to give me permission to continue – characters aren't censors, they don't interfere in what happens to them. But Emilia is not simply one of my characters, she is also a human being, someone I know, someone I run into at Stop & Shop, a friend who has confided in me. Or is she simply someone inside me the way Simón is inside her? Before going out to look for her I remembered the lines of Felisberto Hernández: *One can betray only when one lives with others. But with the body in which I live, no betrayal is possible.* This, Felisberto used to say, is a hopeless situation. I have to clarify things with Emilia, work out where she begins and I end. Not knowing makes me uneasy.

Writing has always been a liberating act for me, the only place myself could roam without having to explain itself. While I write, I let myself go. Only after I have taken a few steps do I think about the boundaries of what I am doing: whether I am headed towards a novel or an essay, whether this is a story or a film script or a profile of the dead. I most often get lost when I try to go beyond the boundaries. Though the boundaries may resist, still I cross them. I want to see what's on the other side of the words, in the landscapes that are never seen, in the stories that disappear even as they are being told. Perhaps if I devoted myself to poetry I might catch a glimpse of this horizon I can never reach. But I am not a poet, something I regret. If I were I would be able to name the true nature of things, unerringly find the centre rather than becoming lost on the margins. What am I going to say to Emilia when I see her?

That human beings are responsible for everything except

our dreams. Many years ago now, before I met her, I dreamed of her and I transformed that dream into the first lines of a story that I have carried with me from country to country, believing that some day I would have the dream again and I would feel the need to complete it. I dreamed that I went into a seedy restaurant where an elderly woman was sitting at one end of a long table staring at one of the people eating with her. At that moment, I knew, with the blinding clarity we have in dreams, that the woman was a widow and the man was her husband who had been dead for thirty years. I also knew that the husband was the man he had been, his voice, his age those of the time he died.

When I woke up, I was excited, imagining the pleasure that elderly woman would feel to be loved, to be made love to by a much younger man. I didn't care whether he was her husband or not. It seemed to me to be an act of poetic justice, since in most stories, the situation is reversed. I started writing, not knowing where my search would take me. I didn't know what the husband was doing in that seedy restaurant, nor why time, for him, seemed to have been suspended. Those thirty years of separation – I thought – somehow echoed the empti-ness of the thirty years I had spent exiled from my country and which I hoped to find, when I went back, exactly as I had left it. I know that it is an illusion, naive in the way all illusions are, and perhaps that was what attracted me, because those lost years will always haunt me and if I narrate them, if I imagine every day I did not live, perhaps – I thought – I could exorcise them. I wanted to remember what I didn't see, recount the life I would have had, looking after my children, loving them, wandering through the cities of Argentina, reading. I wanted the impossible, because I could not have lived oblivious to the torture victims, to the prisoners held without trial, to the slaves in the death camps working for the greater glory of the admiral and the Eel. I wanted to be Wakefield, to disappear completely from the world and come back home one day, open the door and find nothing has changed. I wanted to know what it would have been like, the life of a writer forbidden to write. The questions tormented me, gave me no peace, and in desperation, I set about answering them. The phrase sounds melodramatic, but it is true nonetheless. I wrote quickly, page after page, eager to find out what happened next. I worked at a frantic pace unfamiliar to me. In general I can spend hours agonising over a single sentence, sometimes a single word, but in this book, almost without realising it, the writing consumed me, gambling in a race against death. True to form, death came looking for me. I had written about eighty pages when illness laid me low. In hospital, I began to see things differently. I thought about all the things that disappear without our even noticing, because we know only what exists, we know nothing of those things that never come into existence; I thought about the non-being I would have been had my parents conceived me seconds earlier or later, I thought of the libraries of books never written (Borges tried to make up for this absence in 'The Library of Babel'), but all that remained was the idea, there was no flesh, no bones, a magnificent, lifeless idea. I thought about the Mozart symphonies silenced by his untimely death, about the song running through John Lennon's mind that December night when he was murdered. If we could recover the unwritten books, the lost music, if we could set out in search of what never existed and find it, then we should have conquered death. While I was lying there waiting for death I thought that perhaps this was the way to get my life back. So I abandoned the novel I had been writing, and started this novel, which is filled with what does not exist and at its heart, still, is Emilia, who had taken my hand at Toscana and guided me through her labyrinth. You might say I found her before setting out to look. For her, it breathed new life into her hopes of seeing Simón again; for me, it breathed new life into this book.

I was describing her, bent over her drawing table, over the half-finished map of the *eruv*, when she called to ask me if it was Simón reflected in her mirror. I already said, I think, that I saw only myself and the photo of Simón as a young man on the nightstand behind me. For more than a week now, I have made no attempt to find Emilia. Sooner or later, I feel sure, she will call because the memories I carry within me are her memories too, and she will ask me to leave them where they are. Before I lost her, I thought I saw a light on in her apartment and I rang the doorbell. I must have been mistaken, because no one answered. I looked again and the lights were off.

Sunday night, Emilia orders in Japanese food again and she and Simón eat in silence. On the table is a bottle of sake she bought at Pino's and, without realising, the two of them drink half the bottle. The delicate rice wine enfolds them in a giddiness like marijuana, it is a pleasure Emilia adopted from two late films by Ozu that she watched on DVD. Just as Ozu's women anaesthetise their troubles with sake, Emilia has spent the day letting go her remaining troubles, dealing with the last one on her computer. Before dinner, she sent a brief note to her head of Human Resources at Hammond. 'I need to be out of the office for a few days,' it said, and at the bottom, 'Personal reasons.' She is no longer able to bear the routine of work. She does not want to go back to grid squares of maps, she cannot bear ever to leave this person who has come back to take her away. She has suffered more than she can bear. The world is cruel to those who love, they say. It distracts them, deflects them from the love that is the true centre of life. Why miss out on love and turn towards something else? What to do with all the wasted love that has gone unlived? Now, it does not matter to her to know what happens next. All that matters is that she does not move from the point she has reached. I'm happy, she says to herself over and over, I could go to the depths, the heights of this happiness, but not beyond it.

Simón is very pale. She sees a languid smile play on his lips. It worries Emilia that the smile came to his face just as dusk is blotting out the shape of things and she will lose the image, perhaps forever. This is the trouble with love, she thinks: that cherished expressions disappear, looks which, in memories, could be those of anyone. She gets up and puts on one of Jarrett's concerts. The volume is turned down very low and she would like Simón to touch her. He has been affectionate to her, though she has noticed a certain reserve in his tenderness. Their lovemaking has been better than it ever was; love between them has always been easy, what has been difficult is tenderness. Thinking about it, perhaps this is the price to be paid for the remoteness she too felt in their first months of marriage. Only in Tucumán was she able to surrender herself, to realise that when his body entered into hers, she also entered into his. That one night was also the last: until yesterday. The solitary ecstasy of the past has been repeated and she never wants it to end, she wants to exhaust herself with love as though life were this and only this, the endless orgasm she has dreamed about for thirty years. Let him touch her, then. Simón is now sitting on the bed and she lays her head on his shoulder. 'Touch me, *amor*, touch me,' she says.

But Simón talks about other things. 'When I was far from you I thought I would find you inside a map.' Emilia interrupts him: 'This might sound strange, but I thought the same thing.' Simón: 'I saw you standing in the map. I didn't know where you were because the vectors had been erased. It was a desert with no lines.' And Emilia: 'In that case it wasn't a map.' Simón: 'Maybe it wasn't, but that's where you were.' And Emilia: 'If it was a map with no landmarks, you could have left a trail of names, drawn trees for reference, I would have found you. Once, in Mexico, I followed a trail of white pebbles convinced that, like in *Hansel and Gretel*, when I came to the last one, I would find you. In Caracas, I named all the streets in a neighbourhood so you could find me: Iván el Cobero, Coño Verde. At the top of the hill was a small square. I called it Simón Yemilia. The neighbours thought I named it Simón after Simón Bolívar; I added Yemilia because a lot of girls around there are called Yemila, Yajaira, Yamila, but I knew you would know I meant *Simón y Emilia*, I knew that if you were ever there, ever looked at a new map of Caracas, you would be able to find me. Why don't you touch me?'

Jarrett's music circles around the same clusters of notes, sometimes lingering on a single note, and outside, the night itself has stopped moving; only inside Emilia, as in a dark heart of a volcano, life still ebbs and flows.

She can't remember Simón ever fucking her the way he is fucking her now. Her body is ablaze, she arches herself, raises her body so he can penetrate all the way to her throat, she licks him, devours him, and what she feels is so intense, so overpowering, that she feels coursing from her tongue the foam from the tongue with which he kisses her. Emilia soars so high that Simón's fires reach deeper than her body, they are fires of pure sex, flames that come and go leaving no ashes. By now she has lost count of how many times she's come, they've climaxed, she's orgasmed, how do they say it in other languages, *ancora*, *more*, *encore*, *ainda mas*, don't go, *querido mío*, don't leave. On and on until the first breath of morning seeps through the window, on and on until she can't go on any more and clutches the pillow wet with tears.

The Jarrett concert stays with her all night. The CD ends but she does not notice. She knows the slow final cadences by heart and so the melody slips unnoticed towards silence. She hugs Simón to her, fearful that reality will fade out like the music. The room is still dark, the faint brightness she saw when she woke disappears. Perhaps we can't see the sun, she thinks. A dirty grey day like most of the days this autumn. She doesn't know whether or not to get up. She allows herself to be carried along by the joy of knowing that he is sleeping here, in the room, and that he will not leave her again to waste her life in the maps at Hammond. Why wake him? This body lying next to her is the only map she needs to get her bearings in time. And thinking about it, what need has she of time when time has folded in on itself and now fits inside the body of her beloved. When she first set out to look for him she could not have imagined that there could have been so many circles in her purgatory, nor that when she reached one another would appear above it, and then another. Her eternal noon was an everlasting purgatory.

★ ★ ★

Now, I am the one wondering where Emilia has gone. Nancy Frears phoned the police, who are thrilled to be presented with a mystery in this town without mysteries. Two officers accompanied by the chief of police in person broke down the door of her North 4th Avenue apartment and found not a living soul. The bed was made, the books and CDs neatly organised, the hi-fi and the computer had not even been unplugged. There were no signs of a break-in or a robbery. The only conspicuous detail was that Emilia had not taken out the garbage bag in the kitchen and by now it was beginning to smell. On the table were the remains of some sushi, a seaweed salad and some Chinese fortune cookies. Nancy phoned Chela, but, according to her answering machine, the Echarri family were out of the country. I'm the last person to have seen Emilia and the police asked me to come in and make a statement. As I explained, a fat cop took notes, stopping from time to time to eat the half-finished pizza oozing grease all over the cardboard delivery box. The officer wanted to know if Emilia had been suicidal, suffered from some terminal illness or mentioned that she might be going on holiday. The interview lasted half an hour, and before he handed me the statement to sign, he asked if there was anything else I could think of that might be helpful. I was surprised to hear myself telling him that thirty years ago in my country many people disappeared without leaving a trace and that Emilia's husband had been one of the disappeared. 'She never gave up hope of finding him again,' I said. 'She could never bring herself to accept that he might be dead.' 'What about you, what do you think?' asked the officer. 'I believe he's dead. Emilia's not the only person to hope that someone she loves will come back from the dead; there are thousands like her, clinging to an illusion. Imagine the pain of not knowing where your daughter is, not knowing who took her. And if she were dead, imagine the desolation of not knowing in what dark corner of the world her body is.' 'In this country, it is the job of the police to find out what happened,' said the officer. 'We are paid by the state to do just that. This woman's disappearance might be a crime, a kidnapping, she might have committed suicide, she could have gone away to join a sect. We can rule out kidnapping, since it's been several days and there's been no ransom demand. We can rule out the idea that she's been taken by gangsters running a prostitution ring, since, quite frankly, the woman is too old. Also she has no priors and there's no reason to suspect she was a drug mule or involved in trafficking. She has a perfect résumé, no offences, no problems at work, she got on well with her neighbours. It makes no sense,' the officer went on. 'Here, people don't just disappear into thin air. Give it a week or two and we'll find out what happened.' 'It doesn't always work out that way,' I said. 'You see photos of missing people on milk cartons all the time, kids, old people.' 'Most of them have mental health problems,' insisted the policeman. I said goodbye, left a card with my details on his desk and asked him to get in touch if they found out anything.

The following day, Nancy Frears insisted on seeing me; she asked me to come by her apartment on Montgomery Street. The minute I walked through the door, she threw herself into my arms and started sobbing. 'Where can poor Millie have gone? Have you heard anything?'

'Nothing,' I said.

'I don't know anything either. I drop by the chief of police's office as often as I can. No one there wants to say anything, but you get to hear things around town. If you were a woman, you'd understand. You hear people gossiping at the salon, in the drugstore, over at Jerusalem Pizza. They say someone saw her on the street talking to herself, dressed up like she was going to a party. Someone saw her on Saturday morning at dawn taking the train to Newark. What would she be doing up at that hour? Her car still hasn't turned up. They've issued a description of the car and the licence plate to all the toll routes and hotels for two hundred miles. All the patrol cars have the details too, of course. We should get some news soon. She has to eat, to sleep, to take a bath. Can you wait a minute? I need to go to the bathroom. It's my stomach, I get gas, you know. Never gives me a minute's peace.'

She reappears with a file of clippings. Emilia gave them to her to look after a while ago and she shows them to me to see if I recognise anything. I see the pamphlet again, the samples of Stabilene film which cartographers carried with them everywhere thirty years ago. Inside the pamphlet I see a copy of the 'Rules concerning the making of cartographic documents for the Automobile Club' typed on an old-fashioned typewriter. I don't stop to read it since the predictable articles in it have long since expired. What surprises me is the carefully hand-drawn page at the end. On it there are three squares splitting off like tree branches from a central square. Each space is filled with elegantly calligraphed text. One of them reads: 'Choice and selection of the nomenclature for the colour blue', and the uppermost square reads: 'Rough sketch to scale of Ruta 77 as far as the Abra River'. I assume that it is Simón's handwriting, large, meticulous well-spaced letters. If Simón did write it, it would explain why Emilia has treasured this useless, yellowing scrap of paper all these years. Or perhaps she keeps it because it is the last vestige of his contact with the world: this sheet of paper, his fingerprints on the steering wheel of the jeep, the sketch of the Río El Abra that was taken from them in Huacra, the tremulous signature on the prison register. As I touch the sheet, I barely feel it, it is as though the paper is air; of course I know that my senses are gradually disappearing, I know that my eyesight is failing, that my ears hear only what they want to hear: Kiri Te Kanawa singing Mozart's Mass in C Minor, the voices of my sons, Keith Jarrett playing the piano, the murmur of snow as it falls.

I don't say this to Nancy, but sometimes I think Emilia's senses also disappeared and that is why she is not here. Our senses constantly feed our memory, and beyond that memory there is nothing. The body enters into a continuous present in which pass, one by one, all the seasons of the joys that went unlived.

5

Fame is nothing but a breath of wind

'Purgatorio', XI, 100

I open the cuttings file Nancy Frears gave me and notice that some of them are missing. I know that when she gave it to me there were photos of Emilia with her father at the funeral of the film director Leopoldo Torre Nilsson and at a gala given by the *comandantes* for the king and queen of Spain, but I'm confusing what I see with the things Emilia told me. There are many ant trails in my memory and on this point all of them seem to get entangled. I call one of my doctors and ask if these distractions mean anything. 'We'll know if there's any need to worry after we've examined you. Are you writing?' he asks. 'Yes,' I tell him, 'a novel.' 'In that case, be careful. It's your imagination that's making you ill.' I go back home, and start going over the papers and the notes I have collected.

I started at the end: with the photograph of Dr Dupuy taken in the main studio of Canal 7 during the twenty-four-hour benefit programme in aid of the soldiers fighting in the Malvinas. It is date-stamped in the top right-hand corner, May 20, 1982, with the time, 23.12. Emilia watches from a distance as her father comes onto the set. It looks to me as though at any moment she might turn her back on him. She finds it difficult to hide her hostility, her displeasure. They have not lived in the same house now for three years, and I know that Emilia would have left Buenos Aires if an increasingly slender umbilical cord did not tie her to her mother, whose body is now little more than a sigh. I don't have the dates clear in my head, but I think I remember that Ethel Dupuy died shortly after the programme: she left this world as suddenly as she had entered it. Emilia told me she was cremated in a private, almost secret ceremony and that she herself, 'just me, no one else', scattered her ashes in the Río de la Plata, its waters swollen with all the dead.

In the photo, you can see the programme's presenters in the background: they sit pensively on plastic chairs. I suppose they are charged with keeping alive the patriotic fervour the dictatorship has whipped up in the populace to mask the poverty, the inflation, the sense of imminent ruin. At the start of that year, the *comandantes* of the junta, feeling the country slipping through their fingers, grasp desperately for a lifeline: they invade the icy islands, send soldiers trained in the tropics of the Argentinian north-east where cold is unknown. Those in power are different now, the successors to the admiral and the Eel, though their imaginations are still bleak, empty horizons. The British fleet is on the far side of the world and no one expects them to take the trouble to defend a few shitty rocks inhabited by nothing but cormorants and wind, wind and 2,200 of Her Majesty's subjects, melancholy penguins and wind. Against all expectations, the English launch a counter-offensive; Dupuy calculates that, within eight to ten weeks, defeat is inevitable. Even so, he wants the new *comandantes* to stay at the tiller until the state has weathered the storm. They need to stand firm – but how? When they are as stupid as all the others, as blind to everything that is not white and red and yellow? The stupidest of them are still stealing orphans from hospitals, snatching babies from the wombs of women in labour. There are still many gullible enough to see the country only as the happy, world-beating country depicted by the biddable media. Talk about our crushing victories in the air and on the sea, Dupuy instructs them. Show them photographs of pitiless, corrupt British soldiers. Show them Thatcher with fangs like Dracula. Run the headline: WE'RE WINNING! People are celebrating our armies' victories, pouring into the streets wearing armbands, waving flags just as they did during the 1978 World Cup. Our onslaughts are lethal, the newspapers repeated in unison. Thatcher, they said, is running scared. Professor Addolorato uttered dirges on Spanish radio stations which Dupuy was forced to republish in *La República*: 'My poor country is fighting an unequal battle against the third largest power on the planet, supported by American imperialists. The Argentina waging this war is not what the ignorant and ill-informed call the military dictatorship. No, all of Argentina is locked in this struggle: its women, its children, its old people.' An eloquent opportunist, Dupuy is forced to concede. The British leak the news that Argentinian soldiers are falling at the front without even defending themselves, not from heroism or from enemy shrapnel but because they're dying of cold. They have little ammunition, their rations of food have run out. Dupuy announces that he is going to launch a huge appeal for solidarity. Live on the same television channels that broadcast the World Cup, the greatest artists and celebrities in the nation will take donations: jewellery, money, chocolates, anything and everything, patriotism must be transformed into largesse and, more importantly, into a chorus of praise to the *comandantes*. He is still inspired by Orson Welles's lessons in the art of illusion. What a son of a bitch, Welles, he thinks with a mixture of admiration and resentment. The bastard put him in a difficult position with the Eel and the admiral. Shortly after rejecting his offer to direct the documentary that would have heaped praise on it, he mocked Argentina and filmed *The Muppet Movie*, a pathetic trifle for retarded children. Dupuy has heard that he makes his living falling back on his past as a clown. What he cannot forgive is that it was his voice used in *Genocide*, a tasteless documentary about the Nazi concentration camps in which, in passing, there is mention of prison camps in Argentina. He had better not dare try to set foot in Buenos Aires.

The success of the twenty-four-hour solidarity appeal is beyond his wildest expectations. At precisely 6 p.m. every television in the country is turned on; even those in hospital join in singing the national anthem. The great Libertad Lamarque cries as she recites the poem 'La hermanita perdida'. Famous actors and comedians come down from their pedestals and sell flowers in the streets. The television studios are besieged by old women who have spent sleepless nights knitting scarves and socks for the poor soldiers who are freezing. In a few short hours, there is a staggering pile of jewels, heirlooms, first communion medals, wedding rings. In the grocery shops there is not a tin of meatballs, sardines or beans left on sale – anything that can be eaten has been handed over. '*So that our brave boys can go on fighting*,' sings Lolita Torres to the cameras through the night.

Emilia marches on the television studio with the mothers and wives of the disappeared. Like them, she has covered her head with a white scarf. She hopes her father will see her, will have her thrown out. Nothing would ease her contempt better than a good scandal. But this is something that will not happen, because Dupuy wants only to forget his daughter, to force her, he doesn't yet know how, to go far away. In the streets, the crowds wave flags. In another photo taken in the studio, I can make out Nora Balmaceda. I barely recognise her. I've seen her picture in magazines and in a couple of documentaries, always with her rosebud mouth larded with lipstick and her eyelashes thick with mascara. But what appeared that night on television was her corpse. She is standing, barely able to hold herself up. I don't believe, like so many of the others I recognise in the photograph, she would go so far to hide her story. On the contrary, she would be only too happy to tell it as long as there were cameras pointed at her. She would tell all: the novels she didn't write, her travels, her affairs with famous sportsmen, her affair with the admiral. On her right, an elderly woman, still clinging to her flag, is picking up her false teeth which have fallen on the floor. What patriotic fervour, what religious devotion there is in that photograph. In the last photo, a messenger with slicked-back hair and patent-leather shoes is standing next to Dupuy and whispering something in his ear. He is in civilian clothes, wearing a suit that looks as though he borrowed it, and just this detail is enough to recognise that he is a military orderly. The photo is marked May 21, 1982, at 12.03 a.m. The messenger must be telling Dupuy that the British Army has surrounded the Argentinian troops defending Port Stanley and that the government has ordered them to defend it to the last man.

The war carries on for a few more days, and then it is over. The president shuts himself away in his office, drinking bottle after bottle of Old Parr, and then resigns. On the heels of the invented triumphs comes despair. 'We have lost a battle, let us not lose the country,' Dupuy says in a radio interview. He is the only major figure who dares to show his face. That same afternoon, he meets with the *comandantes* who have survived the disaster and asks them what they want him to do with the donations from the solidarity appeal. 'Is there much?' they ask. 'Oh yes,' he tells them, 'almost sixty million dollars, and 140 kilos of gold which I'd suggest melting down into ingots. There are tons of tinned foods, chocolates, sacred pictures, letters for the soldiers and two whole hangars bursting with winter clothes.' The *comandantes* look at each other, confused. Dupuy sets them straight. 'Almost all of it is rubbish. The scarves and woollen vests are in bright colours and might easily draw attention to the soldiers. The best thing to do is dump it all. Not the gold and the money, obviously. As for everything else, we should ship it out on two Hercules planes, though we'd be running the risk of the British getting their hands on everything, including the planes.' 'What do you suggest, Doctor?' asks one of the *comandantes*. 'I suggest we cover our backs, save face. If anyone asks about the contributions, we tell them we sent everything we could and that, since the islands were in British hands, we don't know what they did with them. We can also say that everything else was put into accounts reserved for the armed forces and the missions. We won't exactly be lying. We have to give up a percentage to dispel any doubts. I would also suggest that this operation be classified a state secret. If it were up to me, I'd order that history books be immediately rewritten to include these heroic deeds before people start publishing all sorts of bullshit. I'd say that London had plans to invade Tierra del

Fuego and that we were merely defending ourselves against the first and third largest powers in the world.' 'Professor Addolorato has already said that,' one of the *comandantes* pointed out. 'In that case, get Addolorato to write the books.' Dupuy was offended. 'All I know, señores, is that when the truth is unfavourable, it must be made to disappear as quickly as possible.' He withdraws, leaving a copy of *La República* on the new president's desk. On page one it reads: 'The time has come for humility. Let us give politicians the opportunity to govern. Let us offer them the wisdom of our military leaders. This country must go on being a country of freedom, of the cross and the sword.'

Some of the other photos in the file sadden me. I see Emilia and Dr Dupuy standing next to the coffin of Leopoldo Torre Nilsson. I read the date: September 8, 1978. The celebrities gathered in the funeral chapel are almost the same as those who, four years later, will be caught up in the fever of the solidarity appeal for Las Malvinas. The same as those who cheered at the World Cup until they were hoarse. The darkest year of that murky dictatorship was 1978. In December, the *comandantes* celebrate their three world triumphs: in football, in hockey and in beauty, when a twenty-one-year-old girl from Córdoba is voted Miss World. I don't think Torre Nilsson would have approved of how his funeral chapel is staged in the photographs: the dark cedar coffin with eight ornately carved handles to carry it, the crucifix that looks as though it might drop onto his head, the wreaths and flowers that shroud him in their heavy perfume, the poster for *Martín Fierro* hanging next to the crucifix (he must have requested the poster: he considered *Martín Fierro* his finest film, I still think it was one of his worst). He would have been ashamed that in death, this most private moment, his wasted, shrunken body should be exposed for all to see.

I met him one night in October 1958 in a restaurant near that very funeral chapel. I was surprised to discover he was even more shy than me – in itself something of a feat – giving up each word with infinite care as though they were joys that he was losing forever. I chattered away, telling him about the deaths I had seen at the cinema and those I had been dreaming about for weeks. 'Some deaths are ridiculous,' I told him, 'and I forget them as soon as the film is over: the living dead, zombies, ghosts. I'm more moved by the personification of Death in Ingmar Bergman's *Seventh Seal*, and the funeral of a village girl I saw recently in Carl Dreyer's *Ordet*.' I told him the scene had made me cry and that later I was disappointed because the girl came back to life. Torre Nilsson smiled magnanimously. 'Ah, *Ordet*,' he said. 'I think in the film Dreyer is denying the idea of death, portraying it as a sort of divergence from life, like an eclipse, after which it is possible to reappear.' 'What is irreparable,' I said, 'is the obscene way in which the dead are put on display. From that there can be no return.' I am remembering that phrase as I look at the photos of Dupuy, the admiral and Addolorato standing before his defenceless body feigning grief.

In another of the photos, Emilia is greeting an actress who appeared in a number of Torre Nilsson's early films and who, for years, had vanished off the face of the earth. The woman looks frightened, as though she has just been caught doing something terrible and wants to hide away. Until twenty years ago, the newspapers carried on publishing stories about what had happened to her, all of them false. Once she was dead, they lost interest and she fell into oblivion. Sometimes I see the startled expression of that former actress staring back at me from a poster in the film club, always the same face, eyes gazing into the middle distance, lips twisted in a foolish smile. Emilia mentioned her in passing that morning we went to see Mary Ellis's grave. She told me that Torre Nilsson had taken her and turned her into a unique character, terrified of sex, constantly afraid of being raped. Later, other directors took advantage of her naive defenceless image to transform her into the perfect victim: a teenage girl who has her virginity taken in a brothel, a country girl who swears eternal love to a rogue in an empty church convinced that, though there are no witnesses, this oath is enough for them to be legally married. Going from one melodrama to the next confused her. One day she woke up not knowing who she really was and ran off the set of her last film. She got on the first bus she saw and disappeared without a trace. She never told anyone what happened in the months that followed. She had no family, only a neighbour she occasionally went out with for pizza. Maybe she was living in a hotel in a small town, maybe she ran away to the beach because when she came back she was very tanned. No producer every called her again. She went back to her old house, to her old routine of going out for pizza with her neighbour and became a dressmaker. Ever since she was a girl she had liked drawing dresses, cutting out patterns, embroidering, making costumes for her dolls. She opened a small shop, took in two stray cats and never spoke about the past again. She emerged from her obscurity only to say goodbye to the director who had discovered her and changed her life. She had intended only to spend a few minutes in the funeral chapel, to leave a flower, say a prayer.

The dead man mattered less to her than that part of her life which had already died. On the huge poster hanging beside the door of the chapel she saw herself, cowering in the shadows of two men. Seeing herself like this, on display, it seemed as though this funeral was hers too and she almost fled. Emilia saw the woman leaving, looking as though she was about to faint, and went to help her. It took a moment before she recognised her. She was no longer the teenage girl in the poster. She was overweight, dishevelled and looked like a middle-class housewife. She had met her long ago in the house on calle Arenales when the actress had come with Torre Nilsson to ask Dupuy to intercede with a reactionary censor who was busy cutting swathes out of the finest films of the day, from Buñuel and Stanley Kubrick to Dreyer and Fellini. Childbirth and kissing, however reverently done, could not be seen anywhere near a church. He had banned two of Torre Nilsson's films and was threatening to bowdlerise a third. 'I don't know what my father said to him,' Emilia told me. 'All I remember is that the girl was crying when she left. At the time, she looked like a schoolgirl – she wore a blouse with a big lace collar and ribbons in her hair. She had the same astonished expression she had in her films, as though her body shifted untouched from fantasy to reality. The trembling woman in the funeral chapel was a different person, she was short and fat with a double chin.' Emilia took pity on her and took her outside for some fresh air. Then she invited her to go for coffee at a cafe on the corner and sat with her until she had calmed down. That was all. Emilia didn't tell me that it was at that moment the photograph I'm looking at now was taken. The rest of the story I know from the notes and cuttings she left in North 4th Avenue.

The more I delve into Emilia's life, the more I realise that from beginning to end it is an unbroken chain of losses, disappearances and senseless searches. She spent years chasing after nothing, after people who no longer existed, remembering things that had never happened. But aren't we all like that? Don't we all abuse history to leave some trace there of what we once were, a miserable smudge, a tiny flame when we know that even the deepest mark is a bird that will leave on a breath of wind? 'One human being is more or less the same as another; perhaps we are all already dead without realising it, or not yet born and do not know it,' I said to Emilia one of the last times I saw her. 'We come into the world without knowing it, the result of a series of accidents, and we leave it to go who knows where, nowhere probably. If you hadn't loved Simón you would have loved someone else. You would have done so joyfully, with no guilt, because you cannot love what you do not know.' She didn't like this idea because she could not conceive of a world without Simón and loving made sense only if it meant loving him. I don't think I understood at all that afternoon. Now, I would say I was an optimist, that the mere fact of existing or loving is enough to give meaning to everything. This is not how Emilia feels, and she is right. I realise this when I find a map among the papers that she left: the map of a city that stretches out in time not in space, and maybe because of that, an impossible city. There are transparent edges with dates beneath which the city is always different. In the centre is a vast palace next to a lake or reservoir. Above the palace, in capital letters, is written the code word to her life, Simón. The map is torn, wet with drool and with tears. It has no edges, sectors, bearing, no scale, and I don't think it is necessary to ask where they are.

★ ★ ★

I have already spent hours unearthing what is hidden in the folds and on the backs of the photographs and clippings given to me by Nancy Frears. Perhaps there is nothing worthwhile here, perhaps that part of Emilia's life I do not know is a lunar desert or an insignificant outcrop like Kaffeklubben. I begin reading one of her notebooks. 'I know D is a dressmaker and I've asked her to make me some dresses . . .' The cellphone I always carry with me rings and I set down the notebook. It is noon. Not many people know I have a cellphone and I don't recognise the number calling. I answer, convinced someone has misdialled and prepared to listen to an apology.

'It's me. Emilia,' says the voice. It's her.

I'm startled. She has taken me so much by surprise that it takes a moment before I react. I don't even remember where I thought she was hiding.

'I've been looking for you all over,' I tell her. 'Nancy was out of her mind with worry – she called the police. You caused a terrible commotion. Where are you? Can I call you?'

'A commotion,' she says. Her voice sounds completely calm. 'There's no reason to be worried. I'm fine, I'm better than I've ever been.'

'I'm glad,' I say. 'But if the police find you, they'll pick you up.'

'I didn't do anything, I'm free to go wherever I like.'

'Of course. It's just that you left without telling anyone. At the police station they asked if you were suicidal, if you'd been depressed. One of the officers thought you might have been kidnapped, that you might even be dead. You took the Altima.'

'What a waste of time. The people in this town have no idea how to fill the lives they don't have.'

'They're looking for your car,' I tell her. 'Sooner or later they're bound to find you. Can I see you?'

'That's why I'm calling, so we can meet up,' she says.

'Sure, just give me a place and a time. I'm free right now.'

'Not now. Tonight, eight o'clock. At Toscana, the restaurant where we first met.'

'Toscana doesn't exist any more,' I remind her.

'It doesn't matter. The best places are those that don't exist, just like on maps. I won't be coming alone.'

'So where then?' I insist. 'I don't want to miss you. Once I've seen you, I'll need to let the police know. I hope you understand.'

'I understand. Eight o'clock then, at Toscana.'

'On the corner there,' I repeat so there's no mistake. 'Who are you with, Emilia?'

'With Simón. We'll both come. Tonight you'll get to meet him.'

I held onto the photos and the clippings for a long time. I don't know what to think. Obviously I'll be waiting for her at eight o'clock on the corner of George and Paterson. Toscana does not exist but there is a point in reality where it does not matter whether or not it exists. Who is this Simón with her? I know that Simón Cardoso is dead, several witnesses testified to that fact. Tortured, a bullet through his forehead: it is all there in the transcripts of the trial of the *comandantes*. Maybe the man I'm going to meet is an impostor, an illusion created by Orson Welles from beyond the grave. If it doesn't matter to Emilia, I don't see why it should matter to me.

I'll give her back the press cuttings tonight, I'll ask her permission to publish what little I already know of her story. I could spend what remains of the afternoon taking notes on some of the other things she's written in the folder. Most of it is unimportant, comments about the soap operas that were on television back then and also an account of the cruel incident which caused the rift between Emilia and her father. On one of the cuttings, I notice a small red circle and, underneath, a line from Dante's 'Purgatorio' in the meek, childlike hand-writing that was Emilia's at the time: *Quel color che l'inferno mi nascose*. I know the line, it is one of the most famous lines of the poem: 'That colour that in me Inferno had concealed'. Nothing in Emilia is chance, which meant that in writing that line she was alluding to a hidden story, one that burned her up inside, but one that she did not want to forget.

I've mentioned that when my cellphone rang, I had been reading one of her notebooks: 'I know D is a dressmaker and I've asked her to make me some dresses . . .' This was just the beginning. At the end of November, the Spanish royal family were to visit Argentina and Dupuy wanted his daughter to accompany him to the gala ball the Eel was planning to throw. The doctor ordered a dinner jacket from his tailor and told Emilia to track down the finest fashion designer in Buenos Aires, suggested she call someone at *Para Ti* for advice. 'I don't trust you to decide what to wear,' he told her, 'and when you are my escort, you can't afford to be anything less than the queen.' He wanted her to wear a dress like the one Audrey Hepburn wore in *Funny Face*, though the only things Emilia had in common with Audrey Hepburn were her long legs and her dancer's neck. 'I want a dress that is simple but unforget-table,' he said, 'and just this once, I'll let you wear your mother's diamond earrings for the evening.' Ethel could not wear anything now, not even the filmy skin that sheathed her body. She was covered with sores from her terrible allergies and even the touch of her nightdress made her whimper like a kitten; for most of the five days she spent in the mansion on the calle Arenales she was almost naked, soothing her tender skin in a lukewarm bath. Emilia did not leave her side: she sang to her as she sang to her dolls as a child, brushed her hair, stroked her head until she finally realised that she would be better taken care of in the home. On the sixth day she drove her mother back and returned to the loneliness and the torment of paying the debt which Dupuy implacably demanded.

Towards the end of 1978, the newspapers and the radio broadcast only what they were allowed. They had been doing so for some time, and by now fear and compliance had become habit. If human beings could disappear, if the houses where the destitute took shelter and the savings of the credulous and the old could disappear, why would inconvenient truths not also disappear? And so readers pretended to know nothing, telling themselves ignorance was bliss. The *comandantes* left it to Dupuy to take care of the unreality and concentrated solely on the armed repression. Madrid and Barcelona were hotbeds for fugitive extremists and it was vital to make the best possible impression on the king and queen of Spain, to give them a glimpse of the happiness and prosperity that flourished in Argentina. Dupuy was not about to permit any dissent from the media, not so much as the flutter of an angry wasp's wing. 'You should go so far as to prohibit making jokes about the royal couple,' the Eel had told him. 'I don't want any gossip, any rumours, any stories about the past.' Argentina was walking on eggshells and Europe was a flank which could not be ignored. The United States had been foolish enough to elect a president who appointed inquisitive, meddling diplomats. He was fanatical about human rights and the subversives were determined to use what little breath they still had to disrupt the royal visit. The honour of the nation was at stake.

Dupuy dispensed with the services of the journalist who had done such sterling work with the European papers before the World Cup. She might be able to pass as the wife of a carpenter, or even as a reincarnation of the Virgin in spite of her weight, but it was unthinkable that he could present her at a royal gala. He needed a journalist who was more ruthless, more refined. The admiral recommended Héctor Caccace who worked for his newspaper and whose manner was as graceful as his prose (officers and lawyers still talked about 'good and bad pens'). Dupuy had never heard of the man and had his people make discreet enquiries. Caccace, his informants advised him, was cunning, a coward, maybe, but deferential to those in power. He was mortified by his surname Caccace – Caca sounded like Shit – and was taking steps to change it. In fact his cousin, Estéfano Caccace, a tango singer who was the toast of *milongas* at Club Sunderland, worked under the stage name Julio Martel to avoid such scatological connotations. Héctor had got ahead by arming himself with an arsenal of literary quotations which he wore everywhere like a whalebone corset. He knew which knives and forks to use, kissed the hands of ladies, effusively praised their gowns with little French phrases. Dupuy called him into his office and within five minutes decided he would do. He was a little affected but his pretentiousness could pass for elegance; there would be no complaints about him at the royal gala. Later, Caccace phoned him. He did not know how to apologise for his discourtesy, he waffled endlessly, infuriating Dupuy, and finally explained his problem to the doctor. 'Having read the invitation, it's clear that formal dress is required, and I don't own a tuxedo.' 'Don't waste my time with such foolishness,' Dupuy interrupted him. 'Go and rent one at Casa Martínez like every other journalist.' Caccace hesitated a moment and then brought up the subject of the starched shirt front, the cufflinks, the shoes. 'They'll cost another hundred thousand, probably a hundred and twenty,' he calculated, 'and I haven't got the money.' 'Come by my house and I'll give it to you,' Dupuy said contemptuously. 'I'll give you the money and a copy of the contract. Just do your job and stop fucking me around.'

Meanwhile, Emilia entrusted the making of her dress to D. She was quick, discreet and talked little. Her speech was peppered with clichés, but her work displayed more originality and talent than many of the fashion houses. She asked Emilia to get her a length of *crêpe georgette* and showed her the design she was working on. It was a tailored off-the-shoulder dress of clean, simple lines with broad straps and a silk trim around the waist. 'What colour would you prefer?' D asked. 'I don't know if I can wear something like that,' said Emilia, 'I'll feel naked. It's so daring, and as you probably know, my husband is not around, he disappeared. I'm more or less a widow.' 'I don't know where my husband is either,' said D. 'They came to our house one night and took him and he's never come back. I spent a year and a half searching for him. This country is a wasteland, a tragedy. Everything fades, disappears. What if I make the dress in black?' 'OK,' Emilia accepted, 'I'll feel more comfortable wearing black. But I'd like the neckline higher, no décolletage.' 'Oh no,' D protested, 'do you want to ruin all my hard work? What about a square neckline? They're very fashionable at the moment.' 'What should I wear over it? It needs to be something light because the weather is getting warmer and by the time the king and queen get here it will be worse.' 'A silk cape would suit you better than a shawl,' said D. 'Or maybe crêpe rather than silk, something you can drape lightly over your shoulders but can take off easily.' 'White? Ivory?' suggested Emilia. D was not persuaded. 'Against a black dress, ivory or white will just look like you bought something off the peg. How about pink? Dusky pink is very popular this summer. If you like I can trim the waist of the dress with dusky pink crêpe too.'

Emilia arrived at the gala like Cinderella in her fairy coach. Her mother's earrings lit up her face with a radiance that seemed to come from another body (she knew from where). Even the Eel came up to greet her, surprised. '*M'hijita*, how pretty you look.' He was wearing a full dress uniform bedecked with medals. Dupuy shook the Eel's hand, bowed to his wife – who was wearing a long blue dress to cover her bloated legs. There was a flight of marble steps up to the main hall. Reality had been left outside with the few families of beggars who scavenged for food in the garbage. The great hall, where a quarter of a century earlier Evita had received the destitute, was a copy of the Grand Hall in the Paris Opera House, the ceiling and the pillars extravagantly and ornately gilded. Inside, the hall was lined with mirrors which endlessly reflected the chandeliers, the jewels, the huge platters of lobster and caviar. Emilia had nightmares about mirrors. Her mother's dressing room had floor-length mirrors, even mirrors on the ceiling. As a little girl Ethel had threatened to lock her in there and ever since she had not been able to shake off the nightmare of being hundreds of Emilias, endlessly reflected, none of them the same, because no reflection was exactly like another. She spotted Caccace in the distance running after a large platter of quails' eggs and popping two and three into his mouth at a time. From time to time he took out a little pad and made notes. The king and queen had not yet arrived, but they were clearly due at any moment because the crowd, forgetting protocol, were elbowing each other at the top of the stairs behind the Eel. Emilia decided to stay at the back of the room near the window where Juan Manuel Fangio, a former racing-car driver, was trying to avoid the stifling heat. Emilia too was beginning to feel suffocated and she draped her cape on a chair between two curtains. She heard applause and moved closer so she could get a glimpse of the king and queen, who looked very young and very happy. The king was wearing a dinner jacket just like everyone else. Next to him, the queen looked tiny. Emilia stopped, incredulous when she saw the dress she was wearing. She had read somewhere that the queen only wore Spanish couture, designs specially made for her by Balenciaga and his disciples. But the dress she was wearing that evening was almost a perfect copy of Emilia's dress. D always insisted that she had very little talent. 'What I do is really simple,' she'd say, 'it's nothing much.' And here was the queen wearing a dress that looked just like the one made by her dressmaker but which had probably cost a hundred times more. It was the same design, subtly tailored with dusky pink trimming about the waist, broad shoulder straps and the same square neckline that Emilia had found so intimidating. The only difference was the colour; the queen's dress was white. The designer at Balenciaga or whoever it was had also given the queen a matching cape: dusky pink crêpe tied with an almost invisible red cord. Emilia didn't know where to put herself; she was terrified the queen would notice the coincidence. She felt embarrassed and ashamed, but at the same time proud of her dressmaker. She was relieved that she had taken off her cape. She watched as the queen, hemmed in by the crowd, fanned herself impatiently, never once losing her smile.

The waiters glided from one group to the next carrying silver salvers which were picked clean within seconds. Caccace came over to Emilia, prattling incessantly. He explained to her who was who, how the room they were in was modelled on the Second Empire architectural style. He went on and on. The queen too seemed to be suffering from all the hand-kissing, the cigar smoke, the terrible humidity, the stultifying heat. She walked towards one of the windows to get some air, taking off her cape and handing it to one of her ladies-in-waiting.

The Eel's wife was sweating profusely. She came over to Emilia, gasping for breath, weighed down by her swollen legs. 'That's a beautiful dress you're wearing,' she said, 'but you really should take your dressmaker to task for copying the queen's dress. He's French, isn't he? An Argentinian would have made something more fitting.' Caccace took a step forward, but just as he was about to kiss her hand and introduce himself, she took a step back. The Eel's wife stumbled and apologised. 'Excuse me, how embarrassing, I think I might faint.' Emilia gestured almost imperceptibly to one of the waiters and together they led her to a chair. Caccace trotted after them, still prattling, still making notes in his little pad. Emilia whispered something in her father's ear as he passed; Dupuy urgently summoned the Eel's personal physician, who within ten seconds had unobtrusively taken her pulse and given her some water to drink. He stayed with her until she got her breath back. Everything happened so quickly that nobody seemed to have noticed and perhaps nobody would have known had Caccace not tactlessly reported it in the admiral's newspaper. Dupuy indignantly phoned the editor and demanded that he immediately fire that childish chimpanzee. Those were his very words; he was proud of his little alliteration.

The king and queen stayed another two hours at the party without anything else worthy of note happening. Just one trivial episode, which went unnoticed, proved the beginning of a secret scandal. On her way back from the toilet one of the queen's ladies-in-waiting stopped, her back turned, to smooth the creases from her skirt and her blouse, and in doing so exposed a glimpse of her hip as she stepped into the hall. Her skin was very pale and above the iliac crest there was an all too obvious, alluring beauty mark. The lady-in-waiting was pretty and also flirtatious. One of the admiral's bodyguards glanced over and smiled at her lasciviously. She returned his smile. This was enough for the guard, in a white dress uniform, to approach her and make a proposition. The lady-in-waiting let out a peal of laughter and, as she walked away, nudged him with her arm. She returned to the great hall, not realising the row she had unleashed behind her. Her gentle nudge had caused the guard, who was drinking tomato juice, to stagger. Not wanting to spill juice on his uniform, he jolted himself upright holding the almost full glass and spilling the juice over Emilia's cape. It looked like a scene from *The Three Stooges*. The guard was probably a new recruit, a midshipman, perhaps simply a cadet, and was appalled at his clumsiness. The admiral was implacable and this blunder could earn him a week in the brig. He was relieved to see that no one had noticed and, not giving it another thought, picked up the cape and put it in his case. He was intending to send it to a dry-cleaner's and then return it to its owner.

Emilia was finding the evening increasingly stifling; she despised the feigned chivalry and was beginning to feel that she was no one, that her place was the nowhere Simón now inhabited. She ached for Simón. She thought how different her life would have been had he not disappeared. Together they would had fled the bloody ruins that the country had become. As soon as her mother no longer needed her, she would take what little money she had managed to save and leave. She didn't know where she would go, but she trusted that Simón would guide her. She went over to her father and told him she couldn't stay a minute longer. 'I've kept my promise,' she said, 'I'm leaving.'

'Don't even think of going out into the street half naked like that,' Dupuy said.

'There are lots of taxis just outside,' she said. Before her father could grab her arm, she headed back to look for her cape. It wasn't where she had left it, but on a chair between two curtains almost at the back of the hall. She slipped it over her shoulders and, relieved, headed outside.

The king and queen moved from one group to another, gracefully acknowledging the bows and curtsies. The air in the hall was increasingly muggy. The ladies' dresses were mercifully light, but the gentlemen, all wearing starched shirts and dinner jackets, were dripping with sweat. Even the king appeared to be exhausted. His brow glistened and he had to mop it. The queen gave him a slight, barely perceptible gesture. The king approached the Eel and said: 'We are extremely grateful, *Presidente*. Argentina is a magnificent country.' The Eel applauded and the crowd followed suit. The queen went to look for her cape but could not find it. She called one of her ladies-in-waiting and asked that it be brought to her. The lady-in-waiting went to the cloakroom but returned empty-handed. 'How strange,' said the queen, 'I gave it to one of you.' 'I left it over here,' said a lady-in-waiting. Everyone in the hall joined the search for the missing cape, as rumours and gossip whirled around the room. 'Someone stole it.' 'I didn't see her wearing a cape.' 'Pink, did you say?' 'Really? The cape she was wearing when she arrived was black.' 'Who knows where she put it.' 'If it isn't found, it will be a terrible embarrassment for the country.' 'I'm sure that some subversive has stolen it.' Within five minutes, the whole room was in uproar. The toilets were checked, the kitchen, the servants, wardrobes; people checked behind curtains and under tablecloths. No one dared to leave. One of the aides-de-camp asked if they might be allowed to check the ladies' handbags; Dupuy dismissed him with a curt gesture. 'This is an honest country,' he said. 'The people here are respectable people. There are no thieves among us.' 'Her Majesty's pink cape.' 'The pink cape!' The words echoed around the room. The waiters and the ladies-in-waiting ran about like headless chickens but nothing was found. In Argentina, so many things disappeared overnight, so many people inexplicably ceased to exist that it hardly seemed surprising the queen's cape should suddenly become unreal – one more sinister trick in the sleight of hand that was commonplace in Argentina.

Eventually it grew late, too late. The queen covered herself with a shawl one of her ladies-in-waiting had been wearing and the guests had no choice but to leave with the king and queen. At 2 a.m., the only people left in the hall were some of the guards, an aide-de-camp and the doormen. They competed with each other, snooping around, interrogating the kitchen staff who were clearing away the platters of canapés. At some point in the early hours, the chief of police arrived with a federal judge who insisted on investigating what was clearly a robbery. This would have been the end of the matter if, shortly before 3 a.m., one of the doormen went up to the judge, clapping his hand to his forehead. 'A pink cape, you said? I think I saw it. One of the ladies left early wearing a pink cape. Maybe it was her own, I don't know.' The man was distressed, pale, he was afraid of losing his job. He described the lady in question, looked at the photographs they showed him of the guests at the gala and finally identified Emilia. 'That's her!' he exclaimed. 'I'm sure that's her.' At 3.30 a.m. the chief of police phoned Dupuy. He apologised profusely for disturbing him at such a late hour and explained that he would be calling at the house on calle Arenales in ten minutes. 'Is it something serious?' asked the doctor. 'I hope not. I'm sure it's just a misunderstanding.'

When Dupuy answered the door to him, Emilia was in bed. The chief explained what had happened and the doctor began to worry. 'My daughter left the reception before I did,' he explained, 'I haven't seen her. She was certainly wearing a pink cape when we arrived. Maybe it looked like the one the queen was wearing. I never pay any attention to such things. But this matter needs to be cleared up. I'll go and wake my daughter.' He burst into Emilia's room, turned on the lights. He would have shaken her, shouted at her, but he did not want the police to overhear. Emilia sat up in bed. Her father's furious tone completely bewildered her. She wasn't worried by his anger, she was sure she had done nothing wrong, and she thought it was a bit much for the chief of police to call at their house at 3.30 a.m. to clear up what was probably just a mix-up, a simple mistake. She saw the cape which D had designed for her draped across the chair next to her mother's bed where she usually read. She saw the black dress lying on the floor. She hadn't had the energy to hang them up when she got back from the party. She had been exhausted and wasn't planning ever to wear them again. 'Look, there's my cape over there,' she said to her father. 'It's mine.' 'Look at it carefully,' Dupuy commanded. 'It's impossible the capes could be exactly the same, that would be too much of a coincidence.' 'Give me a minute, *Papá*, I'm in my nightdress. I'll get up and look.' 'I have no intention of leaving this room,' said her father. 'The police are waiting. Get up right now. I'm not interested in your modesty.' Emilia held the cape up to the light and saw nothing untoward. 'It's mine, I'm sure it is,' she was about to say when she noticed in one of the folds a slender, almost invisible, red cord. The detail made her start, but she remained calm. If it was not her cape, then she would give it back and that would be that. She studied it more carefully. Under the collar was a tiny, exquisitely embroidered escutcheon, the royal Spanish coat of arms with a lion rampant and a three-towered castle in the upper quadrants flanked by the pillars of Hercules and bearing the motto *Plus Ultra*. The needlework was so delicate that, with a magnifying glass, it was possible to read the words. It was not her cape. She had made a mistake. The suffocating heat, her desperate need to get away. Now she remembered that her cape had not been where she had left it and, without a second thought, she had taken the first cape she had seen. She laughed at her gaffe. She would be happy to see the queen and offer her apologies. She would show her that the two capes were like two peas in a pod and the queen would immediately understand. She was sure the queen would say: 'I could just as easily have made the same mistake. I'd like to know who your dressmaker is.' And Emilia would tell her about D. But where was D's cape? Somewhere in the hall, she supposed, with the lost property. She would explain the situation to her father and he would have it tracked down. She had spent her whole life watching him solve other people's problems. She brushed back her hair, smoothed her nightdress. '*Papá*,' she called. Dupuy was still in her room with his back to the bed, his hands on his hips. 'It looks like they were right. The cape I picked up isn't mine. There's a simple explanation – the two capes are almost identical.'

'You dare to say that, as though this were some trivial mistake?' Nothing now could contain Dupuy's fury. 'The police already see this as an act of subversion. It would take very little to trigger a diplomatic incident. Give me your cape too. If they are identical, then we can get out of this mess by showing them both.'

Emilia stammered an apology. 'I can't find mine. I don't know where I left it. I think I must have picked up the wrong cape as I was leaving.'

'Give me the one you've got right now,' said Dupuy, snatching it from her. 'I have people waiting who have been up all night because of your blunder. And don't even think about going back to bed. We need to have a serious talk, I will not have a thief as a daughter.' He summoned up the self-righteous smile he always used in difficult situations and went out to deal with the police. As he went, he concocted the version of the incident which would be published by the papers. Emilia did not deserve his protection; it was his good name that he needed to save.

She sat on her bed waiting for him, her hands shaking. Nothing could appease her father when he was angry. Emilia knew that the only sensible thing to do at such times was to say nothing, to retreat into herself like a tortoise and wait for the storm to pass. She and Chela had long since learned that their mother's anger could be placated with a hug. Her father, on the other hand, did not understand such affection. His feelings, if he had feelings, were like ice and never appeared on his face. On those rare occasions when he touched her, Emilia bristled and felt an irresistible urge to pull away. It was an almost animal instinct which her mind ignored. Dupuy's reactions were unpredictable and the way he was behaving now terrified her. She pulled her legs up onto the bed, hugged her knees to her chest. Simón, she whispered, Simón.

She heard footsteps. Heard him opening the drawers of the cupboards and the wardrobes, slamming them shut, moving the tables in the hall. If her mother had been there, she would have rushed to her side to protect her. But they had taken her back to the home on Sunday. She was alone. At any moment, Dupuy would burst into her room and demand an explanation. She would give him one. As soon as he was calm, she would talk to him. She stared at the glimmer of light creeping through the window. It would be dawn soon. If today was like every other day, her father would soon begin his inflexible routine: the bath, the frugal breakfast of coffee, the round of meetings. It was possible he wouldn't have time to talk and she could go back to bed. She was half dead with exhaustion.

The double doors of the bedroom opened slowly, Dupuy standing between them, filling the space completely. 'Make yourself decent this minute,' he ordered. He gave her no time to take her robe from the hanger but grabbed her by the arm and dragged her to the dressing room which Ethel had used when she was still allowed to make decisions for herself. The walls and the ceiling were covered with mirrors leaving only the parquet floor. It had been one of Ethel's expensive extravagances; she liked to linger there contemplating the fleeting reflection of her body in the world. As a little girl, Emilia had been afraid that the mirrors would swallow her mother up and the woman who emerged would not be the same, but someone who looked like her. One afternoon, finding the dressing room door ajar, she had steeled herself to sneak in to take a quick look. She saw nothing to justify her fears; dresses hanging from a chrome rail flanked by shelves which held hats, shawls, scarves, gloves, bras, silk stockings, lace panties. And everywhere there were shoes, hundreds of them. As she tiptoed out, she was startled to see her night light come on as though the mirrors were a siren song calling to it.

After her mother became ill, the room, like many in the house, fell into disuse. Dupuy ordered that the clothes be given to the Sisters of Charity and had the shelves and the rail removed, postponing until later the delicate task of removing the mirrors, replastering and repainting the room. He would have it done while he was away on business, when he wouldn't be bothered by the comings and goings of builders, the hammering, the paint, the dust.

That morning, it occurred to him that the room could also be used to punish. Very few people have a phobia of mirrors, but in those who do the effect is magical and immediate: a strange and subtle form of torture. Emilia had struggled like an animal whenever Ethel had asked her to go in. To him, and perhaps to Ethel, it had merely been an amusing game. But their daughter's terror was genuine. Mirrors gave her nightmares, made her lose control of her body. He was glad he had not had them removed. Now they would be the perfect means by which his daughter could pay for her crime. He knew her all too well. She was a resentful girl who had thought she could keep the queen's cape as a trophy. This was why she had taken advantage of the crowds to exchange one for the other. She didn't give a damn about the irreparable damage it would cause her father's spotless reputation. If she were not a Dupuy, he would have turned her in and let the police do whatever they wanted, but while she still bore his name he could not do so. The mirrors would break her once and for all and, if he was lucky, turn her into a vegetable like her mother.

Collapsed in a heap next to the dressing room, Emilia no longer struggled. Dupuy pushed her inside, threw a blanket at her and said, as he closed the door: 'You're not coming out of there until the other cape is found. And if there is no other cape, you're never coming out. You're dead to me. And you can forget about your mother.'

Though sounds from outside the room were muffled, Emilia thought she heard him leave. She would not let herself be beaten by her fears. She had already been locked up for a whole night and she had survived. Simón was with her, Simón was her rock. So as not to lose her head, she would keep her mind a blank. No thoughts, no images, like Buddhists. Only the zero that was God. She would die of exhaustion, of fever, of madness, of anything rather than let her father hear her scream or beg or grovel. Her throat felt dry. She would hold out. (The night light was not as bright as her childhood memories of it.) If there was anything of her in the mirrors, she did not see it. She could make out a few blurred images of some other being. In primary school, she had been told to read *Through the Looking-Glass* where reality was reversed. Alice did not disappear, but she was unreachable; no one could catch her. Ever since, she had had recurring dreams about that strange world. On the last page of *Through the Looking-Glass* it says that people in a dream can also be dreaming of us and that if those dreamers should wake we would flicker out like a candle. Emilia did not care whether she flickered out if the dream meant having Simón back. It even occurred to her that Simón might be drawing maps of the infinite in which words and symbols were reversed. She was exhausted, her throat burned with thirst. She lay on the floor of the dressing room, leaned her head against one of the mirrors and gradually fell asleep in the secret hope that the glass and quicksilver would melt into a silver cloud just as it did in *Through the Looking-Glass* and she could leap across the threshold to a place where everything would begin again.

When she woke, she saw that someone had left a bottle of water in the room while she was asleep, a full teapot, some toast and some cheese. Bringing food all this way and bending down to set them on the floor was not something Dupuy would do. If someone else knew she was locked in here, it was a sign that she would not be left to die. But they were obviously not going to let her out either. The mirrors formed a smooth wall with no cracks, concealing the lines of the door. She felt as though she were in a tomb, sealed up forever. Her eyes were now able to make out the empty space weakly lit by the lamp paradoxically called a night light. Emilia ate and drank only what she needed and put the water that remained to one side. She felt more confident. Seeing herself endlessly reflected in the mirrors had a hypnotic effect. She brushed her face against the smooth, indifferent surface. I can see my whole body, standing, she thought. My face sees the whole body, disappears into the mirror and finds paths there, but what about the rest of my body? Why is there no sense of sight in the mind that thinks, the nose that smells, the vagina that pulses? Was she one being or was she many? If many, how would Simón ever manage to find her? Perhaps he could see her from the other side where reality was inverted and was trying to reach her, unable to recognise her among all the reflected Emilias. She remembered a movie with a scene at a funfair, in a Magic Mirror Maze. A man was trying to kill another man; a woman was trying to kill one of the men or maybe both of them, she wasn't sure now, but in the mirrors there were lots of men, whole cities of people, lights that multiplied. Emilia thought that with a little patience she could loosen a block of the parquet, take it out and use it to smash the mirrors. She ran her fingers along the floor, feeling for a crack, but it seemed solid. Near the edge, her fingers chanced upon something unexpected. Taking it in the palm of her hand she saw it was one of her mother's hairpins which had survived being swept up or sucked up by a vacuum cleaner. That something of her had refused to leave was some sort of secret message, a sign that if something persists, endures, it is because it was created to last. She moved closer to the mirror and saw her mother take Simón's hand, saw her walking with him towards the white nothingness, saw them both reflected in the ceiling mirrors calling to her. She wanted to go with them but she did not know how to get to the other side, how to pass through. Desperately, she pounded on the mirrors begging them not to leave. 'I'm coming,' she screamed, 'I'm coming, tell me how to get to there.' They went on walking towards the void, not hearing her, until the whiteness of the other side opened its ravenous lips and devoured them. Suddenly, Emilia saw herself transformed into a thousand hateful people, her whole being waging war on itself, this being that had never struggled to enter reality. 'Wait for me, I'm coming, I'm coming.'

I know that, the day she left the room, Emilia left her father's house and moved back to the apartment overlooking the Parque Lezama where she had lived those first short, happy months as a married woman. She went on working at the Automobile Club and visiting her mother two or three times a week. Lost in the mists of the old people's home, every morning Ethel woke less of a person and went to bed less of a body. She was like Señor Ga, a character created by Macedonio Fernández who has had a lung removed, his kidney, his spleen, his colon, and then one day Señor Ga's valet calls the doctor and asks him to come and see to a pain in his foot; the doctor examines him, and shaking his head gravely tells him there's too much foot and draws a line for the surgeon to cut. Emilia's mother was like the country was back then; what she feared she would be like it would be twenty years later. I know that it was there, in San Telmo, that Emilia got the letter from her paternal aunt saying she had run into Simón in a theatre in Rio de Janeiro, the letter that convinced her to begin her search, to climb the seven terraces of her purgatory of love.

The story was restless, it didn't stop shifting, indifferent to the defeats, the deaths, to the ever more fleeting joys. Back then, I was living in Caracas learning from my reading of Parmenides that non-being is not a half-measure, that what *is not* necessarily *must not be*, I read little Heraclitus because Borges had already used him up, I was rereading Canetti, Nabokov and Kafka, I was working like a dog, writing books that other people signed, this was the life I had been given and since I had no choice I did not complain. Meanwhile, Argentina tried to reconquer the Malvinas, lost the war, the military dictatorship foundered in its own corruption, Raúl Alfonsín won the first democratic elections and Julio Cortázar returned to Buenos Aires to shake the hand of the new president, went back to Paris without managing to get an audience and died alone two months later; Borges, who was ill, left for Geneva and did not want to go back, he was buried in Plainpalais cemetery without ever being awarded the Nobel Prize; Manuel Puig died too, in a hospital in Cuernavaca, but that was much later; all the great Argentinian writers went abroad to die because there was no room in the country for more dead. The last census recorded a population of 27,949,480; housewives wept floods of tears over the misfortunes of Leonor Benedetto in the soap opera *Rosa de lejos*, and Alfonsín put the admiral, the Eel and their most conspicuous collaborators on trial; the Eel spent his trial reading – or pretending to read – *The Imitation of Christ* by the Augustine monk Thomas à Kempis; and three military coups threatened to bury democracy; and Alfonsín was forced to step down before his time because of rampant inflation and because children scavenging in garbage bins for food fell like pollen in the streets; and he was replaced by Carlos Menem who pardoned the *comandantes*, sold off the few assets Argentina still possessed, constantly, vainly, talked about the poor, and let those responsible for the bombings of the Israeli Embassy and the Asociación Mutual Israelita Argentina go unpunished; and Charly García jumped from the ninth-floor window of a Mendoza hotel into a half-full swimming pool, climbed out without a scratch and that night at his concert sang: '*The person that you love could disappear, those who are in the air could disappear*'; and I went back to Buenos Aires intending to stay there forever but I didn't stay. Emilia's cape never surfaced, I reread Parmenides and learned that being also hides in the folds of nothingness.

As I pull up at the corner of Paterson and George it starts to rain. As I expected, Toscana no longer exists. *The house on the corner is no longer a river nor does it weep*, I thought, quoting a poem that came to mind, but the river is still there. I feel sure that when I look out the window I will see a river flowing where once I saw the Pampa of Buenos Aires with cattle grazing, rolling their great eyes upwards now and then to the inclement heavens. Once again I feel that in maps we can be whatever we choose, grassland, Amazonian jungle, ancient city, but also that, inside us, maps can be whatever they choose, aimless asteroids, creatures from the future or the plush bar that now sits where Toscana once was, a bar called Glō which, right now, at eight o'clock, is giving salsa lessons. I stand under the eaves waiting for Emilia for ten or twelve minutes and still the rain does not ease. Finally, I see her calmly emerging from the parking lot across the way. She is alone. I don't want to pester her with questions about her disappearance, about why she has come alone. I am prepared for the unbelievable, since I know that Simón is dead and I realise now that I don't know what happened between them, if indeed anything happened. I gesture to her to explain that it would be impossible for us to have a conversation in Glō. By the door, there is a menacing sign informing us that the salsa class goes on until 9 p.m.

'Let's go to Starbucks, then,' she says. 'For the Aztecs, time is circular, I don't see why it shouldn't be circular for us too. Look around you, the place is full of Mexicans.'

It's true: the river has disappeared and a great dark sun now lours above the street, the Fifth Sun of the Aztecs. It was in Starbucks we first talked, that first Saturday we met, before we went to Toscana; time is gradually running backwards, a slow canon like those of Bach, a *Musical Offering* that leaps backwards in time, in tone, the worm Ouroboros ceaselessly devouring its tail and growing younger; step by step reality returns to its place, plays its last chords here where it played the first, we wander through nothingness with the certainty that it is nothingness and always at the end of the void appears the face of God, the Something.

I tempt fate:

'Hey, Emilia,' I say, 'how is Simón going to know we're not at Toscana, at Glō – how will he know we're waiting for him here?'

'He always knows where to find me. And if he loses me, I know where to find him. We lost each other once. It will never happen again.'

While we wait, I try to forget that I'm anxious. An unfamiliar feeling of vertigo overtakes me and I try to stave it off with tales like the one I am telling her now. 'Years ago I had a dream,' I tell her. 'I was in a seedy dive bar. In the dream, it was noon. By the window, I saw several women about your age sitting at one end of a long table peering into corners in which other creatures came and went like flickering shadows. The shadows called to the women but could not make them hear. The women tried to embrace the shadows but could not touch them. The bar began to empty out, night ushered in the blaze of morning, the sun stripped to become night, and the women and the shadows went on trying to embrace, went on calling to each other in vain until they occupied my whole memory.'

I tauten the string. I say:

'As I told you, I eventually wrote that dream but in an even more dreamlike way. In my story you are all the women in that bar and all the shadows are the loved one who returns: Simón. But I don't see it like that any more. I need to make some changes to those pages. I've read the notes you left with Nancy. I went over the transcripts of the trial of the *comandantes*. I'm going to put the facts back into the reality they came from. Simón is not coming tonight. According to the transcripts, three witnesses saw him murdered—'

'Simón is not dead,' she interrupts me angrily, as though my words could somehow kill him all over again.

'You told me he was with you, that I'd get to meet him tonight. How much longer are we going to wait for him?'

'It's not up to me. He'll do what he wants to do. And I know what I want to do, I want to follow him wherever he goes. I love him more with every day that passes. Without him, I don't exist.'

'I'd like to meet him. Anyone who can inspire such deep, such enduring love is from another world.'

'Simón is the same as he always was. One, continuous and indivisible, motionless, occupying the same space ever since time is time.'

Either I'm not hearing what I'm hearing or Emilia is unconsciously quoting Parmenides. I follow the thread of her memories, decide to go with them wherever they lead. I ask her: 'When did you find him? The last time I saw you, you were still looking for him.'

'Friday, a week ago. We spent the weekend alone in my apartment until Sunday night and then we left together. I was afraid of routine, of reality, of the repetition that destroys everything. He didn't care if life just took its course. He's – how can I explain this? – on the margins of life, watching as things shift, disappear, are reborn.'

Then I listen as she tells me what she experienced. She tells the story as I will write it: the meeting at Trudy Tuesday, the journey back to the apartment on North 4th Avenue in the Altima, forgetting the Altima at the Hammond offices, her surprise at discovering that Simón stills loves her with the beauty and the passion he did thirty years ago. 'Better than it was back then,' she says, 'because now he knows how I think, he can anticipate my every wish.' She tells me about her disastrous wedding night, the joy of her honeymoon, Dupuy's services to the Eel and everything that followed. Her cowed obedience to her father's orders, the cowed obedience of the country to every crack of the military whip. She tells me about her mother's madness, the visits to the old people's home, Simón's stay in an old people's home (perhaps the same one, perhaps another) where he learned the laws of the eternal noon. 'I have everything I ever wanted now,' she says, 'I'm happy.'

The Amtrak station is a few blocks away. I think I heard the whistle of trains several times while Emilia was talking but now I can hear only the bellowing of a passing train which returns us to the night where we never were. She drops her car keys on the table and says: 'Give them to whoever you like. To Nancy, to the police. I've parked the Altima in the lot just over there, on level two.'

'What about you? What are you going to do?'

'I already told you. I'm happy. That's all I want.'

'Where are you going?'

'Simón is waiting for me in a boat by the riverbank. We're going to sail upriver together. Who knows, maybe we'll run into Lieutenant Clay, sailing up the river to find Mary Ellis. We'll fire a harquebus in a salute to Mary Ellis. I've always loved happy endings.'

'The river is very low,' I tell her. 'A lot of boats have been running aground. If you lean out over the bridge, you can see them. You won't be able take a boat anywhere now, certainly not a sailboat. The river's narrow, it's barely a trickle.'

'It doesn't matter,' she says. 'It will grow broader and deeper just for us.'

Notes

7   *kaffeklubben*: a remote island near Greenland.

9   *Rand McNally cylindrical projections*: the 'standard' map of the world in which meridians are mapped to equally spaced vertical lines and circles of latitude are mapped to horizontal lines.

10   *Almendra*: probably the most famous 1960s and 70s Argentinian rock band.

10   *Taoist encyclopedia*: A description of Pangu, the first living being in Taoism. The Mundaka Upanishad describes him: 'This is the universal Self, the Virat; his head is the shining region of the heavens; his eyes are the sun and the moon; his ears are the quarters of space, his speech is the Veda full of knowledge; his vital energy is the universal air; the whole universe is his heart; his feet are the lowest earth.' When Pangu died, his breath became the wind and clouds, his voice the rolling thunder, and his eyes the sun and the moon. His hair and beard became the stars in the sky, his skin the flowers and trees, the marrow in his bones became jade and pearls, and his sweat the good rain that nurtured the earth.

16   *How 'came I in'?*: from Ezra Pound: 'The Tomb At Akr Çaar' (Faber, 1955).

35   *brainless burlesque dancer*: Bataclana (a stripper) – María Estela (Isabelita) Martínez de Perón was a nightclub dancer before she married General Perón. She took power as acting president after his death and was deposed in the coup of 1976.

44   *Raya morada*: this may refer to the Franja Morada – a university-based political movement in Argentina.

52 *'El discurso de Ayacucho'*: A piece of patriotic rhetoric routinely learned by school children, written by Leopoldo Lugones (1874–1738).

92 *Caracazo* (or *Sacudón*): the name given to the wave of protests, riots and looting and ensuing massacre that occurred on 27 February 1989 in the Venezuelan capital Caracas and surrounding towns. The riots – the worst in Venezuelan history – resulted in a death toll of anywhere between 275 and 3,000 people.

100 *Valle de la Luna*: Ischigualasto is a geological formation and a natural park associated with it in the province of San Juan, north-western Argentina.

113 *I want everyone to know*: lines from a poem by Julia Prilutzky called 'Quiero Llevar Tu Sello'.

138 *Montoneros* (Movimiento Perónista Montonero): an Argentine Perónist urban guerrilla group, active during the 1960s and 70s.

138 *People's Revolutionary Army*: Ejército Revolucionario del Pueblo (ERP).

177 *Tiempo de revancha* (1981) is a serious, sober film directed by Adolfo Aristarain about the price of remaining silent during the Dirty War; *La fiesta de todos*, a short documentary directed by Sergio Renán, is a piece of blatant propaganda funded by Videla to hide the 'disappearances' by depicting Argentina as a paradise during the 1978 Football World Cup.

178 *Diario del Juicio*: the testimony given at the 1985 Trial of the Juntas/Juicio a las Juntas, collected daily and published in newspaper form as *El Diario del Juicio* ('The Newspaper of the Trial') by Editorial Perfil, currently republished online at http://eldiariodeljuicio.perfil.com.

181 *a book by Donald Rayfield*: Stalin and His Hangmen: The Tyrant and Those Who Killed for Him (Random House, 2005).

181 *the annoying gaggle of women*: the 'Mothers of the Plaza de Mayo' who for years campaigned about Argentina's disappearance.

186 *'Hail Mary, most pure'*: Ave María purísima is said in the confessional to the priest and is the equivalent of 'Bless me, Father, for I have sinned'; the priest's response being *'sin pecado concebida'*.

195 José María Muñoz, the commentator for the 1978 World Cup.

200 *Horangel*: famous Argentine astrologer.

212 *'Hear, mortals, the sacred cry!'*: the first line of the national anthem.

215   *Carmona*: a character in Martínez's novel *La mano del amo* (1983).
236   *'La hermanita perdida'* ('Little Lost Sister'): a poem (later a song) about the Malvinas/Falklands War.
264   *Señor Ga*: a character in Macedonio Fernández's very short fable, 'Un paciente en disminución'.
266   *The house on the corner . . .*: these lines are from a poem by Juan Gelman, 'La casa de la esquina ya no es un río ni llora'.

The text of this book is set in Bembo. This type was first used in 1495 by the Venetian printer Aldus Manutius for Cardinal Bembo's *De Aetna*, and was cut for Manutius by Francesco Griffo. It was one of the types used by Claude Garamond (1480–1561) as a model for his Romain de L'Université, and so it was the forerunner of what became standard European type for the following two centuries. Its modern form follows the original types and was designed for Monotype in 1929.